THE
COMEBACK
SEASON

Also by Jennifer E. Smith

You Are Here

The Storm Makers

The Statistical Probability of Love at First Sight

This Is What Happy Looks Like

The Geography of You and Me

THE
COMEBACK
SEASON

JENNIFER E. SMITH

SIMON & SCHUSTER BFYR

NEW YORK LONDON TORONTO SYDNEY NEW DELHI

SIMON & SCHUSTER BFYR
An imprint of Simon & Schuster Children's Publishing Division
1230 Avenue of the Americas, New York, New York 10020

SIMON & SCHUSTER BFYR is a trademark of Simon & Schuster, Inc.
For information about special discounts for bulk purchases, please contact Simon &
Schuster Special Sales at 1-866-506-1949 or business@simonandschuster.com.
The Simon & Schuster Speakers Bureau can bring authors to your live event. For
more information or to book an event, contact the Simon & Schuster Speakers Bureau
at 1-866-248-3049 or visit our website at www.simonspeakers.com.
Also available in a SIMON & SCHUSTER BFYR hardcover edition
Cover design by Matthew St Clair
Book design by Jeremy Wortsman
The text for this book is set in Bembo.
Manufactured in the United States of America
This SIMON & SCHUSTER BFYR paperback edition October 2015
10 9 8 7 6 5 4 3
The Library of Congress has cataloged the hardcover edition as follows:
Smith, Jennifer E.
The comeback season / Jennifer E. Smith.
p. cm.
Summary: High school freshman Ryan Walsh, a Chicago Cubs fan, meets Nick when
they both skip school on opening day, and their blossoming relationship becomes
difficult for Ryan when she discovers that Nick is seriously ill and she again feels the
pain of losing her father five years earlier.
ISBN 978-1-4169-3847-7 (hc)
[1. Baseball—Fiction. 2. Chicago Cubs (Baseball team)—Fiction. 3. Interpersonal
relations—Fiction. 4. Fathers and daughters—Fiction. 5. Grief—Fiction. 6. Family
life—Chicago (Ill.)—Fiction. 7. Chicago (Ill.)—Fiction.] I. Title.
PZ7.S65141Co 2008
[Fic]—dc22
2007017067
ISBN 978-1-4814-4851-2 (pbk)
ISBN 978-1-4169-9607-1 (eBook)

TO MOM, DAD, AND KELLY

Acknowledgments

I'm very grateful to my agent, Jennifer Joel, for all the many things she's done for me, and I can't think of anyone else I'd rather have in my corner. I'd also like to thank my editor, Emily Meehan, for being so enthusiastic about this right from the start. Thank you to everyone at ICM for their encouragement, and especially to Binky Urban for her guidance and support. I'm also greatly indebted to Katharine Cluverius, Andy Barzvi, Matt Leone, Jocelyn Maron, Kelly Smith, John Burnside, Justin Cronin, Liz Farrell, John DeLaney, Whitney Smith, Allison Lynk, Chase Bodine, and the many others who have helped along the way. I'm incredibly lucky to have so many friends and teachers who have doubled as readers and listeners, and I can't thank them all enough.

Chapter One

O PENING DAY AT WRIGLEY FIELD ISN'T ALWAYS APRIL 8. It's not like Christmas or the Fourth of July, with their dependable calendar slots, the reassurance of a fixed number. So that it should fall on April 8 of this year—the first of Ryan Walsh's uneven stint in high school—seems reason enough for her to be on a southbound 'L' train at the exact moment she should be taking her seat in science class. The day is beautiful, blindingly bright and faintly breezy, and the Chicago skyline looms a startling shade of silver in the distance. Ryan clutches her backpack as the train lurches from side to side, her forehead pressed against the thick plastic window.

A man in a Ryne Sandberg jersey wafts a foam finger in her direction, and even as she scoots farther toward the window, Ryan's heart beats fast with excitement. There are college kids drinking sweet-flavored vodka drinks from plastic bottles, old men with sweat-stained blue caps, a group of boys trading blue and red markers to finish up a cardboard sign. At each stop, as they collect more fans, as the noise level grows, as they wind their way along Lake Michigan toward the center of it all, she feels it: the fluttery hope, the tentative promise. It is game day in Chicago, the first true day of spring. There is, before them all, a whole new season.

Ryan is not typically reckless in this way. She is, in fact, feeling slightly nauseated at the thought of her impulsive departure after third period. Across the packed train car, she thinks she spots a boy from her math class, the shock of white from a cast on his arm peeking through at elbow level in the crowd. But at the next stop, when the doors open and a new surge of people presses their way inside, he's suddenly gone, and Ryan decides she's only looking for a reason to feel guilty and to think of school.

"Next stop, Addison," the conductor calls out, and the train erupts in wild cheering. Ryan tugs at the drawstrings of her hooded sweatshirt and smiles to herself.

This, after all, is where she feels closest to him. Not when she sits at what had once been his seat at the dinner table. Not when her mom unwittingly sings their song under her breath while she does the dishes. Not when she looks at her younger sister, whose eyes are his: gray-blue and swimming.

No, right here, with the stadium fast approaching and all the possibilities of these nine long innings laid bare: this is where it's easiest to imagine her father still beside her.

She'd been just ten when he was killed in a rafting accident while on a trip to Colorado. Soon after, Mom sold their season tickets—two seats on the third base line, just eight rows back—to help save money while she looked for a job. Emily had always been too young anyway, and Mom was never interested much beyond the novelty of the festival-like atmosphere of Wrigley Field.

But the ivy-covered back wall is the background to most of Ryan's memories of him. She can see his face most clearly when she thinks of him at the ballpark. It was here he'd taught her to keep score when she was only six, patiently helping her fill in the tiny diamond grids across her playbook, and it was here—however unknowingly—she'd begun to prepare herself for his absence. Where better to learn of heartbreak and loss than Wrigley Field? What better place to harden your heart?

At the games, he'd throw an arm across the back of her seat

and lean in. "If the Cubs win," he'd say, "I'll give up chocolate for a whole week."

"It has to be something more important than that," Ryan would say accusingly, as if he didn't care enough to negotiate with something better than candy.

"Not for this game," he'd protest. "It's not even our division."

She'd pull her blue cap down low and frown until he reconsidered.

"Okay, fine," he'd say with a grin. "If the Cubs win, I'll eat only vegetables for the rest of the week."

"How about if they win, you have to give me five piggybacks a day?"

"Five a day?" he'd say, laughing. "You drive a hard bargain."

"It's for the good of the team," she'd insist.

It was a dangerous bargaining tool, this team of theirs. There was always the chance they'd be left with nothing.

Since her dad died, Ryan has only been to three games. The first two with her mom and sister soon after the accident, where they got lost amid the thick crowds and the too-cheerful organ music. Ryan had barely been able to watch the game, instead working to split open peanut shells the way he'd taught her, but they felt dry and dusty in her mouth. Emily cried when someone in the row behind them spilled beer at their feet, and Mom held her close, looking out over the top of her head with a dazed expression, even when everyone else rose for the national anthem. They'd left at the top of the fourth inning, and on their second try a few games later, made it only to the bottom of the fifth. It was soon after that when Mom sold the tickets.

A year later, sitting with a friend and her parents at the third game, Ryan realized she'd forgotten how to keep score the way her dad taught her. She sat with her pencil poised over the scorecard and blinked back tears.

That was five years ago. She hasn't been back since.

But today is different. Today is April 8.

When the train slows to a halt, the passengers shift restlessly until the doors open. Over their shoulders, Ryan can see the huge wall of the stadium rising up against a cloudless sky, and she draws in a breath. The air smells of that peculiar combination of hot dogs and springtime, leather mitts and freshly cut grass, and all of it blends into one scent, one thought, one thing: *Dad.*

"Opening Day programs," a man in red calls out, waving the glossy booklets high in the air. "Cubs programs here!"

Ryan steps off the platform, swept toward the stadium along with the rest of the crowd, and just briefly, she closes her eyes. April 8 may not always be Opening Day, but it *is* always—without fail and without end—the anniversary of the day her father died. And this, she thinks, peering up at the pennants waving lazily in the spring breeze, is reason enough.

Ryan had woken this morning with a dull sense of loss, and when she rolled over to glance at her clock, she remembered and burrowed deeper beneath the covers. Five years ago on this day, she'd been pulled from her fourth-grade classroom and made to sit in the nurse's office until her mom arrived, red-eyed and stunned with her three-year-old sister in tow, to tell her what she knew—that in the chaos of the Colorado River, on the trip her dad had been planning with his college buddies for years, the raft had overturned. Of the group, it had been her father who was tossed in the worst possible direction, where the water was quicker, the river bottom rockier. It was the school nurse who leaned in to clarify the message: "He's gone, honey," she said, and Ryan began to cry.

Sometimes, it seems she hasn't stopped crying since.

This morning, when she came downstairs for breakfast,

Emily was already sitting at the table singing to herself, her legs swinging from the chair as she picked at a blueberry muffin. Her younger sister loves dolls and horses, stickers and puppies, and is so far from what Ryan had been at eight—or ever—that she often has trouble believing they could have been raised in the same family.

Though in a way, they haven't been.

Emily had been too young to remember Dad, and for that, Ryan can't fault her. But her sister's allegiance to Kevin makes Ryan feel like the last survivor of a long-lost era. Their stepfather is a nice enough lawyer who Mom met at the driving range when she decided to take golf lessons a couple years ago. At the real estate agency where she'd started working after Dad died, golf was apparently more than just a hobby. It was the common language. "It's a sport that's actually useful," Mom said, looking pointedly at Ryan. "It's good for business."

Dad had been a sportswriter, and even *he* didn't consider golf a real sport.

Kevin—wearer of ties, believer in rules, hater of baseball— had joined the family shortly afterward, and it is with him that Emily has grown up. Because of this, it's impossible to blame her for not understanding that you don't flip the television channel when the Cubs are on.

This morning, Ryan had looked on wearily from across the kitchen table as Emily folded and refolded a muffin wrapper like a study in origami. Twice, she opened her mouth to say something—to offer some small reminder of the day—but her sister was bright-eyed and ready for school, waiting for Kevin to drive her, waiting for Mom to kiss them good-bye, and Ryan didn't have the heart to draw her into this awful anniversary, no matter how much she wished for someone to share in her sorrow. When Mom came downstairs, she would—as she did each year on this day—hug Ryan just a little bit tighter, linger just a moment longer when she kissed her forehead, smooth back the tangles of hair from her face. They would exchange watery smiles, and without having to say anything, without making any sort of fuss, they would sit down to a breakfast of slightly burned bacon and scrambled eggs—Dad's favorite. Anything more to commemorate the day would be too difficult; anything less, heartless.

But today, Mom came down holding Kevin's hand, the two of them hiding smiles and practically giggling. They stood before the table, Kevin adjusting his tie, Mom with a hand on the back of Emily's chair.

"What's going on?" Ryan asked, frowning. She sat Indian style on the kitchen chair, her arms tucked up inside her sweat-shirt. Mom stooped down to place a hand on top of Emily's, and behind her, Kevin shifted from one foot to the other, bobbing his head of thinning hair and grinning stupidly.

"We only just found out for sure," she said. "I'm pregnant."

Mom looked to them both, smiling hesitantly, until Emily squealed and hopped up from her chair, clapping her hands, and Mom's smile broadened. She raised her eyes over Ryan's shoulder to Kevin, and with that look—the flecks of light in her eyes, the faintest hint of joy—Ryan's heart dropped. *Of all days,* she thought, as she pushed back from the table and pounded up the stairs to her room.

Later, when she heard the knock, Ryan simply tucked her face into her pillow and grunted. She looked up when the door creaked open, and Mom poked her head in.

"Mind if I join you?"

Ryan said nothing, but curled into a ball to make room at the foot of the bed.

"I didn't forget," Mom said, resting a hand on Ryan's ankle.

She tilted her head thoughtfully. "I think, in a way, he'd be happy about it, actually. A new beginning on a day like today. It's just the kind of thing he'd find meaning in if he were here."

"If he were here," Ryan said, staring fiercely out the window, "this wouldn't have happened."

They sat quietly on the bed together, the sounds from the cars outside rising up through the half-open window. Ryan waited for Mom to say something more—to suggest they go downstairs for bacon and eggs, or to tell her she'll never love anyone more than Dad, not Kevin and not even this new baby—but they both remained silent.

Finally, Ryan eyed her stomach. "When's it due?"

"October," Mom said, placing a hand on her belly, obviously pleased by the question. Ryan shrugged, watching the Cubs flag on her closet door flutter in the breeze from the window. It wasn't as if she'd have anything else to do in October.

Chapter Two

YAN DOESN'T CONSIDER HERSELF A TOMBOY, A WORD that makes her think of the girls in her grade who sit together at lunch, broad and bulky, with long ponytails hanging heavy down their backs. Tomboys are jocks. Tomboys are fierce. Girls like Ryan—small and lost and not particularly athletic—shrink toward the wall when they pass.

But the sad fact is that she isn't anything *else* either. She's not popular, and she doesn't get good grades. She's not involved with any extracurricular activities, and she doesn't take part in after-school clubs. Most often, Ryan finds herself drifting through hallways filled with kids her own age who seem years ahead of her in every way. In a school composed of cliques that rotate and shift and absorb and repel one another like molecules in a science experiment, she's left to fend for herself the best she can. Ryan watches her classmates as if from a great distance, observing their march through high school, the certainty in their movements, the subtle confidence that propels them.

It hasn't always been this way. She hasn't always been so alone. After Dad died, her two best friends—Sydney and Kate—had, in all their ten-year-old wisdom, gathered around her. They let her win at board games, handed over the best parts of their lunches, and waved away the cookies she offered in return. They invited her over after school and spoke in soft voices, and when they laughed, it was only briefly, until they all remembered and huddled solemnly together around the swing set in Sydney's backyard. In the afternoons, they'd troop through the ravines that crisscrossed the neighborhood, picking their way along ribbonlike streams, their voices carrying in the deepness of the leaf-covered trenches, making sure no one fell behind.

It wasn't until later that they began to grow in separate directions—which is not at all the same thing as growing apart. That would come with time, but at first, it was a simple matter of Ryan falling out of step.

Shortly after her father's death, in an effort to reestablish normalcy, Mom took Ryan to meet the other two girls and their mothers downtown for an outing that had been planned well before the accident. Just before tea time, they gathered in the lobby of a fancy hotel, and Ryan was startled to see her friends dressed alike in little pleated skirts and shoes that clicked on the marble floors. The other moms arched their eyebrows at Ryan's ensemble: a pair of tattered shorts and sneakers. It hadn't occurred to her to dress up, and Mom—still reeling from the accident—had herself barely managed to shed the bathrobe covered in Emily's cereal that had lately become a uniform of sorts. Embarrassed, Ryan shifted from foot to foot, avoiding her friends' eyes. After a moment, Mom opened her purse, and Ryan reached up and removed the Cubs hat her father had given her, stuffing it into the leather bag beside a tube of lipstick and a brush.

That same baseball cap now sits perched high on a closet shelf, where it reminds her again and again of what she can't possibly forget. It feels to Ryan that no matter how she tries to move forward, a part of her will forever be ten years old. And it seems entirely possible that she will never escape that moment in the nurse's office, crying into her mom's sweater, drowning in a

way, and gripping the edges of the rough blue cap as if it might
be the very thing to save her life.

This afternoon, in the frenzied blocks surrounding Wrigley
Field, the crowds walk just a bit more cautiously and the vendors
glance furtively toward the ballpark, each feeling the pressure of
the new season. This year is different from all the others. In a
history worthy of the most woeful tragedies, nothing has been so
dreaded as the start of the 100th season since the Chicago Cubs
last won a World Series pennant.

It's not that people aren't hopeful, because hope is everything to a Cubs fan. But the years have wound by like the ticking of a clock, and it seems this 100th season must be a year like
no other, decidedly hyperbolic, marked by either great success
or miserable failure. The fans are sure of this. It is only a matter
of time until they find out which.

The Cubs have had successes, of course, since 1908. There
was a World Series appearance in 1945, a winning streak in 1969,
a sliver of hope in 1984, a heart-stopping run in 2003, and the
briefest glimpse of October 2007. But all of these had ended
in much the same way, with disappointments so great that over
the past hundred years, they've snowballed into a sense of sheer
despair. Since 1908, the Cubs have been cursed by a billy goat,
embarrassed by their crosstown rivals, plagued by whispers of
greatness and potential unrealized.

In the past century, glory has found a home elsewhere.
Since their last showing in 1945, every other long-established
team has won a World Series. Their closest allies in campaigns
of loss, the Red Sox and White Sox—both also hapless in their
own ways—have wiped their slates clean with wins in 2004 and
2005 that erased the years since 1918 and 1917 respectively. In
Chicago, the Bulls have made their run, and the Bears have done

their shuffle. Wrigley Field, once home to the greatest team in
baseball and witness to Babe Ruth's called shot, has begun to
crumble. Words like "eventually" and "next year" have become
mantras.

It is without a doubt a demoralizing business being a Cubs fan.
But even so, the fans wait. They hope. They wish.

And none more than Ryan Walsh, who works her way
clockwise around the stadium, overwhelmed after being away
for so long. It's one thing to follow the team from afar, running a finger down the television schedule, checking the score
on the radio, setting timers and recordings, reading newspapers.
But here beneath the red marquee, the huge expanse of Wrigley
Field bearing down on her, she's reminded of what it is to miss
something. She hadn't realized just how much a part of her
this was: the bleacher seats and the press boxes, the men selling
T-shirts and hot dogs and beer.

Today, she feels particularly stuck: her family is moving forward without her, adding new members and forgetting about
the old. Her friends, too, have changed. She's been on the outs
with them since the start of school, for no other reason, it seems,
than her lack of enthusiasm for passing notes and sharing gossip. This new terrain—the cold and endless maze of her high
school—still feels every bit as foreboding as it had eight months
ago, and she has little to show for the past year besides a new-
found propensity for making herself invisible.

And so she is here on her own.

Getting a ticket for opening day—even in the bleachers,
where the sun beats down hard and the fans grow rowdier with
each inning—is practically impossible. Even days, weeks, months
ahead it would have been difficult, but on game day, there's no
chance. Even so, winding her way across Clark Street, Ryan feels
a simple satisfaction in having made it down here at all.

She pauses at the corner of Addison and looks back. Above the stadium and past the waving flags, the jagged rooftops are crowded with people getting ready for the game. Up the street, the bars are filled with fans who have been drinking since early morning, the crowds flowing out onto the street in front of Murphy's Bleachers and The Cubby Bear. Everywhere, there is blue and red, floating Cs and pinstripes.

A man in an old Sammy Sosa jersey clicks his tongue at her, and Ryan feels a small burst of panic, but he only motions at her with a ticket. "Left field," he says in a low voice. "One seat."

She takes a step closer. "How much?"

"Hundred bucks."

"No way," she says, shaking her head. "How high up?"

"There're no bad seats in Wrigley," he grunts. "Everyone knows that."

"Forget it," Ryan says, turning around. But she's only a few yards away when she stops to look wistfully at the entrance, where the ticket people are handing out free baseballs at the turnstiles. Shoving her hands in her pockets as if she might miraculously come up with the money, she remembers the check her mom gave her yesterday for the spring field trip to the amusement park. Ryan had forgotten to bring home the form with the details, so it's still blank. She fumbles through her bag and slips it out from the pages of a book, then turns back to the guy, though when she does, she sees the boy from her math class—the one with the broken arm she thought she'd seen on the 'L'—bargaining for the ticket from beneath the brim of a worn blue Cubs hat.

She stares, blanking on his name. He'd joined their class just a month ago—the only sophomore in freshman precalculus—and Ryan remembers thinking how hard it must be to come into a school at the very end of the year. She's not sure whether his old school was further behind in the curriculum or whether he's simply bad at the subject, but either way, Ryan knows she's in no position to judge. If she doesn't improve her own math grade soon, she could very well share a similar fate next year.

Though she can't remember speaking with him other than to once borrow a pencil, he's the kind of guy you can't help assuming is nice: tall and skinny, with pale freckles and round eyes. He's been wearing the cast the whole time, and like every other kid in school to whom Ryan pays only passing interest, she's come to think of him only in terms of this detail— Broken Arm Kid, Cast Boy, That Guy with the Sling—though admittedly, he seems to have already fared better than she with their classmates.

"One-twenty?" she hears him groan. "Seriously?"

"Not a bad seat in the house," the scalper says, grinning.

"Wait," Ryan says, approaching them, and the boy looks surprised to see her.

"You're in my math class," he says, adjusting his cap.

She nods. "I'm Ryan."

"Hey," he says. "I'm Nick."

The scalper rolls his eyes. "And I'm Don," he says. "Do you want the goddamn seat or not?"

Ryan turns to Nick. "What if we split it?" she asks. "Then we could switch off every couple innings or something."

He shoves a hand into his pocket and emerges with a handful of crumpled bills. "I'm not sure I have enough," he says, suddenly animated. He digs around in his backpack, his broken arm held awkwardly out from his body, his other hand pawing through the bag, a look of fixed determination on his face. The scalper curses at them impatiently under his breath.

"Here," Nick says triumphantly, holding up a few extra bills.

"You don't take checks, do you?" Ryan asks, turning to the scalper, but she finds he's moved several feet away, where he's handing over the ticket to a man in a business suit, who tucks it into his pocket and walks off toward the entrance. The scalper, shuffling a stack of bills, lifts his shoulders when he sees them watching, then heads off too. Ryan's eyes drift over toward Waveland Avenue, the outfield wall where the neighborhood kids gather to listen to the crowd and try to catch home runs or long fouls that may make it up and over to the street. And so—with nothing more to be done—they begin to walk over together, as if that had been the plan all along.

Chapter Three

D AD LOVED TO TELL THE STORY OF HIS FIRST DATE with Mom—a Saturday game against the Mets— where he'd had to explain to her the difference between a ball and a strike. According to him, she'd sat patiently beside him through the whole game, laughing over beers and telling stories between innings, and when he asked her out again, she'd been thrilled. But when she learned that his intention for the second date—and the third and the fourth— was another ball game, she nearly ended it right then. She never fully grasped the game, and even more, his sorry love affair with the team.

"How can you love something so much when they let you down so often?" she asked as they watched the Cubs invent new and heartbreaking ways of losing.

"They'll shape up soon," he said. "Just wait till next year."

Though she never came to love it as he did, she did learn to live with his obsession. She didn't mind when he named the dog Addison and the cat Clark—dubbed for the cross streets where the ballpark sits—though she did draw the line when Ryan was born, using her maiden name for their first daughter. Dad used to tease that they'd named her after Ryne Sandberg—his favorite Cubs player—but Mom messed up on the spelling.

But Ryan's favorite story was of the day he asked her mom to marry him at Wrigley Field. He'd made a sort of reverse bargain, he told her. "As long as she said yes," he explained, "it was okay if the Cubs lost."

"And did they?" Ryan asked.

"Nope," he said with a small smile. "Everyone won that night."

The score is already one to nothing—just two outs into the game—by the time Ryan and Nick make their way around to the back of the stadium. Naturally, the Cubs are losing to the Cardinals, which is particularly painful given the long rivalry between the two teams. Though they don't have the same sort of grudge matches as the East Coast clubs—nothing like the contention between Yankees and Red Sox—Ryan had been brought up to hate everything about the Cards: the stupid mascot, the red of their caps, the fans from St. Louis.

Generally speaking, of course, the Cubs don't need such rivalries. They always seem to do just fine beating themselves.

But it's only the start of the season, and there's still room for optimism in Wrigleyville, where the residents of the neighborhood are out in their yards with coolers and lawn chairs, their radios tuned in to hear the play-by-play from beyond the ivy-leafed back wall. A group of boys is tossing around a dirty baseball, their ears cocked toward the stadium in case someone should hit a home run. T-shirt and souvenir vendors are lined up across the street, waving stuffed teddy bears and authentic jerseys.

Ryan and Nick settle onto the curb—suddenly shy now that they've found a place to sit—and listen to the hollow sounds of the game drifting over the wall on breezes from the nearby lake. Nick leans forward on his elbows, propping his chin up with his broken arm, and Ryan winces.

"Doesn't that hurt?" she asks. "How'd you do it?"

He looks out across the street with clear green eyes, crinkling his nose. "I'm getting it off pretty soon," he says, as if that explains everything.

The block is noisy—kids shouting, airplanes overhead, radios blasting, the uneven cheers from inside—yet the quiet between them feels somehow louder than all of this. Ryan wonders if she should ask him why he's cutting class, what drove him down to Wrigley today without a ticket when he should be in school, but she knows he could be asking the same of her, and she's suddenly grateful for the silence. She gets the impression that he might feel the same way—lost for words that don't include math class or school in general—and so she clears her throat.

"Did you know it's the 100th year since the Cubs last won the World Series?" she asks, tipping her head back to the sky, where an airplane glides by, towing a banner advertising drink specials after the game.

"Of course," Nick says curtly, and Ryan feels immediately stupid for having shared this obvious fact. She's relieved when he smiles at her. "How could we possibly forget?"

"Maybe this'll be the year," she says.

He shrugs, shifting to pull a rolled-up score sheet and stubby pencil from his pocket. Ryan looks on, running her eyes across the columns as he begins copying in the lineup from a stray program left behind on the street. When she leans in too close, he looks up. "Want me to show you how to do it?" he asks, and Ryan shakes her head and chokes out a small "no."

They fall silent as a noise erupts from the stadium. Nick looks over his shoulder at a large man sunk low in a plastic lawn chair, a transistor radio balanced on his lap. He shakes his head miserably and holds up two fingers.

"Two-zip," Nick says, tapping his fingers on the curb impatiently. The man turns up his radio for their benefit, and they wave to him gratefully. "Wish we could see what was going on."

"I don't mind it, actually," Ryan says. "It's sort of nice just to be close by."

A half smile crawls across his face. "I guess so."

"So, have you always been a Cubs fan?" she asks, wondering where he had moved from, what circumstances had brought him to Chicago in the middle of the school year.

"Always," he says. "Even when we lived up in Wisconsin, my parents used to bribe me with Cubs tickets when I complained about the long car rides down here."

"So you've been here a lot?" Ryan asks, hugging her knees. "Do you have family around here or something?"

He doesn't answer, instead staring at the pavement, his face hidden by the shadow of his hat. "No," he says finally. "I only meant that I never liked the Brewers for some reason. Or the White Sox. It was always the Cubs."

Ryan smiles. "Me too."

He bends his head over the score sheet once more, recording the action of the game as best he can with the benefit of half a dozen crackling radios, which tell the story in small bursts of static all around them.

"That last one is wrong," Ryan says, pointing to one of the small diamonds, where he's drawn a *K* in the middle of the box. "He didn't strike out swinging."

"You're right," Nick says, tackling the marking with his eraser. Once he's corrected it, flipping the *K* around backward, he turns back to Ryan, surprised. "Where'd you learn to read a scorecard?"

"My dad," she says quietly.

Something in her face must be giving her away, because Nick clears his throat, searching for something else to say. "That's cool," he says, tapping the scorecard in his lap. "I've never met a girl who likes baseball so much."

"I don't like *baseball*," Ryan says with a grin. "I like the Cubs."

He laughs. "Okay, then."

By the fifth inning, they're down four to one, but the sun is warm on her face, and they've settled into a silence worth keeping. It's as comfortable as anything Ryan has felt all day. There's something reassuring in the way he sits beside her, the utter lack of obligation to talk about anything that matters: school, family, her father, the new baby.

At the seventh-inning stretch, they stand, and Nick dutifully removes his blue cap. They lift their chins and mouth the words—*Root, root, root for the Cubbies!*—looking sideways at each other self-consciously. The blended voices from the stands mount until, at the song's close, they dissolve into scattered shouts of *Play ball!* There's a moment of quivering stillness just afterward, as the game resumes and the fans take their seats, as the halted action of the world eases back to life.

"Actually," Ryan says as they sit down again, "these really aren't the worst seats ever."

Nick readjusts his cap and smiles at her from beneath the brim. "I don't know," he says. "I can think of better."

"Like over there?" Ryan asks jokingly, pointing to where a few kids are perched in the low branches of a tree, straining to get a view over the stadium wall.

"Sure," he says, laughing. "Doesn't get better than that."

"No," she agrees, leaning back on the curb. "It doesn't."

After the game, they ride home together in the yellowish light of the train car, their shoulders just barely touching, their heads tipped back against the seats. They are sunburned and heavy-limbed, weary from the day behind them, but they're also purely and simply happy. The Cubs pulled it off in the bottom of the eighth with a three-run homer, and outside the stadium, where the ball rose up and over the outfield wall—a blurry dot in an otherwise empty sky—the crowd surged and throbbed, shoved and shimmied, until a bald man in a Cubs visor stood tall and raised his hands high in the air: one with the game-winning ball, the other with a sweating can of beer.

They'd both ridden their bikes from school to the train station, and so once they reach their stop, Ryan follows Nick out to where they're propped a few feet away from each other. Her blue Schwinn looks frail beside his bulky black mountain bike. With chilly fingers, they work to unchain the locks in the growing darkness, and once they're ready—wheels pointed in opposite directions, hands gripping the bars—they find that the silence has changed once again. Gone is the closeness of the quiet train ride; lost is the cozy hush that had settled over them during the game. Ryan hadn't ever realized there could be so many different types of *not talking*, so many brands of stillness, as if the quiet itself were a third party to the conversation.

Finally, Nick clears his throat. "So, I guess I'll see you in school tomorrow."

Ryan nods, half-hidden in the fuzzy darkness. They each lift their hands and let them hang in the air for a moment like members of some long lost Indian tribe, before wheeling their bikes in separate directions, the clicking of the spokes echoing in the night.

The game had been a long one, and by the time Ryan gets home, it's almost dinnertime and too late for any excuses about after-school projects or last-minute plans. As soon as she coasts up the driveway, even before she reaches out to brake with her sneakers on the asphalt, Mom appears in the doorway.

"Where have you been?" she yells, a catch in her voice. She steps out onto the front stoop, shuffling her feet on the cold bricks. "You didn't call, and I was worried."

Ryan knocks down the kickstand of the bike, draws her hands into the sleeves of her sweatshirt, and lowers her chin as she walks up the path to the front door. As she passes the window, she can see Emily telling Kevin a story, leaning forward on the dinner table and gesturing with her fork. Once she reaches the door, Ryan kicks at the ground, shoulders hunched.

"You can't just disappear without letting me know where you are," Mom says, shaking her head so that a strand of dark hair comes loose. This is new territory for them, Ryan's tendency toward flight. Out of a combination of boredom and restlessness, she's lately begun escaping to odd places at odd times—the beach near their house before school, the playground after dinner. But this is the first time she's actually cut class, and if there was any hope that Mom hadn't yet realized this, it's now gone. She looks at Ryan with a mixture of anger and worry. "You can't just run off like this," she says, then presses her lips together. "I need to know you're okay."

She seems different somehow, softer in a way, and Ryan wonders whether it's because of the new baby. Had she looked this way for the past weeks, and nobody noticed? Or did this faint glow only come from the *knowing*?

When Dad was killed, Ryan hadn't cried until she heard the news, and a part of her is still—will *always* be—upset that she didn't somehow *know* the exact moment it happened, the precise second he was gone. It seems to her that time should be more forgiving than that. She wishes it were possible to somehow take back those lost hours between the river and the nurse's office, the forgotten minutes between the accident and the telling of it, when nobody was missing him yet. Because that gap is what still hurts the most, a loneliness that presses down hard against her chest each night when she switches off the light.

Now Ryan bites her lip, refusing to meet Mom's eye. From inside, she can hear the high peal of Emily's laughter, and she shoves her hands into her pockets.

If it took only five years to forget this day, then how long until he's gone completely? How long does it take for someone to disappear?

"I get it," Mom says, moving a step closer. "You're sorry." She places a hand on her belly and frowns down at Ryan, who is suddenly and unexpectedly anything but sorry. Everything she'd felt all day at the game is gone now. Standing here in front of their little brick house, she feels suddenly deflated.

"I went to the game," Ryan says quietly, and Mom's face softens. "It's Opening Day. Or did you forget that, too?"

They stand watching each other without speaking. Down the street, the hollow sound of a basketball sets a dull, pulsing rhythm, and as evening falls deeper into night, the garage lights come to life. Neither says anything, and Ryan blinks at the ground.

This silence between them is not anything like the others. It's not pleasant or awkward, not trying or simple. Even now, five years later, it seems somehow determined to last, as if it might be this way always: the two of them out on the stoop, each doing their best not to drift too far. It occurs to Ryan that if there really are all sorts of silences, then maybe death is nothing more than the longest of these; and this, nothing more than the empty space left behind by her father.

Chapter Four

THE NEXT MORNING AT SCHOOL, RYAN IS STANDING BY HER locker when she feels herself spotted by her two former friends. It is an actual physical feeling, a slight bristling, and when she turns her head to confirm it, there they are: Sydney and Kate, hurrying down the hall together like some sort of blond two-headed monster.

They'd made it longer than most, their little crew, surviving the unsurvivable—junior high—before high school did what high school tends to do. Standing with her cafeteria tray on the first day at lunch, Ryan had been astonished to see Sydney and Kate sitting with Lucy Barrett and an assortment of vaguely sneering blond girls, the same ones they'd spent all of junior high alternately envying and fearing. She stood and she stared; she swallowed and she blinked. This was not just a momentary sense of confusion. This was a dramatic shift in all that she knew to be true, a slow and fumbling tilting of the way things were supposed to be. Lucy Barrett—blond and cold, hawklike and calculating, with a collection of bracelets that jangled up and down her arms like a warning bell alerting people of her approach—had not figured into Ryan's equation for the first day of high school.

Completely unsure of what to do, she paused a few feet away, wondering whether she was allowed to do the unthink-able—just waltz over to the table on her own—or whether this required some sort of summoning. Ryan knew even then that this was probably one of those moments that decides more than just lunch, more than simply seating arrangements. But still, she just stood there, her tray quivering in her hands.

When Sydney finally glanced up and met her eyes, instead of calling out, she looked away, and the moment was like the soft rip of an eraser across their shared past. Ryan backpedaled until she bumped into a scowling football player, then wheeled around, scanning the cafeteria for some sort of refuge. She could, of course, have still gone over. She could have sat down with them as if nothing had happened, ignored Lucy's raised eyebrows, eaten her lunch and carried on with her day. But there had been something in Sydney's look that made her feel cold all over, and so she moved away blindly, eventually finding an empty seat at a table occupied by a handful of bored-looking kids with headphones.

Later, Ryan would make a habit out of eating upstairs in the hallway near her locker, the door propped open beside her to create a small space of her own on the cold tile floor. But on that first day, she kept her head down and ate quickly, unable to look over to where her so-called friends were inching their way toward something that didn't appear to include her.

It was true that things had started to change long before then. This shouldn't have been entirely unexpected. But how could Ryan have guessed that the recent differences between them—the subtle shifting of their priorities, the lengthening gaps in conversation—would signal the end of a lifelong friendship?

It was suddenly as if the years leading up to this one had never happened: the sleepovers and secrets, the childhood fights and the long, shaky months after her father died when they'd been so quick to close in around her. Soon, it became clear there was a new set of rules to be followed, an etiquette dictated by one of the flinty-eyed girls at the table Ryan would never be invited to sit at in the cafeteria.

She chooses to believe she didn't make the cut because she didn't want to, because she could see through all the hair-flipping and backstabbing. But this is really only because she has an instinct for self-preservation.

The truth is that although Ryan knows she's pretty enough—she has, after all, been asked by boys to school dances and kissed during the slow songs—it's in a simplistic way, the kind never appreciated by other girls. Which is to say that she doesn't care about makeup or jewelry, and has grown used to getting the once-over for her lack of fashion sense, an up-and-down stare reminiscent of the way her mom studies produce at the grocery store. Ryan prefers ponytails to curling irons, the soapy smell of her shampoo to the fruity ones all the other girls use. She feels most put together when wearing jeans, and she would never trade her flip-flops for a pair of heels.

And mostly, she's okay with this.

But although she's now survived nearly the whole year without friends, it still hurts. Even after all this time, the sting of rejection has not quite gone away, and this is just one of the many things Ryan carries with her to school each day.

She eyes Sydney and Kate now with a great deal of wariness, lingering beside her locker and trying to guess whether they might stop and greet her in the overly nice, pitying manner they have lately adopted, or else rush by without bothering to acknowledge her at all. Either way, math class starts in three minutes, and either way, she'll have to sit in front of them and listen as they make plans without her in barely concealed whispers.

"You missed class yesterday," Sydney says, once they're both assembled beside Ryan's locker. She plays with the end of her ponytail and looks down the hallway with an air of boredom. Kate stares at her feet, and Ryan feels a bit sorry for her. Sydney—tall and blond, utterly certain of herself—was always more likely to be roped in by the popular crowd. But Kate is less secure in the ways that count to these types of girls, prone to second-guessing and worrying, and to Ryan, it seems like an awful lot of effort to keep up.

Sydney raises her eyebrows, waiting for a response, and Ryan tries not to think of how they've forgotten about yesterday, the terrible anniversary. But then, why should this be different than every other day of this awful year? She hadn't exactly expected they'd go for ice cream together—as they had all the other years—or linger afterward, sharing stories from when they were younger, speaking in great looping circles around those things Ryan found hardest to voice, as if childhood memories might somehow bring her father nearer.

She knew enough not to expect that anymore. But she *had* hoped for something more than this: the same unbearable coldness she'd been enduring for months.

"So, what," Sydney asks, "did you ditch or something?"

Ryan shakes her head, unwilling to go into the details of her excursion. This morning's breakfast wasn't yet far enough behind her, where she'd had to listen to Kevin lecture her on trustworthiness, responsibility, and—at the very least—calling home as a courtesy when plans changed. When she'd left for school, Mom had stuck her head out the front door and called after her. "Straight from home to school, then school back home," she'd yelled. "Got it?"

Ryan had only shrugged as she wheeled her bike down the driveway. She hated this sullen version of herself, but lately, her mood had begun to feel like quicksand: alarmingly easy to sink into, with little hope of scrambling back out.

Now, she pushes shut her locker door and sighs. She's almost late for math, and in no mood to tell anyone about her afternoon yesterday, least of all Sydney and Kate. And so, with a small, satisfied smile, she spins around and heads to class on her own, leaving them feeling good and ignored, a surprised duo of open-mouthed girls unused to being on the receiving end of this particular tactic.

When she sees Lucy Barrett leaning against a row of lockers near the door to her math class, Ryan's first instinct is to do a U-turn and find an alternate route. There's something about Lucy that makes her feel overwhelmingly tired, and she's always been happy to avoid the layers of people that seem to form around her. In general, Ryan isn't the type to pore over yearbooks or memorize the starting lineup of the football team, so it's no great surprise that she usually doesn't recognize most of the guys who flock in Lucy's direction. But standing among them now—the big-shouldered lacrosse players and the wiry quarterbacks—Ryan sees, with a small shock, that Nick is there too.

She stares at him, surprised and embarrassed. He looks as he does anywhere else: lanky and loose-limbed, offhanded and disarmingly casual. But among all the other guys, in that sea of square jaws and baseball caps where everyone is trying just a bit too hard, there's an easy confidence that sets him apart. Only last night, Ryan had fallen asleep thinking about all the possibilities of this new friendship. She'd actually imagined herself offering him a seat at lunch—this new kid, this skinny guy with a cast. And she, Ryan Walsh—who was *nobody*—would help *him*, would be nice to *him*, would rescue *him*.

A few more guys join the group, and one of them claps Nick on the back. Ryan wants to move, to dodge into class before someone notices her, but she feels heavy with disappointment. Seeing Nick laughing so easily among the very people she finds so intimidating is completely unnerving, and her mind works frantically to revise her impressions of him from the day before. It had been so long since anyone had been nice to her like that, and she'd been stupid enough to get carried away—to think she might not always be so lonely—when really, yesterday had been nothing more than a friendly gesture at a baseball game they both happened to be attending.

The last bell rings out, signaling the start of class, and Ryan realizes a moment too late that her feet have failed her. She's standing stock-still in the center of the hallway—the easiest prey of all—as the group begins to scatter with obvious reluctance. And she's still there, her ears already burning a bright pink, when Nick looks over. His face breaks into a crooked grin when he sees her, and he lifts a hand in an echo of their parting gesture from the night before. But it all feels different now. Last night could have been weeks ago; yesterday, years.

She ducks her head, alarmed that Lucy might look over, then forces herself to edge around the last few stragglers lingering near the water fountain and slip into class without looking at Nick. Once inside, she sits stiffly in her seat. Sydney and Kate strut past to find their desks behind Ryan, but still, she stares purposefully at her notebook, suddenly intent on the numbers before her.

When Nick sits down just a few rows over, she can feel his eyes on her, but she presses her pencil hard against her paper, scratching out a meaningless equation and refusing to look up. Mr. Davis walks in a moment later, round-shouldered and shuffling, and Ryan sighs. She knows he'll assign a new project today—the last of the year—and it will almost certainly be about variables and integers, a ballet of numbers for which Ryan has no rhythm. Because the class has an odd number, Mr. Davis had—much to her embarrassment—added her as a third wheel to different groups throughout the year. Even Nick, who was new, had managed to partner with another late addition to the class last time, a scrawny kid who'd been out with mono since Christmas break.

She steals a look in Nick's direction, and sees that he's dangling his pencil between two of the fingers that poke out of his cast. It occurs now to Ryan that the cast is probably still white not because he doesn't know enough people to sign it, but because he's too cool for that sort of thing. Without the Cubs hat, his hair is just a little bit long and curls slightly at the back of his neck. Ryan can see the cap propped on the floor beside his backpack, and she feels a small jolt of happiness at the memory of yesterday's game, before reminding herself that it is only that: a memory.

While Mr. Davis begins outlining the terms of the project on the chalkboard, the room has begun to buzz in anticipation of pairing off. Still unable to look up, Ryan flushes a deep red. Worse than not having a partner, worse than not even having a *friend*, would be for Nick to realize all that. Yesterday had been a welcome pause to her life, a slice of time where Ryan was nothing more or nothing less than herself. And now, here in math class, she's back to being the odd man out.

"The point is to center this around a real-life application of the mathematics," Mr. Davis is saying, waving a piece of yellow chalk in the air. "I want you to show me how to put these numbers to work outside the classroom."

Ryan tenses, waiting for the frenzy of activity as fingers are pointed and partners are claimed. She stares at her notebook. She braces herself.

She waits.

"Hey," she hears, and she curls her fingers around the edge of her desk in a white-knuckled grip. She twists, just slightly, to see Nick leaning across the aisle. This is the first time she's allowed herself to meet his eyes, and she's unable to keep from grinning.

"Want to be partners?" Nick asks, and Ryan manages to nod. Mr. Davis wipes the chalk dust from his hands and then motions for them to get started, and all around them, chairs are scraped back as their classmates look to pair up.

But Ryan and Nick sit still, both smiling.

"I already have an idea," she says, realizing it's true as she says it. Nick scoots his chair closer in order to hear over the noise of the classroom. She can feel Sydney and Kate watching, but she suddenly doesn't care.

"Baseball?" Nick suggests, and Ryan grins.

Just like that, it's settled.

Chapter Five

THERE'S A NIGHT GAME ON—THE SECOND IN THE SERIES against the Cardinals—and so Ryan does her history homework on the floor of the family room, her eyes creeping from her notebook to the television despite her best efforts to pay attention. Emily's helping Mom make chocolate chip cookies in the kitchen, and although they're the kind that require virtually no skill or preparation, it's become an enormous undertaking, complete with matching aprons and oven mitts. Kevin's tucked away in what had once been her father's office, paying bills and flipping through golf catalogs.

Ryan's mind is far from World War I and the death of the Archduke. The Cubs are losing three to one in the sixth inning, and their second best pitcher was taken out with a jammed finger. She bends her head over her work, trying to concentrate on the maneuverings of the Balkan states, but she finds herself drifting toward another sort of history. During the commercials, she scratches out statistics in the corners of her notebook, her eyes darting up to the game when the voices of the announcers return. On the floor beside her, she's propped open a book of Cubs facts and is already transferring them onto the page.

She thinks ahead to tomorrow afternoon, when she and Nick have plans to start their project at his house after school. Already, she's looking forward to it, and even before she glances up at the television to see that the Cubs have tied the game with a two-run homer, Ryan is thinking there might still be hope for the season after all.

She'd arranged to meet Nick the next day at the bike rack after last period, but she's running typically late, hurrying down the hallway when she brushes by a group of sophomore girls. As they disappear around the corner, Ryan overhears one of them make a crack about being late for batting practice, and the group dissolves into laughter. She glances down at what she's wearing—a jersey shirt and a pair of jeans—and then straightens her shoulders and shoves open the door.

Ryan will be the first to admit she's not overly talented at anything in particular, but there's no doubt she's an all-star when it comes to feigning deafness.

Outside, Nick is leaning against the bike rack, examining his cast, and she's relieved to see his face split into a smile when he sees her.

"Sorry I'm late," she says, clumsily spinning the combination lock on her bike. She can feel his eyes on her, and her fingers refuse to cooperate. "I had to stay after to talk to Mr. Cronin."

"You're not doing well in English?"

Ryan grins sheepishly. "I'm not doing well in anything."

They wheel their bikes past where their classmates are waiting for their rides, a dozen or so groups arranged in small, distinct clusters, keeping their distance from one another as carefully as if contemplating warfare. Nick takes a few skipping steps and launches himself onto his bike in one motion, and Ryan hurries after him. She can see that Sydney and Kate are watching as she follows him out of the parking lot, past the gymnasium and the tennis courts, and around the bend toward his house. She's not sure whether to be nervous or pleased.

When they reach his house, her eyes are watery and her face stings. The breezes coming off the lake are frozen today, and her fingers are stiff with cold. Nick rides his bike all the way up the walkway to his front door and lets it clatter onto the grass, then watches with interest as she stops short and carefully props hers up on the driveway.

Inside, once her eyes adjust to the light, Ryan laughs, and then—horrified—claps a hand over her mouth.

"It's okay," Nick says. "I pretty much laugh every time I walk in too."

On each wall in the entryway, there are pictures of cows: landscape paintings, cubist portraits, photographs of Holsteins lined up in front of peeling red barns, and Guernseys looking out with big bovine eyes from beneath delicate lashes. On the table in the entryway, there's an assortment of glass cow sculptures and a ceramic dish where you can help yourself to a mint directly from the mouth of a dairy cow.

"They miss Wisconsin," Nick says, kicking off his shoes. "I guess I should at least be happy they're not obsessed with the Packers or something."

"Or cheese," Ryan says, still laughing.

"I don't know," he says. He grabs his math book and she follows him up the stairs. "I think cows might be worse."

Later, they sit with their notebooks spread out on the floor of Nick's bedroom, which is only slightly more baseball-oriented than Ryan's. She leans against his bed, her legs stretched out in front of her with the book of Cubs statistics open on her lap, and though they haven't yet gotten to their project, they've managed to spend an hour talking about RBIs and ERAs. This line of discussion has inevitably taken a detour from the realm of numbers, turning quickly into a debate about this year's team.

"I bet they'll win the division by at least five games," Ryan says.

"That's a pretty bold statement," Nick says. "The season just started."

"It's easier to hope at the beginning of the season."

He shrugs. "I'm more of a stats guy."

"Not me," Ryan says, holding up her math book with a grin. "I'm easily spooked by numbers."

"This coming from my math partner," Nick says, laughing.

"Well, that's the good thing about hope," she says. "It's perfectly unlogical."

"*Il*logical," he says with amusement. "It's perfectly illogical. And I think I'll stick with the numbers."

"So what're they telling you?"

"The stats?" he asks, folding his hands together. "That the wild card's a possibility, but we don't have a shot at winning the division."

"We'll see," Ryan says, arching an eyebrow. "Care to make it interesting?"

Nick shakes his head. "We want the same thing," he says. "Plus, how could you ever bet against the Cubs?"

"You couldn't," she admits. "Especially not while they're doing *this* well."

She twirls her pen and eyes the poster of Andre Dawson hanging over his desk. Below it, there's a miniature replica of Wrigley Field, and Ryan stands and walks over to it, tracing a finger along its edges. His desk is messy, covered in sports magazines and half-torn notebook pages, a flimsy-looking bowling trophy and a picture of him with his parents. She's suddenly very aware of where she is—standing in a boy's room, with the sun dimming outside the windows and his parents not yet home from work—and her hand trembles just slightly.

"Find anything interesting?" Nick teases, and she turns to where he's sitting on the carpet, his knees pulled up, his arms dangling in front of him. He tilts his head at her, and she notices that his hat is slightly crooked. She has a sudden urge to straighten it.

"So how come you moved here?" she asks, settling back down on the floor by the bed. "If your parents miss Wisconsin so much, how come you didn't just stay there?"

"My dad's job," he says, then quickly changes the subject. "So you really think we could win the division by five games?"

"If the Cubs win by five games," she says, the words escaping before she has a chance to stop them, "I promise to do my math homework for the rest of the year."

Nick looks at her sideways. "Huh?"

Ryan freezes, her arms pinned to her sides, her heart straining against her rib cage. She hadn't meant for that to happen. She hadn't meant to say the unsayable.

"Ryan?" Nick says, and she blinks at him, her mind elsewhere.

If the Cubs win, she thinks.

If only, she thinks.

She looks down at her lap and plays with a loose string on her shirt, running the thread between two fingers, trying not to cry. How could she have known it would be so easy, so shockingly uncomplicated, to be reminded of her dad in this way?

Nick is eyeing her as if she might crumble at any moment, and Ryan's aware that she very well might. She takes a deep breath.

"Hey," Nick says quietly, his words measured. "If you can arrange for the Cubs to win, *I'll* do your math homework for the rest of the year."

They're both silent until Nick begins to laugh, and Ryan realizes how tight her whole body had been. She relaxes and lets herself smile, too, somewhat embarrassed that she'd needed rescuing, but grateful that he'd been the one to do it.

Nick inches a bit closer and takes the book from her lap, glancing up at her every few pages as he flips through, checking to be sure she's okay. "Wouldn't it be cool to be general manager of a team?" he asks, and Ryan gets the distinct impression he's trying to buoy the conversation once more. "I mean, can you think of a better job?"

Ryan pulls her knees to her chest. "Is that what you want to be?"

"You mean when I grow up?" he asks with a faint smile. "Maybe." He ducks his head and takes his cap off, running a hand lazily through his hair. "What do you want to be?"

The truth is that Ryan has no idea where she's headed. Unlike other kids her age, she's always been reluctant to consider what the vast and terrifying future might hold for her. She's not like Sydney or Kate, with all their many plans, their schedules and preparations. Their logic is maddeningly simple: get an A in Pre-Algebra and you move up a level next year, which puts you on the fast track in math, which gets you into a good college, which turns into a good job, which means you'll have a good life. It's an equation in itself, with no room for incorrect solutions. There's only one way to move forward, and Ryan hasn't yet learned the right technique. Given the choice between future and past, she would always and without hesitation choose to move backward, and for years she has lingered through her life in this way, loitering and meandering, a wanderer with the most aimless of intentions.

But before she has a chance to answer him, there's a knock on the bedroom door, and Nick's mom—a small woman with large eyes, exactly the type inclined to collect dairy cow memorabilia—appears when it opens.

"I didn't mean to bother you two," she says quickly, and Ryan notices Nick shoot her a pleading look. "You must be Ryan," she says, her face brightening. "I'm Mrs. Crowley."

"It's nice to meet you," Ryan says politely. Mrs. Crowley stands for a moment with her hands clasped in front of her, holding a small pill case.

"Nick," she says, "I just wanted to make sure—"

Looking pained, he springs up and takes the case from her hands. "It's okay, Mom," he says quickly. "I've got it."

Towering over his mother now that he's on his feet, Nick puts a hand on her back and ushers her toward the door. "It's okay," he says again, and she nods, patting him on the arm and waving good-bye to Ryan as she leaves. Nick closes the door behind her, and then turns around, red-faced.

"They're just for my arm," he says, holding up his cast. He looks around the room, as if for a glass of water or perhaps an escape, and shuffles his feet. This is the first time Ryan has seen him the least bit ruffled, and he finally shrugs helplessly and laughs. "I just—"

"Hey," Ryan says, before he has a chance to go on. He looks up gratefully, waiting for her to continue, and she's pleased that in some small way, she can rescue him today too. "How about this?" she says. "If the Cubs win ninety-five games this season, I promise to do my math homework all *next* year too."

"That's a pretty steep bargain," he says, rattling the pills in his hand.

Ryan thinks of her dad, the way he used to lean forward in his seat during those rare and wonderful days at Wrigley when the wind blew just the right way and the flags pointed out toward the lake and the world aligned itself just so. *This is not a team to stake your life on,* he'd say. *But that's the only way to do anything that matters.*

Nick is watching her across the room, and Ryan is thinking, *if only.*

After a moment, when she still hasn't responded, he tries once again: "You drive a hard bargain."

"That's the only way to do it," she tells him.

Chapter Six

THE FOLLOWING WEEK, THE WEATHER TURNS UNCHAR-acteristically warm for mid-April, and during the lunch hour, everyone spills outside onto the huge lawn that borders the blacktop behind the school. Ryan spots Nick sitting with a handful of sophomore boys, most of them wolfing down their sandwiches to leave time to play basketball. Nick's face is tilted back to the sun, and Ryan can't help watching the scene with a sense of detached wonder. Beside him, Will O'Malley—the school's star basketball player—is tossing peanuts into the air and then catching them with his mouth, and a few other guys are mock fighting with fists raised and knees bent. Among them, Nick looks completely at ease, and Ryan even notices Lucy and her friends—Sydney and Kate included—casting meaningful glances at the small group on the lawn. Nick has only been at the school for a month, but through some mysterious mixture of friendliness and indifference, he seems to have already won over everyone who matters.

Ryan wanders over to the old swing set, which stands empty at the corner of the blacktop. She's only spoken to Nick a few times since working on the project at his house last week, always waiting for him to approach her first. When she's with him, it's easy. But when she watches from afar, across the hallway or the classroom or the lunchroom—she by herself, always by herself; and he with his new buddies—the idea that they might be friends seems a possibility too unlikely to consider.

Ryan never used to be so unsure of herself, but this is what the last year has done to her. This is how loneliness can change a person.

Now, she rocks slowly back and forth on the swing, circling the metal chain with one hand and using the other to unwrap her peanut butter sandwich. There's a note in the bag from her mother, the same one she sends every day—*Missing you till 3 P.M.*—and Ryan crumples it into a ball and sends it flying toward the metal garbage can. It hits the edge and bounces across the woodchips. Nick appears as if from nowhere, stooping to pick it up.

"Don't read it," Ryan says, swinging in small circles.

"Love letter?" Nick suggests, tossing it into the garbage and then walking over to the second swing. "Diary entry?"

Ryan makes a face at him. "Very funny."

She can't help wondering why, of all things, he'd choose to be here with her, sitting quietly on the peeling swing set, though she knows she'd never ask him. Whatever this is between them, this fragile new friendship of theirs, Ryan is reluctant to rattle it. There's a questionless ease to their time together, and she finds it amazing that she can feel so drawn to someone without knowing much about him beyond his favorite baseball players. But the way she sees it, there's plenty in life that's complicated already. She's more than happy to keep this off the list.

"So," Nick says, offering her a pretzel as he swivels around on the swing, his long legs planted in the wood chips. "What's with all the looks?"

Ryan freezes, worried that he might have noticed her watching him earlier. But before she has a chance to explain, he lifts his chin in the direction she'd most hoped he wouldn't, to where Sydney and Kate are gathered with the others beneath an oak tree.

"You're keeping an eye on them," he notes.

"So?" she asks, bristling.

"Former friends or future friends?"

"It has to be one or the other?"

Nick shrugs.

"Former, then," Ryan says, sighing.

He seems satisfied with this answer, licking the salt from his fingers once he's finished his pretzels. "I only asked because you sort of tiptoe around them."

"I don't really," she says much too quickly, then adds, "it's really only Lucy."

"The little blond one on a power trip?"

Ryan laughs. "That's her."

Across the lawn, the other girls are standing now, doing some sort of jokey dance, and most of the guys have drifted in their direction. Ryan sees Will O'Malley put his hand on Sydney's back and lead her around to the other side of the tree. The sound of their laughter carries clear across the blacktop, and Ryan takes a small bite of her sandwich and tries very hard not to listen.

"So," Nick says. "I have a new theory."

"Which is?"

"The Cubs are relying too much on their big hitters," he says, reaching up to flip his hat around so that it's now backward, a small tuft of hair sticking out of the gap in front. "They can't always depend on hitting the ball out of the park no matter what."

"No danger of that happening," Ryan says.

"Yeah, but that's why we lost the series against the Astros this week," Nick says with a little frown. "I think the key is to play small ball."

She raises her eyebrows. "Small ball?"

"Yeah," he says. "One hit at a time, one out at a time. So that you let each individual play build up to the next."

Ryan hears someone call Nick's name, and she looks over to where his friends are now scattered on the soccer field, tossing a baseball among them. She stares apologetically at her lap, suddenly worried she's keeping him from whatever else is out there: friends, laughter, games, all the things she's missing out on. But he just waves at them, unbothered, and then turns back to Ryan.

"You have to admit," he says, "it's a good theory."

"So if you were in charge . . ."

He sits up and grins. "Small ball," he says. "Small ball all the way."

"Okay," she says agreeably. "But I'm not so worried about strategy."

"Let me guess," Nick says mockingly, tapping his chin in thought. "You have a feeling?"

"I do," she says matter-of-factly. "I have a good feeling."

"Well, then," he says, tossing his lunch bag in the garbage can and pushing back on the swing. "Forget statistics and strategy, Ryan has a feeling!"

She begins swinging, too, pumping her legs until she's high as he is, and after a minute, they fall into the same rhythm. When she looks over, he's right there beside her, the sky behind him cloudy and close.

"Just wait and see," she says, her words whipped away by the wind.

On her way to biology, Ryan runs into Kate, who's hanging up posters for the spring dance with one of her new friends, a girl named May or June or something equally ridiculous. Ryan ducks her head and tries to hurry past, but Kate calls out to her, and so she backpedals reluctantly.

"Aren't you *so* excited for the dance?" Kate asks. "April and

I are going with Dylan and Heyward, and did you see that Will O'Malley just asked Sydney at lunch?"

Other than Will, Ryan has only the foggiest idea about who those boys are, and she shifts from foot to foot, more concerned about why Kate's bothering to talk to her than she is with April's date for the dance. "That's great," she offers.

Kate tacks another poster up on the wall. It's bright pink, with thick black letters that spell out the time and place. Ryan guesses that nearly every other student must be counting the days until the dance, but the truth is, she's barely even thought of it. She makes a move to walk away, knowing what their next question will be, but Kate puts a hand on her arm. Ryan stares at her, trying to find the face of her old friend beneath this new, horribly sweet smile.

"Do you think anyone will ask *you*?" Kate asks, and April giggles.

"I'm sure I won't go," Ryan mumbles, backing up.

"Why?" April asks, perfectly pleasant. "Because you'll have to wear a dress?"

Ryan chews on the side of her lip but says nothing.

"I saw you sitting with that new guy at lunch," Kate says, her tone purposefully casual as she turns to hang another poster. "That sophomore? Nick something?"

"We're doing our math project together."

Kate raises her eyebrows, and April lets out a sharp little laugh. Ryan's face is burning, but she takes a deep breath and remains silent.

"You *do* know . . ." Kate begins, but then pauses. "We're out of tape," she says to April. "Would you mind grabbing some?"

Looking somewhat annoyed, April disappears into a nearby classroom, and Kate takes a step closer to Ryan. "I just wanted to make sure you realized that Lucy sort of likes him," she says.

Ryan swallows hard. "We're only friends," she manages to say, even though she wants to ask *why?*, to say *no*, to throw her head back and yell *of course!* Because hadn't she known, on some level, that this might happen? Hadn't she learned that things like this only happen to girls like Lucy?

"Of course," Kate says, as if Ryan and Nick being anything more than just friends were a notion too ridiculous to consider. "I only wanted to make sure you knew."

"Thanks," Ryan says, forcing a smile.

Kate hands her a flier for the dance. "And here," she says. "In case you change your mind about going."

Ryan holds the pink piece of paper at arm's length, staring at the words. She nods to Kate, then backs away, eager to leave. But as soon as she turns the corner, she crumples up the flier and tosses it into the nearest garbage can, pleased to have at least made the shot this time.

Later, during math class, Nick leans across the aisle while Mr. Davis works out an equation on the board. Ryan tries to ignore him, aware of Sydney and Kate behind her, observing the interaction with keen interest. She can't help feeling terribly on display.

"Hey," Nick says, tapping his pencil on the side of his desk to get her attention. "Ryan."

She sighs, keeping one eye on the back of Mr. Davis's balding head. "What?"

"The project's due next week," he says, laughter behind his eyes.

Directly behind her, she can sense Sydney listening, and Kate is covering her mouth. Ryan lifts her hands to Nick. "So?"

"So, I don't think we can get a good read on the numbers from here."

Mr. Davis turns to look for a straightedge, fumbling around

on the desk while he continues his discourse on prime numbers. Ryan smiles at Nick, catching on.

"What'd you have in mind?" she whispers, knowing the Cubs have a home game this weekend against the Cincinnati Reds. Her mind is already springing ahead to the ride downtown and the crowd outside the stadium. She's suddenly far from the classroom, from the girls leaning forward on the desks behind her, from all the rumors and gossip and talk of school dances.

Nick winks at her. "I'm thinking we might need to do some fieldwork."

"I think you're right," she tells him, hiding a smile with her hand. Behind her, the girls begin to whisper, but Ryan doesn't notice. For her, it is already Saturday, and she is already miles away.

Chapter Seven

THEY GO FOR PIZZA BEFORE THE GAME AT A NARROW restaurant tucked beneath the Addison Street stop, the whole place shuddering with each train that goes by, a series of miniature earthquakes that cause the framed photos of former athletes and local celebrities to jiggle and dance on the wall. Nick stands ahead of her in line to order, and Ryan scans the menu, wondering whether they'll share a pizza or each get their own slice. This seems to be a decision of great significance, and she's relieved when Nick turns around to inquire as to her feelings about pepperoni.

"In general?" Ryan asks. "Or with respect to pizza?"

He grins. "Both."

"In general, I'm pretty ambivalent."

"But on pizza?"

"Definitely."

When it's their turn at the register, Nick orders for them both, and though Ryan pulls a few dollars from her pocket, he waves her away. She tries not to read too much into this gesture, but her cheeks go hot anyway.

They find an open table in the back that's sticky with soda and littered with used napkins, which Ryan relays to Nick, who tosses them into the garbage can. The restaurant is warm and dark, and seems an impossible distance from the crowded streets just outside. Nick sets the plastic number for their order on the table between them, then leans back and yawns. There's a small television set angled in one corner of the ceiling, tuned to a twenty-four-hour sports station. The commentator is recapping yesterday's ball games, and when the White Sox score flashes up on the screen, Nick makes a show of wrinkling his nose.

He leans forward with his elbows on the table and nods at Ryan. "So," he says, his face utterly serious. "Cubs or Sox?"

She frowns at him. "What kind of question is that?"

"A dumb one," he admits. "But I'm just warming up."

"To what?"

"Coke or Pepsi?"

"You had to warm up to *that*?"

"You can't start cold with this game," he tells her, shaking his head in mock disappointment at her ignorance of these sorts of things. "You have to throw a gimme in there to kick things off."

"Okay," she says, playing along. "Diet Coke, then."

"Interesting," he says, rubbing his chin.

"How's that?"

He shakes a finger at her. "I know your type, Walsh," he says. "Not much of a rule-follower, kind of a rebel."

"Well, I didn't like either of the options," she says. "Try me again."

"Black or blue?"

"A bruise?"

He narrows his eyes at her. "Very funny," he says, tapping the plastic number against the table and looking pleased with himself. "That was a trick question anyhow. To see if you're really a Cubs fan. If you'd said black"—and here, he runs a finger along his throat—"it would have been a red flag. White Sox colors."

Ryan rolls her eyes. "How come *you* never had to answer the first one?"

"Cubs," he says.

"No," she says with a laugh. "Coke or Pepsi?"

"Pepsi."

She points to the counter. "You just ordered a Coke."

"I'm trying to keep you on your toes," he says, wiggling his eyebrows. "I'm being unpredictable."

They both sit back as their pizza arrives, the cheese still bubbling so that each time they reach for it, they're forced to draw back, laughing. Ryan burns her mouth on a piece, then finishes off her glass of water.

"You don't seem that way," she says, eyeing Nick across the table. He folds a slice of pizza in half, then tilts his head sideways to take a bite.

"What way?" he asks around a mouthful of cheese.

"Unpredictable."

He lowers his pizza, and Ryan looks on absently as he busies himself unwrapping a straw. When he's torn off half of the paper wrapping, he brings the straw to his mouth and blows the other half across the table, where it hits Ryan squarely on the forehead.

"Bet you couldn't predict I'd do that," he says, grinning.

Ryan balls up her napkin underneath the table, then raises a hand to launch it at him. It glances off his shoulder, but he only smiles at her.

"That," he says, "I could have predicted."

"We should really try to get actual tickets sometime," Nick says later, as they make their way down Sheffield, past the rows of vendors. He hangs back every few steps to make sure she hasn't gotten lost, and Ryan elbows her way through the throngs of people to keep up.

"Definitely," she says, watching a father with three kids try to get chocolate ice cream off a brand-new Cubs jersey. "This summer for sure."

A four-man jazz band in blue top hats have set themselves up outside the back entrance to the stadium, and the brassy sound of their instruments rings out brightly in the cool spring air. Ryan gets squeezed back in the crowd by a couple with oversized blow-up bats, which they're thrusting in the air as they march toward the stadium as if about to wage battle with the Reds themselves. Ahead, she can see Nick scanning the crowd for her worriedly, and when he spots her, his face slackens with relief. Wordlessly, he reaches for her hand when she catches up, and she follows him, his grip heavy and certain, her hand folded into his.

They pass the knothole—a gated opening where people gather for an outside view of the field—but it's already thick with layers of people, and so they continue to walk around until they come to the spot where they'd sat on Opening Day. The first notes of the national anthem are already playing, and the motion outside the stadium slows until the song is over. A man selling Cubs pennants strolls by, and Nick raises a hand, then pulls out two crumpled bills and hands them over.

"Here," he says, handing her the flag, and Ryan stammers out a thank-you. She holds the thin wooden rod so tightly that she worries she might break it.

At the end of the third inning, Ryan offers to get them bags of peanuts, but Nick, shifting around on the curb, puts a hand on her arm.

"Wait a sec," he says, avoiding her eyes.

"Not a fan of peanuts?" she jokes, but he seems to have lost his usual composure, and only shrugs. It occurs to her that maybe he wants to ask her to the dance, but she tries to ignore the tiny flip of her stomach, reminding herself that things like that don't happen to her, and especially not with someone like Nick.

He opens and then closes his mouth. "I was just wondering," he begins, his words muddled. "If maybe, if you're not already . . ."

A peanut vendor passes through the crowd in front of them with the effortless ease of a salesman, tossing a giant blue bag from hand to hand and calling out the price. Nick hesitates, and then—looking somewhat relieved—stands up and flags him down.

"We'll take two," he says, and Ryan—realizing she'd been holding her breath—exhales. While Nick fishes a few dollars from his pocket, the vendor, a grizzled man with a reddish beard, hands her a bag of peanuts, then winks.

"This a date?" he asks, and without looking at Nick, Ryan quickly shakes her head, anxious to prove that she has no such expectations. She stares hard at the ground, and the vendor grins. "Sure looks like one to me."

When he leaves, they fall silent once more, concentrating on the stubborn peanut shells. After a few minutes, Ryan turns back to Nick.

"What were you going to say before?" she asks, but he only shrugs and claims he doesn't remember.

Sometime in the seventh inning, a group of visiting fans wanders over to their area. There are four of them, college kids with Cincinnati caps and brown paper bags, and their eyes are already rimmed with red, their faces heavy with alcohol and confidence. Their team is up by six, and their lips curl with this knowledge as they weave their way through the many Cubs fans that sit just outside the stadium, rooting hard, unwilling to give up on their team just yet.

They drop to the curb a few feet away from where Ryan and Nick sit pressed close to each other with a pile of peanut shells at their feet, and begin to cheer loudly for their team. There's a small radio propped in their midst, tuned to the national broadcast rather than the local one that every other radio is playing.

Nick jerks his head at them. "Typical Reds fans," he says, tossing a peanut shell in their general direction. "Assholes."

"Who cares?" Ryan says. "We've got more important things to worry about."

A few plays later, the Cubs leadoff man is up with two men on base, and they can hear the announcer on someone's radio proclaim that it's now or never for the Cubs to stage a comeback.

"So much for small ball," Ryan says.

The first two pitches are balls; the third, a swinging strike. Ryan's and Nick's eyes are on the stadium wall, but their ears are cocked toward the radio. A half beat later, they hear a loud cheer, and the commentators' voices go up several octaves as they yell— *It's going back, back!*—until the crowd outside the park gets to its feet to watch the ball sailing up and over the wall.

"It's right there," Ryan says breathlessly, and Nick jogs to the left, zigzagging along with the rest of the mob as they all try to gauge where the ball might meet the ground. He darts over near the Reds fans, his heavy cast swaying, his eyes to the sky. A moment later, the ball lands in the center of the pack, a scrambling pile of grown men and older boys pawing at the ground. Ryan stands on her tiptoes on the curb, craning her neck to spot Nick amid the flurry of fists and elbows.

The brawl widens out along the street, rings of red-faced souvenir hunters scraping at the ground in a tangle of limbs, shoving one another to get to the little white ball in the center of it all. Ryan backs away as a few people jump in to break it up, and a man backs out of the scuffle with a sharp yell, clapping a hand over his eye and limping off. When the rest of the crowd begins to disperse, she sees a guy in a jersey emerge with the ball. Bruised and grinning, he dusts himself off, then trots over to his buddies to display his prize, and when Ryan looks back over, she sees Nick holding one of the Reds fans in a headlock with his one good arm.

"Hey," she yells, running over to where a new sort of crowd has arranged itself around them, a few boys excitedly chanting *fight!* around its edges. Ryan pushes through the gathering of eager spectators, her eyes widening at the scene before her. The three other Reds fans are staring menacingly, unsure what to do, and the guy Nick has pinned to the ground glances at them with wild eyes, his teeth bared.

"Get him the hell off me!" he shouts, and his friends look to one another.

"You want us to hit a kid with a broken arm?" one says.

Ryan stands frozen, staring at Nick's face. His eyes are focused and stony, and he's trembling with a kind of fury Ryan hasn't before seen in him, as if it comes from somewhere deep inside, all the way down in his bones. His eyes are on the guy, his arm tight around his neck, but whatever is boiling up inside him has given him a faraway look, like an anger without end. Ryan takes a small step toward him.

"Nick?" she says. Out of the corner of her eye, she can see some kids motioning to the two police officers posted near one of the gates, and she lays a hand on his arm. "Nick," she says again, more urgently, and she feels his muscle relax. "Let go."

He blinks at her, and his face changes. When he releases his grip, the guy in the Reds hat coughs and spits, then gets to his feet. The crowd has begun to pull back now that the show has ended, and the guy rubs at his neck, at a loss for words. He spits once more, and it lands near Nick's foot, but then he turns and walks off with his friends, shaking his head and grumbling under his breath. Ryan grabs Nick's arm and pulls him away before the police officers can pick him out of the crowd, and they're all the way to the 'L' stop before he says anything.

"I'm sorry," he mutters, not sounding at all sorry. "That guy pummeled me in there. It was a cheap shot . . ."

He trails off, and she looks at him sideways. He's still breathing jaggedly, but there's something sorrowful in his eyes now, and Ryan's suddenly sorry not to know him better, not to be able to understand the way he ticks, what awful reasons or frightened impulses might have caused him to fight like that, as if out of sheer panic, as if for his life.

"What're you so angry about?" she asks, almost to herself, as they sit down together on a bench. Nick doesn't say anything; he just leans forward to peer down the empty track, his mouth set and his eyes lowered as they sit waiting for the train that will take them home.

Chapter Eight

THE NEXT DAY IS EMILY'S NINTH BIRTHDAY, AND RYAN has been drafted to help out with her party at the local bowling alley. She and Kevin carry the balloons from the car, while inside, Mom spreads a plastic tablecloth out onto the card tables in the party room and lines up the goody bags.

"How's that math project going?" Kevin asks as he struggles to wrangle the helium-filled balloons from the back seat. Ryan stands a few feet away, playing with the edges of her fleece jacket. When she doesn't answer, Kevin hands her a bunch of balloons and pushes at his glasses. "We can still get you a tutor, you know."

"I'll be fine," she says with a sigh big enough to leave no question of her annoyance at the conversation. She tucks a wrapped gift under her arm and heads inside.

Discussions about math and grades—anything of importance, really—are supposed to be Mom's territory. It's not that Ryan has a problem with Kevin, who's been unfailingly nice to her since he joined their family. But though Mom loves him, and Emily adores him, to Ryan, he'll never be more than a stand-in, an actor struggling with the part of her dad. When he'd first moved in after the wedding, Ryan made a point of offering him her usual seat at the dinner table. Mom's eyes watered at the significance of the gesture—how kindly her daughter had welcomed her new husband into their home—but the truth is, Ryan only did it out of selfishness.

She didn't think she could bear seeing him sit in her dad's old spot.

At three, the kids begin showing up for the party, twelve third graders who sprint between lanes and climb over the scoring machines and giggle at Kevin's attempts to show them the right way to roll the ball. Emily asks Ryan if she wants to be on a team, and when she says she'd prefer to just watch, Emily frowns.

"Why didn't you invite a friend?" she says. "Mom said you could."

"It's not *my* birthday," Ryan snaps. "Go play."

She wanders back to where Mom is counting out the tiny wax candles. Her growing stomach has just recently started to show, and Ryan watches with fascination as she moves around the tables, straightening plates and smoothing out napkins. Despite all the chaos of the party, she looks relatively peaceful, and it occurs to Ryan that maybe she's imagining future birthday parties for the new baby growing inside her.

"Mom," Ryan says, and her mother pauses, candles in hand, and smiles. "Do you need any help?"

She scans the room. "I think we're okay," she says. "I'll go back out with you."

Kevin is monitoring the kids, pacing back and forth to make sure nobody drops a ball on any toes or goes sliding up the greased lanes. Emily has just managed to down six pins, her ball zigzagging off the bumpers at least a dozen times as if that were the point of the game. She jumps up and down and raises her fists in the air. Ryan and Mom sit down just behind the scoring area.

The bowling alley is crowded for a beautiful Saturday afternoon, and Ryan longs to switch the channel on the TV set in the bar to the Cubs game, but Kevin has already beaten her to it, and so the Masters is on instead. Ryan crosses her arms, left to wonder if her team is winning or—more likely—losing.

At the counter behind her, she's surprised to recognize Sydney's voice requesting a pair of bowling shoes. Dismayed, Ryan twists around and sees that she's here with Will, the basketball player. She's relieved to discover that none of the others seem to have come along, but this doesn't stop her from sinking a bit lower in her seat.

Mom pokes her arm. "What are you doing?"

Ryan groans.

It takes only a minute for Sydney to spot them. "Hi, Mrs. Graham," she calls out, waving, and as much as she hates the sound of Kevin's last name used to address her mom, Ryan hates it that much more coming from Sydney. She sits up in her seat and smiles weakly.

"Sydney," Mom says, getting up to give her a hug. "I haven't seen you in ages!"

Her mom knows little about what happened between them, other than that they no longer spend any time together, though Ryan suspects she must be able to guess who was left behind by whom. It isn't terribly hard to figure out.

"Ryan," Sydney says, smiling hugely. "You know Will, right?"

Will lifts a hand, his face unchanged. Ryan manages a feeble hello.

"How's everything with you?" Mom asks Sydney. Ryan finds this completely humiliating, standing here with her mother, talking to her ex-best friend as if nothing has changed. She looks toward Emily and Kevin, wishing she could take Mom by the sleeve and drag her away.

"Everything's great," Sydney says, positively beaming. "Except it's been so busy that Ryan and I haven't gotten to see much of each other lately."

Ryan resists the urge to roll her eyes. Mom's nodding hard,

probably sympathizing with Sydney's busy schedule. Will looks anxious to get away from the conversation, his eyes roaming the room.

"Plus Ryan's always with that cute new guy," Sydney says, winking at Ryan as if they share some great secret. "They're practically inseparable."

Mom raises her eyebrows. "Really?"

"Just the guy I'm doing my math project with," she says quickly, and Sydney pats her on the arm condescendingly. Ryan feels like she's about six years old. She smiles politely at them, then looks to her mom. "We should get back."

Sydney loops her arm through Will's. "What a cute party," she says. "Hope you guys have fun. It was great to see you, Mrs. Graham."

As they walk away, Ryan steering them fast toward the bumper lanes, Mom looks at her with interest. "So who's this boy, anyway?"

"Just a guy," she says, shaking her head.

Unsatisfied, Mom presses for more information. "What's his name?" she asks. "Is he cute? Is he nice? What's he like?"

Ryan shrugs. "I don't really know him that well."

There's only one conversation taking place at school the following week. Nobody's talking about math tests or biology experiments. Nobody's even interested in discussing the weekend's winning football game. There's little interest in the state of the world or global affairs. The collective mind of the school is, for the moment, on one track. And the topic drifting through the hallways is singularly focused on the upcoming spring dance.

This, as it happens, is the one thing Ryan isn't in the mood to talk about.

Nick hasn't said a word about it since chickening out at the game, and so, as the committees meet and the posters seem to multiply in the halls, Ryan chooses to pretend the whole thing isn't happening—though what had been effortless only weeks ago is now more difficult. She's having trouble admitting to herself just how much she wishes Nick would ask her.

At lunch on Monday, he finds her sitting alone on a bench outside.

"Want to come over tonight to finish the project?" he asks, joining her.

Ryan lowers her sandwich. "Aren't we pretty much done?"

"Yeah, I guess," Nick says, adjusting his cap, and Ryan immediately regrets having said anything. Other girls would have seen this as an opportunity to spend more time together, but somehow, Ryan always manages to figure these things out a beat too late. Now, they'd probably finish up the project at lunch one day, adding the final touches over peanut butter sandwiches beneath the watchful gaze of the entire cafeteria. And once they finished, that would be it. No more math project, no more Cubs games, no more lunches together.

"Hey," Nick says, watching her carefully. "You okay?"

"Fine," she says with a little nod.

Ryan realizes that now would be the time to say something about what had happened at the game the other day, but it's not an easy subject to broach. After the fight, Nick had been sullen and quiet, staring out the window of the train and grunting in response to her questions. After a while, she'd given up and inched away, watching the flickering lights of the train car cast shadows across the floor. A part of her can't help feeling that something had been lost that day. Where before she thought they understood each other perfectly, Ryan now gets the sense that there are too many stories they each guard too closely.

They sit for a few minutes in companionable silence, side by side on the bench, their backs to the rest of the world: the soccer field and the lawn, their classmates in all their various activities. A few crows pick at the remains of someone's sandwich, and a squirrel circles a nearby garbage can appraisingly.

"Listen," Nick says, tossing a piece of his bread crust on the ground at their feet. "I've been meaning to ask you . . ."

Ryan feels her face flush, unable to look at him as she waits. But a new voice breaks the quiet between them, a sharp intrusion from the forgotten motion of the lunch hour behind them. She hears Lucy before turning around to see her standing above them, Sydney at her side.

"Hey there," Lucy says. She punches Nick's shoulder playfully, and winks—actually winks!—at him. "What're you doing all the way over here when there's a basketball game going on?"

Nick cranes his neck to where the other sophomore guys have started their daily pickup game. "I'm not much of a basketball player," he says, holding up his cast.

Lucy rocks back on her heels. "Well," she says, letting her gaze fall on Ryan. "We're always under the tree over there if you want to hang out once they start playing."

"Thanks," Nick says with a polite smile. "Good to know."

Sydney opens her bag and rummages through intently, searching for something Ryan's sure isn't there. She's not particularly hard to read: she's nervous near Lucy and wary of her interactions with Ryan, and because of all this, she needs something to do with her hands. When she catches Ryan watching, she zips the bag, then crosses her arms and looks to Lucy.

Lunch is nearly over, and people are already beginning to shuffle inside. The squirrel disappears behind the garbage can, and Ryan flings the rest of her sandwich in its general direction. Without looking at her once, Lucy steps back toward the school and waves to Nick. "You're welcome anytime," she says, falling into step with Kate and April, who stroll by just then as if the timing had been choreographed. Sydney hurries after them, and Ryan bites her lip.

"That was nice of her," Nick says, leaning back on the bench.

Ryan, unsure whether he's being serious, can't resist chiming in. "Yeah," she says. "She's known for that, actually."

Nick laughs. "Being nice?"

"The nicest," Ryan says. "You probably wouldn't know, being new and all. But Lucy Barrett is practically a saint."

"Ah," he says. "Good thing I have you around to fill me in."

The lawn is almost empty now, and Nick tosses his lunch bag in the garbage, then stands waiting for Ryan to collect her stuff. They walk back inside without talking, and Ryan wishes he'd finish the question he'd started to ask earlier. At the door to her biology class, they pause.

"So we'll add the finishing touches to the project tomorrow then?" he asks.

"Sure," she says, tripping on her shoelace as she tries back-pedaling to the safety of the dark classroom. "Tomorrow's fine."

"We'll give the team a chance to up their stats a little bit at tonight's game," he says with a laugh, then walks off to his next class. Ryan stands at the door for a moment, then turns to find her seat in the classroom. The teacher is late getting some slides together, and so she sits very still at her desk, holding her breath against the antiseptic smell of the dissection tables. A moment later, Sydney slips into class unnoticed, scrambling into the seat just across the aisle from Ryan.

"Hey," she whispers, as the teacher begins pointing out the different organs of a frog. "You must have good taste."

Ryan raises her eyebrows.

"Lucy *never* asks guys to dances," Sydney whispers, her voice tinged with giddiness. "I mean, every guy always wants to ask *her.*"

"Good for her," Ryan mutters, turning back to the front of the classroom.

Sydney continues, unfazed. "You might be interested to know that we just ran into your buddy, Nick," she says. "And Lucy asked him to go with her."

Ryan looks up sharply, her mouth falling open.

"That's what I thought you might say," Sydney says with a little laugh.

The teacher dims the lights in the room to show a slide of a frog's intestine, and Ryan is grateful that nobody—especially Sydney—can see her face, which she's sure must be giving her away. She rests her forehead in her hand, pretending to study her notes, and after a moment, Sydney loses interest and turns back to her own papers. When the lights go back on, Ryan rubs her eyes and takes a deep breath.

Once class is over, she waits for everyone else to trickle out the door before pushing back her chair. She's so concentrated on trying to keep herself from crumbling, right here among the dead frogs and the petrified wood, that she doesn't notice the boy who is waiting—the one who wears Hawaiian shirts every day and controls the lighting for school plays and is at least two years older than anyone else in the class—until he is standing right in front of her.

"Hi, Ryan," he says, tugging at his flowered shirt.

"Hi," she says wearily, having forgotten his name.

The next words, she knows, are inevitable. "I was wondering if you'd want to go to the dance with me," he says, then wipes the sweat from his upper lip as he waits for her answer.

Ryan—who has zero interest in going to the dance at all anymore—presses two fingers to her forehead. The clock on the wall lunges forward, the sound loud in the empty classroom. The boy shifts from one bulky leg to the other, waiting.

"Sure," Ryan says, utterly miserable. She tries to keep the hollowness out of her voice, forcing herself to smile. "That sounds great."

Chapter Nine

THE NIGHT OF THE DANCE, RYAN SITS PERCHED ON the toilet seat while Mom helps her curl the ends of her hair. She's still wearing pajamas and trying hard not to think about the evening ahead of her, which will begin in just a half hour when Robert—the junior in her freshman biology class—is set to pick her up. Emily's balancing on the bathroom counter near the sink, carefully observing what's happening with Ryan's hair.

"I wish I could go too," she says.

"Want to take my place?" Ryan offers, and Mom shoots her a look in the mirror, then turns to Emily.

"You'll go someday," she says, switching off the curling iron. She bends down to kiss Ryan on the cheek. "Tonight is Ryan's night, though."

After she changes into a simple pink sundress with a white ribbon around the waist, Mom and Emily clap their hands, and Ryan eyes herself in the mirror. Despite what others might think, she doesn't mind wearing dresses, and tonight, especially, she knows she looks pretty. For a moment, she's pleased at the thought that Nick will see her too, but then she remembers who he's going with and feels deflated once again. There's no competing with someone like Lucy Barrett.

Since the day she found out Lucy had asked him, Ryan has been avoiding Nick. It wasn't something she planned, but when she'd first seen him in the hallway before math class that same day, he'd been awkward and stammering, and rather than wait around to hear what she already knew, Ryan told him she'd forgotten something in her locker, and then made her escape.

And so it had gone for the past few weeks.

They'd finished their math project at the end of class one day, scribbling down the last few additions to their findings, then hastily binding the whole thing together. Ryan saw that he'd printed a cover with the Cubs logo on it, and sitting there beside him in the empty classroom, she felt suddenly like crying.

"Not bad," he said, admiring their work with a rueful grin.

Ryan nodded, but then scraped back her chair before he could say more. "I have to get going," she told him. "I'll see you later."

During lunch, she often noticed him heading in her direction, but Lucy and her friends began intercepting him on his walk over, and so Ryan started spending the period on the floor beside her locker as she had in the past—a far better option, it seemed, than having to watch Nick get drawn into the frightening whirlpool that had so far claimed every good friend Ryan ever had.

She glances at her watch now, then slips on her shoes. Downstairs, Kevin insists on taking pictures, and so Ryan waits patiently until he's gotten enough, then hovers in the kitchen until she sees the headlights from Robert's car graze the windows. Mom gives her a hug, and Ryan waits for the doorbell to ring.

"Mom," Ryan begins, turning around.

"*Yes*," Mom says before she has a chance to finish. "You have to go."

Robert smiles when she opens the door, and though his suit looks a size too small, she's relieved to see that at least he's not wearing a Hawaiian shirt. "Wow," he says, handing her a small white flower. "You look great."

"Thanks," she says, then forces herself to add, "You too."

Robert opens the door of his parents' car for her, and they spend the short ride to the school in silence, except for the sharp sounds of the radio as he searches for a station. When they pull up to the gym, Ryan gets out of the car and stands staring at the hordes of her classmates funneling inside, a sea of familiar faces in unfamiliar attire, all sparkles and ribbons, flowers and silk. Robert offers his hand, and Ryan pretends not to have noticed as they walk to the door, a small distance apart from each other.

Inside, the gym is decorated like a jungle—this year's theme for the dance—and they make their way toward the punch bowl, moving past a cellophane waterfall and a wall plastered with green-construction-paper trees. There's a disco ball on the ceiling that makes Ryan feel silly somehow, the flecks of light passing over them dizzily. She hides her face in a cup of punch.

"I'm not much of a dancer," Robert apologizes.

"Me neither," Ryan says, relieved.

Across the gym, she spots Lucy and Nick, and something inside of her grows heavy at the sight. Nick had gotten his cast off the week before, and his hair is neat and combed. His face looks pale against his suit. Lucy's wearing a strapless red dress with her hair drawn up from her face, and could easily pass for a college student. Ryan suddenly feels about eight in her sundress.

She watches as Lucy grabs Nick's hand and pulls him toward the photo area, where she motions for him to bend down to tell him something while they wait. Ryan turns back to Robert, who's telling her about a joke the tech guys once played on the drama teacher.

"That's funny," she says, doing her best to sound convincing.

Robert shrugs modestly. "We thought so."

When Nick and Lucy have finished taking their photos,

Ryan can see Sydney and Kate trying to gather up the rest of their friends for a group shot. They walk by, leaning in close to whisper once they've passed Ryan. She ignores them, glancing over to the punch bowl where she spots Nick. A few random guys grin and slap him on the shoulder as they walk by, no doubt congratulating him on his date.

Ryan feels Robert's hand on her back, and she sidesteps away, pretending to have dropped something from her purse. She crouches on the gym floor, making a show of feeling along the ground, and when enough time has passed, she stands up again. They've been joined by two of his friends from the tech group, dressed in all black, dateless, and in charge of the lighting for the evening.

"Do you mind if we borrow your date?" one of them asks, a short kid with a mop of reddish hair, and Ryan is momentarily terrified that they're talking about her. But then she realizes there's a problem with the blue lights on the fake waterfall.

She pats Robert on the arm. "Go save the rain forest."

There's a lull in the music, and Ryan presses her back against the cinderblock wall of the gym, kicking at a fallen piece of cellophane with the toe of her shoe. When she looks up again, Nick is standing a few feet away, looking quite suddenly shy.

"You look nice," he says, his hands shoved in his pockets.

It takes her a moment to find her voice. "You too."

He sweeps his eyes around the gym, then takes a few steps toward her. "Listen, Ryan," he says, but she stops him.

"Could we not talk about Lucy?"

He bobs his head. "Sure," he says. "Of course."

"Okay, then," she says.

He nods. "Okay, then."

They stand shoulder-to-shoulder against the wall, half-hidden by a cardboard elephant, watching their classmates across the dance floor. Ryan finds herself wishing Robert would never come back, that Lucy might never find them. She'd like nothing more than to stand here for the rest of the night.

"Do you think maybe we should dance?" Nick asks without looking at her.

Ryan widens her eyes at him. "What about your date?"

"What about yours?" he teases her.

He sticks out his hand, and she takes it, following him out to the crowded dance floor. She can't help looking around to see who might be watching, but once there, the song changes to something slower, and Ryan forgets about everything else but her hand inside of his. They're unsure of themselves, bumped by couples moving to the slow beat of the music, but then Nick circles his arms around her, and they sway stiffly until they find an uncertain rhythm. The back of his neck is warm where Ryan's hands are knotted together, and she can feel his breath on her shoulder.

She opens her mouth, trying to think of something to say, but the music is too loud anyway, so she just leans against him, resting her chin on his shoulder as they move. They turn small circles in the darkened gymnasium, their feet sliding across the wooden floor, and Ryan lets her eyes flutter shut. Here together, clinging to him in the darkened gymnasium, Ryan gets the feeling she doesn't ever need to know him more than this, his hands on her back, her head on his shoulder.

When the song ends, they disentangle themselves, and she realizes he's still holding her hand. Another song comes on, something faster. A few boys begin jumping straight up and down, and soon others join in until the whole building seems to be bobbing, the floor creaking beneath them.

Ryan looks around the sticky gym and the sweaty dance floor, suddenly desperate to be anywhere but here. She scans the crowd for Lucy or Robert, and when she doesn't see either one, she turns to Nick. "Want to get away from the music for a minute?" she yells over the noise, and he nods, leading her past the DJ booth and the small group of chaperones out toward the hallway. She notices Robert sitting around the re-lit waterfall with the tech guys, and she's happy to see that he also looks like he's having more fun now that they've lost each other.

Once outside of the gym, their ears are still ringing, and when Nick leans in to say something, it sounds muffled and muted. "What?" she shouts.

"I said," he says, laughing, "let's go outside."

There are a few couples sneaking cigarettes out behind the school, and Ryan and Nick see Mr. Davis fulfilling his chaperoning duties by shooing them back inside. They duck around the corner, Ryan's heels sinking into the soft grass of the playing fields. The night is beautiful, more summer than spring, and the air feels soft against her bare legs.

"You know what we could do?" Nick says, adjusting his hand on hers.

"Stay out here all night?" Ryan suggests. Now that they're outside, the thought of returning to the stuffiness of the dance—the rising noise still throbbing faintly in her ears and the probing eyes of their classmates—is wholly unappealing.

"Or we could go back to my house," Nick says.

Ryan looks up at him sharply. "What about Lucy?"

He laughs. "What about Robert?"

"Not funny," she says.

"It's a little funny."

Ryan looks toward the entrance to the gym. Lucy must be furious by now. She's not the type of girl who gets left behind by her date, and Ryan hates to think of just how much more miserable she could make their lives if Nick doesn't reappear by her side in the next few minutes. But standing here beside him, her fingers entwined with his, she's having a hard time caring.

"The Cubs are on the West Coast tonight, so the game's just starting," Nick says. "We could go hang out in my basement and watch it."

Ryan lets go of his hand, trying not to look disappointed. Maybe this is all he wants, she thinks: someone to talk shop with him, to debate over lineups and argue about strategy. She looks down, playing with the ribbon on her dress.

"We'd probably have more fun on our own," he says, and Ryan feels somewhat better. "Unless you don't want to leave. . . ."

"No," she says after a moment. "That sounds nice."

Nick's house is just two blocks away, and they cut across the soccer fields behind the school, the grass already wet with dew. She stops at one point to slip off her shoes, and when she straightens, one finger hooked around the straps of her sandals, Nick is standing just beside her, watching.

"What?" she asks, but he only smiles and ducks his head.

"Nothing," he says.

At his house, he puts a finger to his lips because his parents are already in bed. They make their way downstairs to the base-ment quietly, Ryan first, Nick's hand on her waist, and once there, they collapse onto the couch. Nick passes her the phone, and she calls her mom to say she's going to a party after the dance, that she'll sleep over at one of the girls' houses, so she won't need a ride home.

Tomorrow morning, they'll wake up early and Nick will walk her the three blocks back to her house before anyone is up. They'll stand on her lawn in the first hours of light and things will be different. They will already be going over the night's events in their minds, worrying over what might have changed, what the summer might bring.

But tonight they are happy to be in the cool of Nick's basement, lying under a blanket in front of the TV as the Cubs take the lead against the Dodgers. Her head is on his chest, his arm hooked around her shoulders. Tomorrow, her dress will be wrinkled and the curls will have come loose from her hair. But tonight, she presses herself closer to him beneath the blanket, and they fall asleep together in this way, drifting off long before the game comes to an end.

Chapter Ten

O N THE LAST DAY OF SCHOOL, RYAN TIPTOES around the breakfast table in the kitchen, wary of the array of jams and jellies that all pose potential danger to the white tablecloth laid out for the occasion. She's the first one downstairs, and so she sits alone at the table, resting her chin in her hand. It's also Emily's last day of third grade, and Mom is upstairs curling her hair the way she'd done Ryan's for the dance just the week before.

Ryan was fairly old before she realized that not every family makes such a big deal out of the last day of school. But it had become a Walsh family tradition, spurred on by Dad, the great proponent of commemorations and celebrations on even the smallest of occasions. On her last day of first grade, they'd had a picnic in the backyard. After second grade, it had been a trip to the batting cages. In years past, there had been field trips of all kinds: the red trolleys in the city, a sailboat ride out on the lake, even an afternoon at a strawberry patch, where they'd eaten more than they picked, their mouths turning red from the berries.

The year he died, on the day Ryan's fourth-grade class had let out for the summer, she'd arrived home to find Mom preparing homemade ice cream sundaes. As they filled little bowls with sprinkles and chocolate chips, Ryan asked why he'd made such a big deal of the day, when he'd always hated endings so much.

"He didn't see it as an ending," Mom told her. "It was the beginning of summer, his favorite season. That was always reason enough for a celebration, I guess."

This morning, Ryan surveys the table, relieved that summer has finally arrived. There's nothing in her that's sad to leave freshman year behind. Even before this mostly miserable year, she'd never felt a drive to preserve these sorts of memories, all the things her classmates write about in their yearbooks. She knows enough to hope that these aren't the best days of her life, just a middle ground, a fleeting phase between the years with her father and the years ahead. She'd always had the feeling she was just passing through—though to what, she isn't yet sure.

If her dad were here this morning, he'd have made her wait to get dressed until after breakfast. "I'm going to put enough syrup on these pancakes that you can depend on coming out of this sticky," he'd have said. He would have whistled on the drive over to school, said something corny about how fast she was growing up. He'd have met her afterward with an enormous grin, trying not to give away whatever surprise he had waiting, whatever he might have come up with to properly observe the day, the start of a new season.

Ryan swallows hard, blinking back tears. She looks at the table, and her eyes fall on an envelope sitting above her plate, half-hidden by a pitcher of orange juice. She reaches around and picks it up, turning it over in her hands. Her name is written across the front in her mom's handwriting, and when she nudges open the flap, she sees the tops of two Cubs tickets peeking out.

Before she leaps up and shouts, before she runs up the stairs and hurtles into her mother's arms to thank her, before she lets herself look forward to the game itself, she sits very still, alone at the kitchen table, and bows her head. She doesn't wish that Dad were here to go to the game with her, and she doesn't wish the day had turned out differently. What sense is there in wishing for the impossible? But she does, for the briefest of moments, allow herself to imagine that the tickets had been his to give. That sitting here on the last day of this awful year, her dad might have been the one to leave such a gift. And when she closes her eyes, she can almost believe that he has.

After the last class lets out, everyone lingers amid the explosion of locker doors. Ryan tiptoes through the torn notebook pages and empty binders that litter the hallway, keeping an eye out for Nick. She sees Sydney and Kate posing together for a picture and dodges past, hoping they haven't seen her. In the week since the dance, neither has so much as said one word to her. Ryan senses a tiny bit of sympathy in their looks, which makes her all the more unsettled. Each time she's run into Lucy, the girl's mouth curls into a small smile, and Ryan can't seem to hurry away fast enough. She suspects the last day of school doesn't at all mean the last of Lucy, and she hates to think of when they might next cross paths.

Around the corner, Ryan spots Nick shaking hands with one of their teachers, who smiles at him in a way no teacher will ever smile at Ryan. Once she leaves, Nick puts his hands in his pockets and rocks back on his heels.

"Hey," she calls out, and he gives her a lopsided grin.

"Hey, yourself."

Ryan adjusts her backpack and scans the hallway before approaching him. "Listen," she says. "My mom gave me two tickets as sort of a last-day-of-school gift."

He folds his arms across his chest. "Tickets to what?"

"What else?"

His face brightens, just briefly, before he seems to readjust with some amount of effort. "When is it?"

"In a couple of weeks," she tells him. "It's against the Pirates."

"I can't," he says, flicking his eyes away. "But thanks for thinking of me."

The hallway is nearly empty now. Everyone has spilled out onto the front steps or the lawn or the parking lot, where they're huddled together making plans for the afternoon and the summer beyond it. Nick shuffles his feet and studies the floor.

"Why not?" Ryan demands.

"My summer's going to be kind of hectic, I think."

She grins conspiratorially. "Too hectic for the Cubs?"

They hear the soft slap of sandals down the hall, and both look up to see Lucy. She leans over to take a sip from the water fountain, then glances over at them. Even from a distance, Ryan can see her raise her eyebrows before she spins around to march back outside. Nick stares at the place she'd been standing even once she's gone, and when he turns back to Ryan, he seems almost surprised to find her still there.

"My family's going up to Wisconsin for most of July," he explains.

"The game's at the end of June."

"I just don't think I can go," he mumbles, and when she doesn't say anything, he finally meets her eye. "Look, Ryan—"

"No, it's fine," she says, shaking her head. "I'm sure someone else—"

He puts a hand on her shoulder to stop her. "I'm really sorry," he says, and she can see that he is, though for what, she isn't entirely certain. It feels like they're talking about more than just the game, and Ryan tries to hide her confusion as all her hopes for the summer, all the plans and possibilities, begin falling away.

Nick seems about to say something more, but instead leans down to kiss her on the cheek. "I'll see you," he says, though it feels less like a promise than an excuse.

He's halfway down the hall when he turns to wave at her.

Ryan lifts her shoulders in response, left alone in the empty hallway to watch this strangest of escapes, this most puzzling of disappearing acts.

Twelve days into it, Ryan's summer has assumed an alarmingly depressing shape, each unhurried day opening into the next like rooms in a railroad apartment. In the mornings, Kevin drops Emily off at camp on his way to the office, and Mom leaves for the real estate agency where she still works part-time, while upstairs, Ryan shoves her head under her pillow to ward off the light. Once she manages to get out of bed, the balance of the day is spent trying to appear busy, something that has itself become nearly a full-time occupation.

The main audience for this—her always hectic, though never eventful one-man show—is her mother, who would surely find cause for concern if she knew how completely and utterly bored her daughter is fast becoming. Ryan's too old for camp, but too young for most jobs, and she'd passed on every activity her mom had wanted to sign her up for—first, because she'd hoped her friends might come around, and later, because she'd been counting on hanging out with Nick. All her classmates will be whittling away their summers at the nearby beach, while Ryan—friendless and alone—is left to fend off Mom's latest idea of summer school.

And so her days are spent flipping through newspapers with a look of utmost concentration, walking purposefully around the neighborhood, studying the flowers in their backyard garden as if there were nothing more important than the well-being of the petunias. She's become a master loafer, a brilliant loiterer, a rambler of the first order. She spends so much time working to convince others of how busy she is, that occasionally, she manages to fool even herself.

But not often.

Since the last day of school, Ryan has left two messages with Nick's mom and a third on his answering machine, and this isn't counting the half dozen times she's hung up after letting it ring. A few days ago, she'd mustered up the nerve to walk over, crossing the streets with her head down, dodging stray baseballs and scooters as the neighborhood busied itself around her so effortlessly. Standing in front of his house, she leaned with one hand on the cow-shaped mailbox and kicked at the curb, angry with herself, and with him, too, for ruining whatever it was they'd had. It wasn't the dance she regretted, and it wasn't just being with him that she missed. It was something bigger than that. It was something far more important.

Ryan is tough. She's survived this type of thing before. But this hurts in a way the past year hadn't. Being ignored by her girlfriends was a matter of gossip. Being left behind by Nick feels like being cut loose. It's like drowning, but not quite. Like throwing a stone, letting it skip out in wide arcs, seeing it shiver across a lake, like magic, like glass, and then watching it sink.

She's waited until today—the day before the game—to think about the second ticket, hoping that in the span of these two endless weeks, Nick might resurface. Whatever had happened between them—and truthfully, Ryan still doesn't know—surely this must be bigger. What better truce is there, what happier peace offering, than this: a day spent in the friendly confines of Wrigley Field, perched high on their green plastic thrones, presiding over the infield as if their presence alone might be enough to change history. As if wanting something enough could make the difference.

But she still hasn't heard from him, and she tries not to think of how much it hurts—this failure of his—as she helps Mom set the table for dinner, avoiding the question on both their minds: *Who will she take to the game?*

Ryan clicks off the burner on the stove and then clears her throat. "So would you want to go with me tomorrow?" she asks Mom, and without turning around, Ryan can sense that she's paused. "It's an afternoon game, so we could be home by dinnertime."

"I wish I could," Mom says, putting a hand on her shoulder, which makes Ryan feel worse. "But I have my doctor's appointment tomorrow."

"That's okay," Ryan says quickly. "It's no big deal."

"What's no big deal?" Kevin asks as he strolls into the kitchen, his face hidden by the business section of the newspaper.

Mom very nearly bounds over, then thumps him on the shoulder a couple of times. "Why don't you take Kevin?"

"Take me where?" he asks, pleased to be included.

"Ryan needs a date to the Cubs game," Mom says. "Wouldn't it be fun if you two went together?"

If Mom were to ask, Ryan would say that Kevin is the last person she wants to take to the game with her, but "last" implies that there are many, and the sad truth is that Ryan can't think of anybody else who might want to spend the afternoon with her.

The two tickets are beginning to seem as cursed as the team itself.

Kevin takes off his glasses and rubs the bridge of his nose. "Aren't I supposed to go to a doctor's appointment or something with you tomorrow?" he asks Mom, who shoots him a look.

"I'm fine on my own," she says, beaming at Ryan. "You guys will have *such* a great time together."

Ryan tries to imagine Kevin—whose favorite beverage is hot tea—with a twenty-ounce beer at the ball game. She pictures him wiping relish off a hot dog with his napkin. She knows he'll compare batting stances to golfing alignments, and she dreads having to explain to him why the old-fashioned scoreboard at Wrigley is better than the flashy, pixilated ones used for nearly every other sport.

"Sounds like fun," Kevin is saying, nudging her companionably with his elbow.

If they were to ask her, Ryan might say she'd rather not go at all. But nobody does, and so she just nods and grabs two water glasses, walking over to set the table, looking busy enough to fool them all.

Chapter Eleven

RYAN HAS ALWAYS LOVED NIGHT GAMES BEST. There's something about seeing the field bathed in white, the sky above hazy and glowing as if the whole world is focused on this one block in Wrigleyville.

Chicago doesn't have a long history of evening games. The stadium lights, which were meant to be ready for the 1942 season, were instead donated to the war effort, and the idea wasn't discussed again until the 1980s when the Tribune Company bought the team. The issue was tied up for years by grumbling neighbors and officials, who worried over the volume level of the neighborhood on summer nights. "Noise pollution can't be much of a problem," one state representative argued. "There's nothing to cheer about."

Apparently, enough people agreed with him. In 1988, the first night game was played, and—predictably—rained out after three and a half innings.

The last game Ryan and her dad attended was on a warm night in September, when the air was still sticky with summer and an orange moon appeared low in the sky toward the start of the ninth inning. With no shot at the postseason, other teams might get lazy and other cities might despair, but not Chicago; the team hustled in the outfield as the close of the game drew near.

It was the tail end of the season, and for once, the wait-till-next-year philosophy wasn't all wrong; the following year, 2003, would be their best in nearly two decades.

But this—this pitiful string of games—was the last season Ryan's father would ever see. He rested his elbows on his knees, leaning forward in the seat, and pointed as the Cubs' shortstop lunged for a ground ball, throwing his body into the dirt and just barely managing to snag it. "Look," he told Ryan. "The game's basically lost, the season's almost over, but that—*that!*—is what being a Cub is all about."

"Catching the ball?"

"That," he said, "and getting dirty."

Ryan slumped into his side, rubbing her eyes. The stadium pulsed and rang with ninth-inning cheers, the last desperate calls of a dying season. Dad was wringing his hat in his hands, his eyes bright. He nudged Ryan to her feet as the crowd rallied around them. Everyone yelled until they were hoarse, until all the shouting, all the cheering, all the screams became one rising sound, a symphony of noise beneath the white-hot bulbs that bore down on the field like spotlights.

"I wouldn't be a Yankees fan for all the money in the world," Dad said, shaking his head. "If you win that much, it takes all the character out of it."

"So you like it that we lose all the time?" Ryan asked, and he playfully swatted the brim of her cap.

"Nobody *likes* to lose," he said. "But there's some good in it too."

Ryan considered this. "Like how it makes you want to win more?"

"Like how it makes it that much better when you do."

"But what if we don't?" she asked. "What if they don't ever win?"

Dad looked out over the field, the milky lights of the stadium, the navy dome of sky above. The players moved across the grass like actors, the whole field a stage.

"We just have to be patient," he said, smiling. "There's always next year."

It was true; the following season, the Cubs would come maddeningly close to the World Series. They broke records and defied expectations, and those fans who thought it wasn't possible to yell any louder than they'd been doing all their lives found a whole new volume.

But not Ryan's dad.

It could be argued that he was saved from having to watch them come so close only to break his heart once again. But Ryan knows differently. He should have been there beside her, shouting his head off for their team, stomping his feet and whistling. He missed those last few nights of misfortune—the infamous foul ball, the futile efforts to turn things around—but he also missed a whole season of hope, an entire summer of promise and possibility.

Ryan doesn't remember that the Cubs lost that last ball game they'd gone to together. All she remembers is the rumble of the crowd, so loud she had to cover her ears with her hands until Dad lifted her onto his shoulders to see. She doesn't remember the last few outs, and she doesn't recall the final score. She has no memory of the ride home after the game.

All she remembers is that of everyone there that night—over thirty thousand roaring fans—it was her dad who was cheering the loudest. And if this was not actually so, then it was, at least, the way it seemed. It's the way she will always remember it.

It takes Kevin nearly forty minutes to find a parking spot he deems suitable for the sky blue convertible he's had since before marrying Mom. This would be unforgivable if they were running late, but since he'd insisted on leaving nearly two hours early, they still have plenty of time. When Ryan used to come down with Dad, they always took the 'L' train. He'd been of the opinion that no die-hard Cubs fan should drive to Wrigley. It's the sure badge of a tourist, an infrequent visitor to the land of Cubdom.

Kevin inches along the crowded streets in Wrigleyville— street parking being out of the question for a whole litany of reasons that Ryan has only half-listened to—until they come across a far-flung lot with two harmless-looking attendants.

"We may as well have walked from home," Ryan says with a sigh as they catch up to the mob of people drifting toward the stadium. Kevin doesn't hear her. He's looking over his shoulder at the car they've left behind, no doubt worrying over the golf clubs in the trunk.

"You know," he says, as they cross Clark and make their way up to the entrance, "I've never been to a Cubs game before."

This doesn't surprise Ryan in the slightest. "Have you been to *any* game before?"

"I think I once saw the Phillies play when I was a kid," he says. "Or maybe it was the Steelers."

"The Steelers are *football*."

"That's right." Kevin laughs. "Then I guess it was the Phillies."

Once they're standing in the hollow underground of the stadium, their voices tinny against the concrete floors, Kevin hands over her ticket stub. "Want to keep it as a souvenir?"

Ryan shakes her head. She still carries the one from her last game with her dad in her wallet, and there's nothing in her that wants to continue collecting them.

They wait in line to get hot dogs and Cokes, watching the pregame show on the little TV sets angled in the corners of each booth. Dad never would have bought food beforehand. He always found a distinct joy in waving down the vendors, in the camarade- rie of passing your money across the aisle and then watching the change come back the other way. It was part of the experience.

Their seats are along the first base line, and Ryan's grateful
to be on the opposite side of the stadium from where Dad's had
been. She can see them now from where she's sitting—high on
the second tier with the press boxes to their left and the lake to
their right—and she's able to make out the fuzzy forms of two
old men in the spot where she'd watched so many games with
her father. Across the outfield, the sun glances off the bleachers,
and the giant green scoreboard stretches wide against the sky.
The back wall of Wrigley is lower than most stadiums, so the
brownstone buildings lining the block have views from their
roofs, and most of them are already filled with people barbecuing or hosting parties before the game.

Kevin balances the cardboard box with their hot dogs on his
lap and hands her an enormous pile of napkins. "So are the Cubs
good this year or what?"

"Or what," Ryan answers, turning to face the field. After a
promising start, they'd lost two consecutive series on the road
and had dropped down to fourth place in their division. Today's
matchup against the Pirates, although still early in the season,
is a division game, and so an important one, and Ryan can't
help wondering what Nick is doing instead of sitting here
beside her.

She feels a small flush of anger at the thought of him watching it on television. There's no good reason for him not to be
here right now. If he'd decided to come and they hadn't spoken
the whole ride down, then that would have been just fine. If he'd
had a problem with her and they argued through the first few
innings, then so be it. If there had been a long, awkward silence as
the game wore on, then still, it would have been better. Because
nothing should matter as much as this: being at Wrigley on a perfect summer afternoon with the team running out onto the field
below to warm up, their uniforms bright against the grass.

Kevin finishes the last of his hot dog and leans over. "Are we white or gray?"

"White," Ryan mutters, resting her elbows on her knees, her eyes drifting over to the two seats on the third base line, where all those seasons ago she'd watched the Cubs lose beneath the dusky lights. The whole time—through warm-ups and the national anthem, the start of the game beneath a white-hot sun—Ryan's eyes keep coming back to that spot. It's easy, in this way, to go back in time. It's the simplest thing in the world.

Beside her, Kevin points at home plate as they move into the bottom half of the first inning. "Look at the screwy way that guy's standing," he says, and Ryan sees that the Cubs' left fielder is up to bat, a guy with an odd habit of turning his knees inward at the plate, whittling away his strike zone by crouching so low. Before she has a chance to explain this, Kevin folds his arms and nods sagely. "Now if he were a golfer," he says, "that would really cut down on his range of movement. . . ."

But Ryan has stopped listening. She watches the pitcher throw two more balls, and the batter rips off his glove and jogs to first base, where he throws his head back to laugh at something the Pirates' first baseman is saying. If she were with her dad, he would be doing his best impression of the conversation right now, using a high, girly voice for the player on the opposing team: *What an outrage,* he would mimic, as if he could hear from across the field. *The most deserving team in the whole league has gone the longest without a championship.*

That's not what he's saying, Ryan would giggle.

Dad always arched an eyebrow. *It's what he* should *be saying.*

But not in that voice.

Fine, he'd say, sighing dramatically. *If you're going to be a stickler about the facts.*

The catcher for the Cubs is now up to bat, and he hooks a

long shot to right field, the ball coasting up toward where they're sitting, and for a moment, Ryan thinks it might come close. But it arcs past them into the next section, where a man gets hold of it off the first bounce and hands it to his son. Kevin raises a hand to flag down a vendor selling popcorn, and Ryan stifles the urge to tell him this is not a movie theater.

A few innings later, there's still no score—Ryan feels sorry for the guy behind the scoreboard lifting all those zeroes into their slots—and the Pirates pause the game to replace their pitcher.

"I can see how this could be a fun tradition," Kevin says, fumbling through the box of popcorn. "A good thing for fathers to do with their kids."

Ryan bristles, keeping her eyes on the field.

"Maybe someday when the baby's old enough, we'll take him or her down here," he's saying. "The same way your dad did for you."

Something wells up inside of Ryan then, a sadness so profound it feels as if her heart is actually being twisted. She knows he's only trying to be nice, but she can't help thinking of what she'd give to have her father here today instead of Kevin. She struggles to keep her eyes from the two seats that stick out so sharply, so readily in a stadium brimming with people.

Kevin's cell phone begins to ring from his pocket—a merry little tune that makes Ryan want to cry—and he sets down the popcorn to answer it.

"Hi, honey," he says, covering his other ear with his hand. "How'd it go?"

Ryan takes a deep breath. The Pirates throw out a Cubs player at second base, and the next batter springs from the dugout and walks to the plate.

"I thought we were going to wait," Kevin says, frowning,

and Ryan watches the player tap his shoes with the bat and spit at the ground.

"No, I'm not mad," Kevin's saying, ducking his head against the noise as the batter steps into the box. "I'm sorry if it seems that way, I'm just—" He stands from his seat, several pieces of popcorn falling from his lap, and shrugs apologetically at Ryan as he squeezes around her and past four other people out into the aisle. She watches him pace back and forth along the railing, the crowd around him rising to their feet as the batter slices one into a pocket just past the shortstop. The whole of the stadium is up and hollering as he safely overruns first base.

Ryan stays sitting, as if bracing herself.

When the noise dies down and the fans collapse back into their seats, she sees Kevin skip up the stairs, nudging his way along the row and past Ryan to sit back down. He holds up his cell phone.

"So," he says, grinning broadly. "It's a boy!"

Below on the field, when nobody's watching, the runner steals second. And even though she's happy for the Cubs, the other team's pitcher looks so forlorn that she almost feels sorry for him. He paces the dirt on the mound with a sort of dazed air about him, as if wondering how the play had slipped so quickly from his grasp.

Ryan thinks she knows how he feels.

Chapter Twelve

THAT NIGHT AT DINNER, RYAN SITS SLUMPED IN HER chair, picking at the cooked carrots on her plate while Emily peppers Mom with questions about the new baby.

"Will his eyes be open when he comes out of your tummy?" she asks, her own eyes large and round at the thought. "Will he have hair already?"

Ryan's about to make a snide remark about Kevin's gene pool, something witty about the growing bald circle on the back of his head—now a bright shade of pink after the day's excursion—but she manages to bite back the words. There is something undeniably permanent about what had happened today. *It*—whatever had been growing in Mom's stomach—was now a *him*. What had before been something vague and shapeless was now a tiny boy, a little brother. And no matter what, he would always be a part of Kevin, too.

Riding home from the game, Ryan had rested an elbow on the window and watched the buildings slip by against the lake. Kevin fiddled with the radio, flipping past the Cubs postgame report—no doubt a lament on the afternoon's sorry performance—and eventually settling on an oldies station. Ryan wondered whether the new baby would like this kind of music, too. She couldn't help marveling at the idea that soon, there would be a new person in the world that came from her mother without any part of her father. Would he look like Kevin? Would he be musical and culinary and good at math? Would he have a long face and a nice smile and a tendency of rubbing at his forehead when he's worried?

Ryan tried to think of herself like a recipe—one part Mom and one part Dad—without much luck. She had her mother's dark hair and her father's small nose, Mom's green eyes and the same lopsided smile as Dad. But it was more than just the way she looked. Ryan had inherited Dad's hopeless tendency toward dreaminess, his lack of interest in the facts. He'd always been firm about everything happening for a reason, and even now that he's gone and there's no reason Ryan can see for that, she still struggles to follow his example, moving from one day to the next with a hope like a habit she's unable to break.

But Kevin is as stable and steady and grounded as Mom, and Ryan wonders about the lack of balance, how this baby will move through life without those ingredients that had so far kept her from floundering completely. Mom is high-strung and worried and careful—all things that make her a good mother—but Dad had been wistful. He'd been impulsive. He'd been funny. And where would the baby be without all of that?

Emily kicks her from underneath the table, and Ryan looks up, startled. "What's your pick?" she repeats, her hair—dark as Mom's—in two braids, and her eyes—gray as Dad's—asking a question Ryan isn't sure how to answer. "For a name?" Emily says, prodding. "For the baby?"

Name him after Dad, Ryan wants to say. But instead, she surprises even herself by saying "Kevin," and the word is the biggest gift she can offer right now. It is wistful and impulsive and funny all at once. It's the part of her that is her dad, and it's the best she can do.

Kevin smiles at her across the table, and Mom laughs.

"It's a nice thought," she says, reaching out to place a hand on Ryan's. "But I don't think we need that sort of confusion around here."

"My grandfather's name was Percy," Kevin suggests, and Ryan coughs.

"No way," Mom says, winking at her. "We can do better than that."

"I know," Ryan says. "I'm not worried."

In the morning, they drive through grassy subdivisions and neat rows of houses to drop Emily off at day camp. Mom keeps one hand on the wheel and runs the other through her hair, humming a soft, lilting tune while Ryan fidgets in the front seat.

"Why doesn't Ryan go to camp, too?" Emily asks, leaning forward between the seats. Her backpack is balanced on her lap, and her shoes are already untied.

Mom stops humming and gives her a grave look in the rearview mirror. "Ryan flunked archery one summer," she says, shaking her head.

"For real?" Emily looks unconvinced.

Mom's about to say no, but Ryan cuts in. "The goal is pretty much *not* to hit other kids with an arrow."

Emily's mouth falls open. "You hit someone with an *arrow?*"

Mom shoots her a look across the front seat. "You're worse than your dad."

Ryan tries not to look quite so pleased with herself.

They wind along a tree-lined road that slopes south as it cuts away from the lake, and at the end of the street, a few dozen kids in camp T-shirts are milling about on a brownish soccer field. Ryan squints out at the assembly of campers, those ready for the day and those already waiting for it to end, and hands Emily her brown lunch bag.

"Have fun at archery," she says, patting her on the back.

Afterward, Mom turns out onto the main road to run the errands that Ryan had agreed to help with out of sheer boredom.

They park in the center of town beside the village green, and at the dry cleaners, Ryan stands dutifully with a pile of clean shirts, the plastic sticking to her arms in the heat, waiting while Mom chats with the owner.

When she's done, Ryan agrees to drop the clothes off at the car and meet Mom in the grocery store, but as she makes her way across the green, fumbling with the bulk of Kevin's shirts and trying to see from behind the billowing plastic, she notices Sydney and Kate. They're both sitting on the edge of the fountain, their legs dangling, their faces tilted back to catch the sun. They haven't yet seen her, and Ryan stands frozen for a moment, suddenly weary at the thought of the ensuing conversation. She knows what will happen as surely as if it were already a memory.

"Ryan Walsh," Sydney says, swinging her head around. She says her name casually enough to leave no question of it being anything other than ironic. Sydney has developed a rare ability to make even the most ordinary interactions feel like she's doing you some great favor. As if by simply deigning to talk to you, she's somehow being charitable.

Ryan tries to tamp down the dry-cleaning plastic without much success as she stands rooted a few feet away from the fountain. It's almost worse when the rest of their posse isn't around. However illogical, it's harder to bear when they're not at school, when there isn't an audience or a peanut gallery to observe their interactions. Without the benefit of a stage, the drama of it all feels silly. It's when they're alone together—all the distractions, all the maneuverings and calculations stripped away—that she remembers most clearly how things had once been between them.

"How's your summer so far?" Kate asks.

Ryan wills herself to take a few steps forward, and she finds herself standing at knee level with the two girls on the fountain.

"Good," she manages. "What about yours?"

"My parents are in France for most of it," Sydney says, sliding down and flashing Kate a meaningful smile. "So you know what that means."

Ryan can guess it means a series of parties supervised by some bored college kid Sydney's parents have paid to keep her out of the alcohol cabinet. It probably means afternoons by her pool, boys huddled around the ping-pong table, cheap beer in cardboard cases and pizza deliveries at midnight.

Sydney shifts from foot to foot, and Ryan stares dumbly at her jeweled flip-flops and painted toenails. Kate hops down too, and the three of them stand together without speaking. Ryan feels like they've graduated from one level of un-friendship to another. Now that the boundaries are clear, now that they've boxed her into a new category of person to be dealt with and she's proven her ability to adapt to this new set of rules, they're able to relax in their efforts to exclude her. She feels a bit like a trained animal. If she doesn't ask about the party at Sydney's house, they won't have to voice what is already understood: that she's not invited.

"So, have you been hanging around with that guy at all?" Sydney asks, utterly transparent. "What's his name again?"

Ryan clears her throat. "No," she says. "I haven't seen Nick."

Kate raises her eyebrows at Sydney, and they both struggle to keep their faces blank. Ryan's desperate to know whether Lucy's seen him at all, but she refuses to ask.

A few kids whisk by them, chasing after a rubber ball, and Ryan shifts the shirts in her arms. An old beat-up car—a red bug so faded it's nearly pink—lurches around the corner, lumbering noisily across the cobblestone streets that line the green, and without thinking, Ryan shouts "Punch buggy!" and gives Kate a light knock to the shoulder. Before she has the chance to be horrified, she notices Sydney's hand balled up as well, and Kate points at her, laughing.

"She beat you to the punch," she says. "Literally."

Sydney smiles ruefully, but Kate is nearly doubled over at the humor of it all—their old joke, the trigger instinct—and after a moment, Sydney and Ryan are laughing, too. Across the green, Ryan sees her mom struggling with her shopping bags as she emerges from the grocery store, and she wipes at the corner of her eyes and adjusts the laundry in her arms.

"I should go," she says, and Sydney stops laughing abruptly and stiffens, not the least bit unclear in her message: that she could care less whether Ryan stays or goes.

"See you around," Kate says. Sydney only lifts her chin as she turns to leave, but Ryan doesn't mind. She can see the situation as if she were a bystander, as if she were somewhere outside of herself. She can see the differences between herself and the new girls they hang out with, can see the way she's become a social liability. Ryan knows she should feel worse about it all, but the truth is, she can understand what they're doing. And she doesn't really blame them.

But sometimes, she *does* miss them.

Chapter Thirteen

WHEN KEVIN MOVED IN WITH THEM, THE BASEment where Ryan used to watch the games with Dad had been turned into a makeshift storage space. In the debate over what pieces of furniture to use where, Mom won nearly every argument, and as a result, the basement is now littered with the remnants of Kevin's bachelor life—an oversized globe, a treadmill that hasn't worked in years, a portable putting green, a corduroy couch, and three mismatched pieces of wooden furniture that block the television set.

Once, before the basement had grown dusty and dank, there'd been a dartboard and a small refrigerator with cans of pop. The ping-pong table hadn't always been used to stack laundry, and the couch hadn't always housed Kevin's music collection. The walls are still covered in Cubs paraphernalia—a replica of the Wrigley marquee, a clock with the mascot, a CUBS ONLY parking sign they'd stolen after one memorable game from the lot near the field—but most of these have grown faded, or have tilted on their pegs so that the room now has an off-balance, slipshod look about it.

Ryan has learned to be content with watching the games upstairs in the den, wrestling Emily for the remote or waiting for Kevin's interminable golf tournaments to end before she can switch the channel. But today begins what is arguably the most important series of the season, and though the TV in the basement only works occasionally—often going staticky or blurry without reason—Ryan decides to risk it. This, of all games, deserves better treatment than most.

Call it what you will—the Windy City classic, the Red Line

rivalry, the crosstown showdown—but the series against the White Sox is a battle for far more than just a couple of afternoon ball games. It is this series, more than any other, that brings the city of Chicago to its feet as the Northsiders and Southsiders begin the fiercest staring contest of all across the line that divides them so decisively.

It is, in Chicago, the closest thing there is to all-out combat.

It's a form of warfare. It's a call to arms.

In the fall of 2005, the White Sox had won their first World Series pennant since 1917—a hefty nine years short of the Cubs' last win in 1908, but still, a long time to wait. Up until then, the balance of power in the city had been clear. The home of the White Sox—Comiskey Park, and then later, U.S. Cellular Field—sat half-empty most days, dotted with green where the vacant seats stood out in the dwindling crowds. A few years ago, over six thousand seats—the entire upper deck—were simply lopped off to reduce the appearance that nobody was coming to the games.

"If they played the way we do," Dad once said, "they wouldn't have a single fan. It's only because they're halfway decent that they draw any crowd at all."

"And what about us?" Ryan had asked.

"We've spent nearly an entire century losing, and look at Wrigley Field," he said. "Not an empty seat in the whole place. That's what you get as a Cubs fan: a lousy team, but a great view."

Despite breaking their long losing streak, the White Sox have yet to get rid of the chip on their shoulder, the inferiority complex that comes with being second place in a city whose heart belongs to the Cubs. And the Cubs—forever looking to shake the curse that has followed them for so long, the awful streak that trails them like a ghost—see the series as their chance to prove themselves. There's always a possibility of tilting the balance, a whirling, dizzying hope that this moment might be the one to change all those to follow.

But the Cubs have fallen to last place in their division, and the Sox are first in theirs by several games, and to Ryan, the series feels less like an impending duel than a potential massacre. She and Nick had talked—back when they used to talk at all— about heading downtown for the matchup. They'd joked about heckling Sox fans, writing GO CUBS across their cars with shaving cream during the game—things they'd never actually do, but liked to imagine they might. But now, since this is clearly not about to happen, Ryan surveys the dusty furniture in the basement, thinking wistfully of Dad's old version of the room.

"Sure you don't want to watch up here?" Mom calls from the top of the stairs, and Ryan can hear Emily and a friend of hers running through the kitchen, their footsteps heavy on the ceiling. "Kevin won't be back from golf for a while."

"I'm fine," Ryan says, shoving a few boxes off the old couch.

By the time the pregame show begins, she's carried down a bowl of peanuts and pulled a score sheet from an old book of Dad's. When she was younger, he used to insist they use red or blue markers to chart the game, and if the Cubs won, they tacked the sheets up on the unfinished plaster wall beneath the basement stairs. Most of them are still there, yellow and brittle, with Ryan's bubbly grade-school handwriting scrawled across them. When Mom uses the washer and dryer on the other side of the wall, they tremble and flutter like flags.

She finds a pencil to use now on the clean sheet of paper, no longer sure of herself. The couch sighs a small cloud of dust when she sits down, and the room has a vacant feel to it, neglected and abandoned. When the game begins, Ryan feels flustered and unprepared. She moves the bowl of peanuts to a different corner of the table. She runs back upstairs for a can of pop. She pushes the couch back a few inches, then changes her mind and shoves it forward once more. After the first two pitches, her pencil still hangs in the air uncertainly. She balls the score sheet in her fist and stuffs it between the couch cushions.

Emily pounds down the stairs sometime during the third inning, pulling her friend Annie along behind her. The Cubs are down five to nothing already, and Ryan sits with her arms folded, frowning at the screen from beneath the rim of her cap.

"Annie saw your hat from the stairs and thought I had a brother," Emily announces, and Ryan flicks her eyes toward them briefly before returning to the game. "I told her you're not a boy, it's just that you really like sports."

"My mom watches tennis a lot," Annie offers.

Ryan sighs. "You guys can only hang out down here if you want to watch the game," she says. "This isn't a tea party."

Emily hesitates, and for a moment, Ryan's surprised to find how much she wishes they would stay. The basement feels dim and gray, not at all as she'd remembered it, and the Cubs are limping through the game one inning at a time. She thinks she might be able to stand some company, even if it's only her little sister and her friend.

"I'd rather watch *golf*," Emily says, giggling, and Annie laughs, too. Ryan knows she's only joking, but the statement is probably somewhat true. She wonders for the thousandth time—the millionth, the trillionth—how things would be different if Dad were still around, but then the White Sox hit a home run and Emily and her friend skip up the stairs, and Ryan is once again left alone in the basement with her floundering team.

By the seventh inning, she's started to grow restless. The Cubs have managed to fumble through each of the last two innings in quick succession: three batters up, three batters out. And then, just for good measure, they begin the seventh with an astounding display of Cubness, in which the team's left fielder loses sight of an easy pop fly against the sun-laced clouds, letting it bounce off the top of his cap before it lands in the outfield grass with an embarrassing thud.

"Aw, don't do that," the television announcer cries involuntarily, before righting himself with some quick statistics on errors for the day.

Ryan pulls a pillow over her face and groans.

They're down ten to nothing.

She stands up and looks around the basement. There's a commercial on now, and Ryan uses the time to shake loose the dust from the pillows, sneezing as she claps them together loudly. After that, it seems only logical to keep going, and so she grabs a few dishrags from the laundry pile and sets about mopping at the thick layer of grime coating the framed photographs on the walls. The coffee table has only three good legs, propped unsteadily by a cracked coaster with a picture of an old Cubs player on one side. It had once been angled in a different direction so that they could put their feet up during the games, and she shoves at it now until it finally gives way, then moves the last few boxes of Kevin's stuff into a corner near the washing machine.

On the screen, the seventh-inning stretch has begun, and some clownish, middle-aged movie star is leaning over the edge of the press box in a painful rendition of "Take Me Out to the Ball Game." But Ryan's too busy to notice, dusting and shuffling and cleaning and organizing. And when she's finally done, she steps back to admire her work. She knows that no amount of rearranging can restore things to the way they'd once been, but it still feels nice to have created a room of her own, a place both comfortably familiar and entirely new. The basement feels sunnier already, less dingy, and when Mom comes down to change a load of laundry, she pauses at the bottom of the stairs with the basket propped against her hip.

"Wow," she says. "It looks great down here."

"It really needed it," Ryan says, remembering Saturday afternoons spent helping Dad clean up, how he used to use the broom as a microphone, mouthing the words to whatever song was on the ancient radio still tucked in the corner.

Mom circles the basement, running a hand across a photograph of Ryan and Dad at the stadium. When she turns back, her eyes are bright. "Well, you did good."

Ryan smiles as she sits down on the newly arranged couch. "I didn't do anything Dad hadn't already done," she says, and Mom kisses her on top of her head before heading back upstairs again.

She's only been gone a minute or two when the Cubs hit a double. Two men score, and Ryan leans forward in her seat.

Even the most disillusioned of fans can sense when a rally is starting.

As stadiums go, Wrigley Field is a moody one. It sits tight against the breezes from nearby Lake Michigan, prone to shifting energies and ever-changing weather in the windiest of cities. From where the batter stands, looking out past the whipping pennants and the dated scoreboard to where the ballhawks pace along Waveland Avenue, the wind can carry you or kill you. On certain days at Wrigley, there's no such thing as a pop fly: there are only the foul balls with their unintended curves or the long-sailing home runs, products of luck as much as skill.

Even from the basement, down below where only a few shafts of light angle their way in through the shallow windows, Ryan can feel the winds shift.

It happens in quick succession after that: a single, then a triple, followed by a two-run homer. On the screen, the crowd is on their feet, their fists pumping the air, their mouths open in mingled cheers. Ryan sits on her hands so she won't bite her fingernails. The announcer's voice echoes around the empty basement with barely disguised surprise.

"Sox leading ten to six," he says, stifling a small, giddy laugh. "No outs in the bottom of the seventh, and it looks like we have ourselves a ball game."

The color commentator can't help himself. "At least by Cubs standards."

But there's a sense of rolling energy now, a momentum like a storm, and each time the Cubs step to the plate to stare down the scowling pitcher, they seem surprised by their luck, half-hopping the bases as the shortstop hits a two-run homer, followed by a single shot far over the ivy-covered wall by the catcher. They are one run away with no outs, and much to Ryan's frustration, she finds she isn't thinking about who's up next. She's wondering what its like outside of Wrigley right now, imagining she's there with Nick as if it were more than simply pretending. As if it were a wish.

Playing it safe, the Sox pitcher walks the next man up, the big first baseman for the Cubs, who steals second shortly after, then stands tapping his foot and eyeing home plate like he's running late for an appointment there. The next two hitters strike out, and then there's only one out left, and Ryan claps her hands over her eyes.

It's only the seventh inning, she reminds herself. *Nine innings is a lifetime,* Dad would have said back. *And there are at least two left to go.*

She takes a deep breath.

If they win this series, she thinks, *I'll stop moping this summer. I'll try to make new friends. I'll try to be normal. If they just win. If they could only just win.*

"What an inning," the announcer says, stalling as they wait for the Sox coach to have a word with his pitcher, who looks relieved when they replace him with someone else, someone younger and with a fresher arm.

But it doesn't matter. His first pitch is hit wide and long, a ball with no chance but what its intention had been: a home run to put the Cubs ahead by one.

Ryan falls back against the couch cushions and sighs happily, scanning the room once more with pride. Upstairs, she can hear Kevin coming in through the back door, and a moment later, his heavy footsteps on the basement stairs.

"Hey," he says, maneuvering a golf bag through the narrow space. "Looks like you did some work down here."

Ryan shrugs, her eyes on the TV. "Just some rearranging." Kevin hefts the golf bag into a corner and then raises his eyebrows. "Don't sell yourself short," he says. "I'd say it's more like rebuilding."

"Rebuilding," she repeats, then smiles. "I guess so."

The White Sox score once more in the ninth to tie it up, and the game limps along, scoreless, into extra innings. The afternoon sun comes through the basement windows at a slant now, and Ryan hugs her legs to her chest, watching the game over the tops of her knees. They move from the tenth inning to the eleventh, then twelfth, and it isn't until the bottom of the thirteenth that the Cubs finally hit a solo shot far into left field, sending the long-suffering crowd into a flurry of noise.

Ryan smiles as the game ends and the fans file out of the stadium. The Cubs' manager is being interviewed on television, scratching his head as he attempts to explain the strange momentum that had grabbed hold of his team.

"I think the winds were just in our favor today," he says, smiling into the microphone. "And that last home run was what really counted."

But Ryan knows better. It wasn't the extra innings or the

weather or the long shot to left field to end the game. It wasn't even the final score. It was, she knows, the possibility of a comeback. That last reservoir of hope, when what may or may not be out of reach suddenly seems so very reachable.

Ryan turns off the TV and eyes the crumpled score sheet, wedged between the couch cushions. She pulls it back out, then spreads it on the table, smoothing the angry creases with the flat of her hand. She considers the pencil on the table, but changes her mind and finds a blue marker in an old box of art supplies, and then—though the progression of the game is lost to her now, and though she feels a bit like she's cheating—Ryan marks down the win in big letters at the top of the page. When she's done, she tacks it up on the wall beneath the stairs, where it hangs—wrinkled and incomplete, but somehow important nonetheless—beside all the others.

"Ryan," Mom calls from upstairs. "Dinner will be ready in twenty minutes, okay?"

"Okay," she yells, her eyes still on the wall. "I'll be up in a minute."

"Did they win?"

Ryan grins. "Yup."

"Imagine that," Mom says, laughing.

Imagine that, Ryan echoes, and the importance of the game, that one magical inning, balloons up inside her. *Imagine that.*

She runs into Emily at the top of the stairs, who points at the kitchen. "Your turn to set the table."

Ryan looks at her watch, then at the front door. "Tell you what," she says. "I'll be back in ten minutes. I'll do it then."

"Where are you going?" Emily asks, but Ryan's already out the door, walking fast down the front path and then unable to help breaking into a run as she rounds the corner of their block. An older man is out watering his flowers, and he swivels as she sprints by, weaving around a few kids making chalk drawings on the gum-stained sidewalk.

Ryan isn't sure what she's doing. She only knows that the Cubs won, and the importance of this, the enormous significance, is dampened only by the fact that she has no one to share it with, no one who understands in the same way she does how much this game had meant.

They won, she thinks—is *all* she can think—as she runs the streets between their houses. *They won, they won, they won.* And if they won this, they can win anything. If they won this, they can win it all.

Her sandaled feet slap the ground as she jogs around the final corner toward Nick's house, her breath jagged now. At the end of the driveway, Ryan stops, resting her hands on her knees and breathing hard. The sun has slipped behind the houses now, and the evening light is soft and pink. She hears someone call their kids into dinner, and the neighbor's dog throws his head back and barks. Nick's house looks quiet, dark except for a few lights on near the front door, and Ryan takes a step backward, rethinking her impulsive decision.

What if he's not even there? He could be up in Wisconsin or out to dinner with his parents. He could be out with his friends, or even with Lucy. Ryan is suddenly embarrassed to be so terrifically exposed, standing alone out on the sidewalk in front of his house. But then she sees the flicker of a television set in the window of Nick's bedroom, and she's sure he's been watching the game too. She breathes in, partly angry, partly hurt that just blocks away, he'd been seeing what she had seen—the impossible rally, the unexpected comeback—and hadn't been moved to call her, hadn't come running over to find her the same way she'd been compelled to come here.

She takes a few steps up the front path, her eyes fixed on

the wavering light in Nick's window, and Ryan feels her anger loosen its grip. They had won, and she'd come here to share that with him. If there was ever a time to mend things between them, it would be now. If there was ever a person who would understand that, it would be Nick.

The front door of the house is propped open, swung back to let the summer breezes in through the screen. Ryan stares at the pinecone wreath in the entryway. She can hear Nick's parents in the kitchen, the low sizzle of something on the stove and the bright sounds of silverware, a reminder that she needs to be home soon. She shifts from foot to foot, her mouth set in a straight line. When she finally raises a hand to knock, she bites her lip with indecision and then lowers it again.

If she were to have to chat with his parents right now— endure pleasantries and invitations to stay for dinner, polite questions about life and school—Ryan knows she'd lose her nerve. She feels impatient and surprisingly bold, made brave by the events of the day behind her—the rediscovered basement and the astounding comeback—which have all conspired to propel her forward. Even as she reaches to turn the knob on the screen door, she's surprised by her actions, as if watching herself from afar. But the door opens easily, and she tiptoes inside, pressing it closed behind her with a click. The eyes of a dozen cows follow her as she climbs the carpeted stairs, her heart thrumming hard in her chest, her hands shaky on the banister.

The door to Nick's room is open just a crack, and Ryan stands before it for a moment, trying to collect herself before knocking. When he doesn't answer, she knocks again and calls his name softly.

It occurs to her to leave. To turn around, steal back down the stairs, and slip out the front door as if this had never happened. But she's already here, and she can hear the muffled sounds of the postgame show on the television in his room, and so without thinking anymore, she pushes open the door to peer through.

"Nick," she whispers, blinking into the dim room. The curtains are all open, letting in the pale evening light, and the TV casts an uneven glow around the stillness of the room. "Nick?"

On his dresser, she can make out a tray with a small cluster of orange pill bottles arranged beside a water glass. Ryan keeps a hand on the doorknob but leans in farther, and she sees that Nick is curled up in bed, napping, with his face turned away from her, his legs pulled up beneath the covers. He shifts restlessly, the sheets rustling in the quiet room, and Ryan's stomach tightens. She begins to back away, embarrassed to have found him asleep, mortified at having come here at all, when the postgame show ends and the nightly news begins with a too-bright display of graphics and loud music. Ryan feels disoriented and confused, eager to get home.

"And here are our top stories for tonight," the announcer booms with a plastic smile. "More tension in the Middle East: what the government doesn't want you to know."

"And later," says his coanchor, beaming at Ryan from across Nick's bedroom, "have scientists found a way to slow cancer cells in mice?"

Ryan freezes, her breath caught in her throat. She looks once more to the pill bottles on the dresser, the horrible order of the arrangement, then back to Nick, who coughs and then sighs in his sleep.

She closes her eyes and takes a step backward.

Please be okay, she thinks as she hurries back down the stairs.

Please let it not be that, she says without saying it, closing the front door behind her and picking up a run just outside the house. The air is now cool, the skies in the neighborhood hurrying toward night. Ryan runs hard, her legs numb, her arms strangely limp.

"Please let him be okay," she whispers to no one in particular, to the sidewalk spread before her, to the last bits of light in the western sky. She tells herself not to jump to conclusions, and she tells herself to quit being dramatic. She tries to stop overthinking, but her mind keeps returning to the worrying stillness of his bedroom.

And in the end, without fact or knowledge, without certainty or assurance, there is only one stubborn thought that emerges from all the rest. She walks home with her head lowered, repeating it over and over like a mantra, childish and ageless all at once, the worst bargain of all.

It's okay if the Cubs never win again, she thinks, *if only he would just be okay.*

Chapter Fourteen

OME MAY CALL IT SUPERSTITION—THIS FERVOR THAT all Cubs fans inflict upon themselves—while others see it as a necessary bowing to whatever illogical spirits may still preside over the sport of baseball. But whatever its root and whatever its outcome, the fact remains that it all began because of a goat.

The history of the Cubs is rich with curses, hexes, and spells of all kinds, but the worst and most enduring of these was born in October of 1945, on a cool autumn day at Wrigley Field. The Cubs were leading the Tigers two games to one in the fourth game of the World Series—the last, as it turns out, they'd see—when William "Billy Goat" Sianis showed up outside the stadium.

The owner of the local Billy Goat Tavern had brought along his pet goat, Murphy, as a good luck charm for his favorite team, and though they allowed him through the gates, he was galled by their attempts to stop him from taking his seat once inside. After a heated argument—he had two tickets, after all: one for himself and the other for the goat—the owner of the Cubs, P. K. Wrigley himself, was summoned.

When he decided that Billy would be allowed in as long as he left his goat behind, Sianis grew upset. "Why not the goat?" he asked, and Wrigley shrugged.

"Because the goat stinks," he said.

Furious, Sianis stormed away, goat in tow, but not before placing a curse over the Cubs: They would never win a National League pennant or play in a World Series game so long as the goat was not allowed in Wrigley Field.

That night, the Cubs lost game four, and as predicted, went on to lose the rest of the Series in a similar fashion. Billy Goat Sianis sent P. K. Wrigley a telegram the following day. All it said was "Who stinks now?"

And so began the curse.

Over two long decades later, in 1969, the Cubs took the lead in their division, and it seemed possible that this might finally be their year. But during the second game of a crucial series against the Mets, a black cat darted out onto the field, briefly eyeing Ron Santo—the Cubs' beloved third baseman—before disappearing into the stands.

On the heels of so many losing seasons, there was a growing suspicion in Chicago that their baseball team might be haunted.

The first time a goat was allowed back inside Wrigley Field was during the Cubs home opener in 1984, when the owners—in an act of sheer desperation—invited Sianis' nephew, Sam, along with a floppy-eared, head-butting descendant of Murphy named Socrates. The pair walked out onto the infield and, lifting his hat, Sam proclaimed the curse to be over. The city of Chicago held its breath, hardly daring to hope as the team romped through the regular season and into September, having won their first Eastern Division title ever. But two games into the National League Championship series, a ground ball slipped between the first baseman's legs, and the Cubs crumbled from there.

On the heels of so many losing seasons, there was a growing suspicion in the city of Chicago that their baseball team might be haunted.

They were closest in 2003—just five outs away from their first World Series appearance in 58 years—when they began to unravel. Heading into the eighth inning, the Cubs were up three to nothing. The fans stood, hands clasped together, throats tight with emotion. It was October at Wrigley Field, a thing rarely

seen, and the ivy was tipped with red against the back wall. But
as the winds shifted, there was a general feeling of helplessness,
a spiraling sense of doom. The Florida Marlins made play after
play, racking up eight runs in a single inning When a Chicago
fan reached out for a foul ball, skimming the glove of the Cubs'
left fielder so that they both ended up grasping nothing but air,
something seemed to snap. There was a palpable sinking of spirits as the fans glared across the stands, their eyes flicking back and
forth to the giant green scoreboard, the white floating numbers
that had somehow tipped off balance.

There is no surprise ending to this story. That night, the
Cubs lost the game, and the following night, their chance at the
World Series. A few months later, the foul ball was blown to
pieces in the hopes that curses might be so easily destroyed.

But there was no such luck.

In 2007, after clawing and scrabbling their way into the
postseason, the team was cast aside neatly and efficiently by
the Arizona Diamondbacks, swept away in three uninspiring
games, a Cubbie-style collapse to go down in history beside all
the many others. It seemed the worst joke in all of sports—this
99th season of futility—but to Cubs fans, it was just the new-
est addition to a long chain of gut-wrenching losses. And so
once again, they did the only thing they could: they shook their
heads and lowered their chins, they muttered and prayed and
cursed and wished. They settled in for the long winter.

They waited for next year.

A storm sweeps through the following day, and Ryan watches
from her bedroom window as the rain flattens the flowers lining
the stone path up to the house. She flips onto her back and stares
at the ceiling, having spent most of the night in a similar position. After her trip to Nick's house, Ryan had endured dinner

silently, eager to retreat to her bedroom.

"I thought the Cubs won," Kevin said, watching her pick at her food.

"They did," Ryan told him as she stood to drop her plate in the sink. "I'm just tired."

But the truth is, she isn't sure why she's so shaken. The more she recalls it, the less she finds odd with the scene in Nick's bedroom. It's entirely possible that he was just tired and took a midafternoon nap. But still, there is something deeper—a nagging instinct—that worries her. And she can't seem to shake it.

By game time, the rain hasn't let up, though it's lightened to a steady sprinkle. Ryan watches on the basement television as the groundskeepers roll back the giant blue tarp that covers the field, and the game begins beneath a hazy veil of rain. The players squint and blink into the spray of it, wiping their eyes against the pelting drizzle.

Whatever spark they'd had yesterday seems to have disappeared, and the Cubs plod through the game as though afraid of the rain. By the ninth inning, they're down six to two, and they still look half-asleep, losing predictably and comfortably, as if eager to return to normal after yesterday's fluke of a win. When the last batter strikes out to end the inning, Ryan switches off the TV and heads back up to her room.

The following morning, it's still raining, and she wakes to the dull pulse of water against the gutter outside her window. It's Sunday, and the final game of the tied series, but Ryan isn't much in the mood for baseball. She considers skipping the game entirely, though there isn't much else to do, and so she dwindles away the morning helping Emily with her art project—a charcoal drawing of their house—while she waits for the game to start.

Kevin paces the kitchen restlessly, annoyed over his canceled golf outing, and Mom is upstairs napping. Emily smudges a blackened finger against her forehead while she tries to remember the details of the house: how many windows there are, whether there are three front steps or four.

"This would be easier if we had a picture," Ryan says.

"It's not raining that hard anymore," Kevin says, peering through the blinds in the next room, "if you want to go out and check."

Emily crinkles her nose.

"I'll go," Ryan says, pulling up the hood of her sweatshirt.

Outside, the rain has turned soft and scattered. Ryan closes the door behind her, then half-jogs down the path, the stones cool and damp against her bare feet. At the end of the walkway, she turns and looks back at the house: perfectly proportioned, small and square and brick, with mint green shutters and two round windows on either side of the door that look a bit like eyes. Ryan is amazed at how you can see something every day for fifteen years and still not be able to recall the littlest thing about it from memory. She makes a mental note of the rest of its features, her eyes running over the slant of the roof, the tree that bends near Emily's window, the lightpost near the front door.

She's still standing there, barefoot and wet, when she hears Nick call her name.

"What're you doing?" he asks as she whirls to face him. He's wearing a blue slicker, but the hood is down and his wet hair has fallen in his eyes. He looks just as pale as always, and somehow younger without his baseball cap, but he holds his shoulders straight and his chin high as he regards her with amusement.

Ryan looks down at her feet. "I'm helping my sister with her art project."

"Performance art?"

"Not exactly," she says with a sheepish grin. "Do you want to come in?"

He shakes his head, but takes a few steps closer.

"How are you?" she asks.

"There's a game today," he says, without answering her question. "Tiebreaker."

Ryan sucks in a breath. "I know," she says. "I've been watching."

"So," he says, lifting his shoulders. "Should we go?"

"Downtown?" She stares at him to see if he's kidding, but despite the smallest hint of a smile, she can tell he's completely serious. "I'm sure it'll be rained out."

"It might," he says. "But it might not."

She looks back toward the house, then wipes the water from her face and takes a few steps toward him, realizing they've been yelling over the rain. She's beginning to grow cold, and can tell he is too, by the way his jaw is set. "I don't know," she says, hugging her arms to her chest. "I don't think it's a very good idea."

They are close now, and there's something in his eyes that makes her go quiet.

"It is," he says, then lowers his voice. "Please."

Ryan opens her mouth, then closes it. She pulls her eyes from his and looks around the yard, the rain falling steadily on the slabs of stone, the grass wet and curling. She wiggles her toes against the ground and shivers.

"Okay," she says after a moment. "Let me just grab a coat."

Chapter Fifteen

BY THE TIME THEY GET DOWNTOWN, THE RAIN shower has turned into a thunderstorm. Ryan pulls her hands into the sleeves of her raincoat and ducks her head as they get off the 'L', looking to Nick. But if she'd expected him to suggest going home, to hop back on the next northbound train, she'd been wrong. They'd ridden the whole way in silence, and something about the look on his face kept Ryan from trying to start up a conversation. There's something purposeful about his manner as they stand now beneath the dripping overhang of the Addison train stop, the sky around them curdled and blackened, the thunder trembling in their ears.

The game is undoubtedly delayed, if not canceled entirely, and the area around the stadium is quiet. A homeless man in a brown garbage bag approaches them, and Ryan digs in her pockets for a dollar. When he shuffles away, they are once again alone, and it takes everything in her not to ask Nick what he plans to do next.

"Let's go find a spot," he says, jerking his head toward the stadium. "I bet this'll pass."

Ryan stares at him as another fit of thunder shakes the platform around them. A spike of lightning splits the sky, and she pulls her hood tight around her face. "There's no way this is passing anytime soon."

"It's just a summer storm," he says. "C'mon."

She has no choice but to follow him as he makes his way down the stairs and out toward the stadium, which looks dreary and forlorn beneath the spitting rain. Ryan wipes the water from her nose and lowers her head, trying her best to avoid the puddles as Nick leads them past the entrance and alongside the ballpark toward Waveland Avenue. There are a few vendors trying to untangle plastic tarps to cover their merchandise, but other than that, the street is nearly empty. Even the old fire station at the corner is shuttered against the storm. Ryan stops walking, and Nick turns around when he realizes she's no longer behind him.

"What's wrong?" he calls out.

"This is crazy," she says. "Let's go find a coffee shop or something."

He tips his head back and squints at the sky. Ryan jumps at an explosion of thunder, then stamps her feet against the chill. A car rounds the corner, passing between them on the street and throwing up small waves of water. Ryan takes another step back and shakes her head.

"This is *not* passing," she says.

Nick motions to the rows of brownstone homes lining the street. The nearest one has a small front porch with a stone overhang. "C'mon," he yells, and Ryan follows him reluctantly, climbing the stairs and keeping an eye on the front door.

"What if someone comes out?"

Nick shrugs as he slides down onto the stoop. "Then we'll move."

The overhang doesn't provide much shelter, and the rain comes in at them sideways, stinging Ryan's face. She sits down across from him and gathers the ends of her jeans in her hands, doing her best to wring them out.

"What exactly are we doing here?"

"Waiting," he says.

"For the apocalypse?"

He smiles as he shakes the water from his hair. There's a

steady drip from the ceiling that collects in a small pool between them. She presses herself closer to the door, moving away from the storm. The sky above the stadium is leaden and heavy, a grayish mess of clouds and rain. Ryan peers out, shuddering. When she turns back to Nick, hunched in the opposite corner of the small vestibule, she finds him watching her.

"I'm sorry I haven't called," he says, his green eyes intent. "It was a dumb thing to do."

Ryan settles back against the wall. "What?" she asks. "Disappearing?"

"I didn't disappear."

She knows. She may have only seen him once, may have only stumbled upon an afternoon nap, may not *really* understand any of this at all, but even so, the tiniest part of her knows that something is wrong.

Nick folds his hands together and looks out at the rain. Ryan can feel what's coming next, something unnamed and foreboding, the kind of thing that divides time into a before and an after. She has a sudden childish impulse to clap her hands over her ears, but instead, she stands abruptly and steps from beneath the overhang.

"What're you doing?" Nick asks.

Ryan lets the rain slide down her nose. "Let's go get something to eat," she says. "There's a diner around the corner."

Nick doesn't move.

"Come on," she says, a desperate tinge to her voice. "We can still salvage the day."

"I don't know," he says, with a small smile. "This doesn't look like it's passing."

The wind picks up, lifting the rain in great sheets of water, but Ryan stands her ground. Nick gets up and follows her out into the open, settling down on the lowest step. He looks somehow small against the weather.

Relenting, she walks over and sits beside him, folding her arms across her knees. "So," she says again, her voice softer now. "What are we doing here?"

"What are we doing here," he repeats, throwing his head back to catch the rain. "You should know this is the last thing I want to be talking about right now."

Ryan understands this is her cue to ask *what*, but she can't bring herself to voice the question.

"I didn't tell you at first, because it didn't feel important," he continues. His eyes are hard now, bright behind the curtain of rain between them. "But it's starting to feel like lying—not talking about it—and so here we are."

"I know," Ryan says, her voice flat. "You're sick." She blinks at him, surprised by the statement, which had come without warning, though she realizes now that she must have known this for some time, maybe since she first met him.

Nick's face doesn't change. "I was," he says. "And could be again."

"I know," Ryan says again, without really knowing anything at all.

"We didn't just move here because of my dad's job," he says. "The only reason he ever looked for work here in the first place was because of me. Because of the doctors here."

The rain is softer now, and the few people passing by on the sidewalk lower their umbrellas and peer up at the sky. Ryan holds out a flattened palm and watches the slow drops fall on her hand, working out how to ask her next question. When she can't come up with anything gentler, she decides to be straightforward. "What's wrong with you?"

He surprises her by laughing. "I'm sorry," he says, holding up his hands. "But you look so serious right now."

She makes a face and punches him lightly on the shoulder, then draws back, a new thought occurring to her. "It's the broken arm, isn't it?"

"One of a few, actually," he says.

"But why?"

"Bad luck?" he says with a grin. "Clumsiness?"

Ryan isn't sure whether to laugh or not. She feels horribly slow right now, her mind churning to no effect. There are a million questions that need answering, and she's fairly certain this is not how a conversation of this sort is supposed to go. Bad news, to Ryan, has always been like being thumped on the head by something heavy. It comes all at once, without shades or degrees. The world goes from white to black in an instant.

But this is different.

Nick, seeing that she hasn't spoken, takes the opportunity to kick at a puddle between them, splashing water onto Ryan's already soaked-through rain jacket.

"But what's—"

"What's wrong with me?" he asks, and he holds out one hand, spreading his fingers wide. As he talks, he ticks them off one by one, and Ryan holds her breath. "It's called osteosarcoma, which is a type of bone cancer that kids get." He raises his arm. "This is the third time I've broken this one. We didn't know why until they found the first tumor a couple years ago. I went through surgery and chemo, both last year, to take care of this guy"—and here, he pulls up his sleeve to point at a scar on his shoulder that Ryan had never seen—"and missed practically the whole school year, which is what landed me in your math class."

When he's finished, he tugs his sleeve back down, then shrugs. There are a thousand questions Ryan wants to ask, a thousand worries caught inside her. She rests her forehead in her hand, feeling dizzy, then realizes the pose might seem too defeatist, and straightens up, trying her best to look upbeat. But her face refuses to cooperate, and her mouth twitches with the effort, falling at the corners. She takes a deep breath—the first half of a sigh—then remembers herself and holds it, worried that he'll notice.

Ryan has experience with this kind of business. She, of all people, understands that worry can look an awful lot like pity if you're not careful.

"I finished treatments about six months ago," he says. "I'm okay for now."

She shifts around on the wet stoop, her hair sticking to her face, her toes clammy and cold, trying to assemble the different strands of information. She wishes Nick would tell the whole story at once, from Point A to Point B, from back-then to here-and-now, without sidebars or detours, just pure chronology, methodical order. Later, she will worry. Later, she will bury her face in her pillow. Later, she will stomp through her backyard and kick at the ground as if it were the grass's fault. There will be time to be irrational and upset and inconsolable, if that's what is to come. But now, she understands, should be for collecting facts. It is a simple matter of staring down the next few waterlogged minutes, the uneven conversation that will—that must—follow. Ryan feels it's up to her to find out just what it is they're up against.

"If you're okay now," she asks, "how come you still had to move here?"

"My dad applied for the job back when I was really sick," Nick says. "But he didn't find out he got it until right after I broke my arm a few months ago."

"And so you moved anyway."

He flicks his eyes away, but doesn't answer. The rain has

mostly stopped now, the last drops filtering through the trees, though the sky is still a deep, gunmetal gray. The traffic has picked up around the stadium and people have begun circling tentatively, watching and wondering and waiting to see if the game might be played after all.

"Don't look at me like that," he says with a wry smile. "It could be worse."

"How?" she asks mechanically.

He tilts his head back, mouth open. "The game could get rained out."

Ryan shakes her head. "Nick."

"I'm sorry," he says. "It's just strange having this conversation with you. Sometimes, I feel like talking to you is the same as talking to myself. Like you already know all there is to know, so there's no point in explaining."

"But I don't," Ryan admits, trying to keep her voice from wobbling. "I just . . ."

"Just want to know whether I'll be okay."

She manages to nod.

"I don't know," he says.

She wants to be nearer to him, to close the gap between them, but she suspects that to move would be to upset the fragile balance of the conversation. And so she sits very still, cutting her eyes out across the street to where the fans are once again emerging onto the abandoned pavement, shielding their eyes against the still-trickling sky.

"This is much easier without the rain," Nick says, and Ryan ventures a sideways look to see that he's smiling. "Bad weather's a little melodramatic, don't you think?"

His eyelashes are still wet, and he looks genuinely content right now, his eyes busy with the awakening world around the ballpark. She knows somehow that this is how she'll always think of him: sitting here on the stoop of someone's brownstone, soaking wet, the two of them like a pair of beggars.

"I guess you were right," she says. "About the storm passing."

"I'm sorry I didn't tell you before," he says, standing up. He stretches a little, then shakes the water from his sneakers. They make slushy noises as he steps down onto the sidewalk. He offers a hand, and Ryan pauses before grabbing it, and then he pulls her up too. When he lets go again, she feels very far away.

"So," he says. "Any other questions, or can we get on to more important things?"

Ryan glances over at the stadium, which looks a pale yellow in the breaking light. A few people are dragging chairs out onto the lawns around them, and the street is suddenly crowded, as if there had never been a storm at all, as if they had only ever imagined it.

Her next question, which is for now to be her last, is the hardest. She lowers her eyes. "Why now?" she asks. "Why are you telling me all this now?"

He glances down at his left arm, still pale from where the cast had been for so many months. "In cases like mine," he says quietly, "there's a better chance of another tumor growing when the bone's broken."

Ryan hesitates for only a moment, then takes his hand. "Let's go," she says, and together, they make their way out onto the street. They move wordlessly toward the stadium—past the ticket booths and the scalpers and all the many gatekeepers to the game—and then continue beyond to find a spot on the outskirts of it all. Even once the rain starts up again, she keeps her hand in his, unwilling to let go.

A short time later, the storm stops almost as swiftly as it had begun, but by then, Ryan and Nick have already given up on the day. And the Cubs—even once they find a patch of sky long enough and clear enough to play—manage to lose anyway, slouching and slinking through each inning as if losing were nothing but a way of surviving until tomorrow, when another game can be played.

Chapter Sixteen

NICK HAS PLANS TO GO UP TO WISCONSIN WITH his family for the Fourth of July, and then spend the rest of the month at his grandparents' lake house, swimming and sailing and barbecuing. None of this should come as a surprise to Ryan, but somehow, the idea that they could be up there carrying on as if nothing were wrong is deeply perplexing.

She'd had a similar feeling after her dad died, a sense of astonishment that the world could still hum along at exactly the same pace, that such a great loss could hardly cause any interruption. But this is different: Nick is still here. And while he spends the month sitting on the edge of a pier, all they can do is hold their breath and wait and hope that another tumor won't show up on his arm. Ryan feels nearly mad with frustration that there's nothing that can be done to prevent it, this possible cancer, this potential disaster.

That afternoon, Nick had walked her home from the train station in silence after the ride north from Wrigleyville, neither willing to be the first to speak, to break the quiet between them that felt somehow safer than words. After she'd taken a hot shower and put her wet clothes in the laundry, Ryan spent a few hours circulating her house like some sort of distressed ghost, until Mom finally pointed to a chair.

"Sit," she said. "Talk."

This struck Ryan as a good idea, though she realized it wasn't Mom who she needed to talk to, but Nick. She backpedaled out of the family room—away from the troubling normalcy of the scene before her, where Mom and Kevin and Emily sat around the television unaware that anything had changed today—and left for Nick's house.

His mother answered the door, and though Ryan attempted a greeting, her tongue was thick in her mouth. "He's upstairs, honey," Mrs. Crowley said, and Ryan thanked her, then hurried up and knocked on the door to his bedroom.

"I have a few more questions," she told him when he appeared in the doorway.

He stepped back to let her in. "I sort of thought you might."

They spent the evening sitting on the floor of his room. There were no more jokes, no more long pauses. He answered her questions dutifully, as distantly as if he were talking about someone else.

"What are the chances it will come back?" she asked.

"I don't know," he said. "It either will or it won't."

"But if it does?"

"*If* it does, it would depend on how bad it is," he said evenly, his words measured in the quiet room. "And whether it's self-contained or not."

"What happens if it is?"

"Same thing as before, probably."

"Surgery?"

"And chemo."

"But if it's worse?"

"It could spread to the rest of the bone or my lungs," he said, and this was the first time Ryan thought she could detect a hint of alarm in his eyes. Or, at the very least, the first time he'd failed to hide it.

"But this is all just a big maybe," she said. "Right?"

He nodded. "Hopefully the worst of it's behind me."

Ryan pulled her legs beneath her and watched him, unsure

what more to ask, afraid to unsettle the frail architecture of trust between them.

"Would it be weird if I asked you not to mention this to anyone?" Nick asked.

"Not at all," she said, smiling dolefully. "It's not exactly like I have a lot of people to tell anyhow."

"It's just been nice," he said. "Not having anyone here know."

As they talked, the square of sky in Nick's bedroom window fell dark, and Ryan noticed this with surprise. It could have been seven o'clock as easily as ten; she felt somewhere beyond time right now, firmly outside the mundane constraints of dinner hour and curfew.

"What can I do?" she asked.

"Pretend like I never told you?"

"I don't know if I can do that."

"Then pretend like it'll all turn out okay."

She tried to keep her voice from wavering. "It *will*," she said. "Of course it will."

"Look at that," he said with a humorless little laugh. "You've got the hang of it already."

This year's Fourth of July begins with the sound of Mom throwing up in the bathroom down the hall. Ryan waits outside the door for a few minutes to be sure it's just the usual morning sickness before climbing back into bed. She has no plans for the holiday other than to avoid all the places where her classmates are sure to be gathered for the day's festivities. With Nick out of town, she has nobody to go with to the parade or the fireworks, and after last week's conversation, these things now seem small and silly anyway.

When Kevin knocks on the door to her bedroom, Ryan opens one eye.

"Your mom's not feeling well," he says, from out in the hallway. "She asked if you and I would take Emily into town for the parade."

Ryan stumbles out of bed and pulls open the door. Emily's standing beside Kevin, decked out in red, white, and blue and clutching a miniature flag. "Hurry up," she says, hopping from one foot to the other. "We don't want to miss the beginning."

"Fine," Ryan says. "But I'm not wearing something patriotic."

"Wear anything you want," Kevin says. "As long as you're ready soon."

"It's not like she doesn't have a million Cubs shirts with those colors," she hears Emily say as the two of them head downstairs.

The parade, led by the volunteer firemen in their noisy trucks, runs through the center of the village, circling the small green and then winding alongside the shops. The show doesn't vary much from year to year, and as they pick their way through the curbside spectators, trying to find a spot, Ryan can see the same familiar floats from when she was little. There are marching bands from area high schools, local political figures in antique cars, members of the garden club with their watering cans.

Mixed among the families with plaid blankets and lawn chairs, dozens of kids from Ryan's school wander through the crowd. She notices a few boys from her history class smoking cigarettes behind the post office, and others are gathered just down the block. Lucy's there too—wearing a little red-and-white dress with a blue head-band—the only one of the whole group dressed in the colors of the day, yet she somehow manages to make everyone else look dumb for not thinking of doing the same. One of the boys hands her a blue cup with a drink he's mixed for her, and Lucy stands on the edge of the curb, observing the parade with a look of mild interest. Sydney and Kate are, of course, there beside her, tucked back on a blanket with a few of the other girls.

Not one of them would be caught dead with their parents right now, much less a stepfather wearing an American flag pin and a little sister with red, white, and blue ribbons in her hair. Ryan couldn't possibly feel less festive as they settle onto the curb beside an elderly couple straining to see the next float. When a church group marches by tossing candy for the kids, she gets hit in the head with a lollipop.

"We're not staying for the whole thing, are we?" she asks Kevin, who laughs as if she's made some sort of joke, then offers her a juice box. Ryan stabs her straw into the top of it, watching a group of kids on bikes, their wheels decorated with streamers like pinwheels. She used to ride every year too, with Sydney and Kate, and Dad had always led the small procession dressed as Uncle Sam—complete with star-spangled top hat, shiny striped pants, and a fake beard—while Mom stood off to the side and clapped.

He loved nothing more than holidays, but the Fourth was always his favorite. One year, he built a catapult out of a funnel and some rubber tubes, and after the parade, he'd organized a contest to see who could launch a water balloon the farthest. At the block parties, he was always the one in charge of the barbecue, and later, when the evening grew dark and the fireworks had yet to start, he was there to pass out sparklers, helping even the littlest kids light up the small piece of night around them.

Ryan watches Emily now as she creeps up to the street, craning her neck to wait for the next float as the brassy sounds of a band die away.

"The lawn mower guys are my favorite," she says, bouncing up and down on her knees as a disheveled group of middle-aged men pushing lawn mowers marches by dressed like the Statue of Liberty.

"They were Dad's, too," Ryan tells her, and Emily turns around. "And mine."

This makes her smile. "We have good taste."

"Yeah," Ryan says. "We do."

All four of them make it down to the beach later for the fireworks, after Mom emerges from her room feeling better. They spread a blanket out onto the sand, which is peppered with families like their own, gathering together as the light begins to fail over the water.

While Emily helps Kevin assemble dinner, Mom and Ryan take off down the beach, their feet sinking into the soft sand as the color continues to disappear across the sky. Mom clasps her hands behind her back, and from the look on her face, Ryan can tell she has something to say. But they move along in silence, dipping in and out of the water as the surf creeps up the beach. A few kids run past with buckets, and a bit farther down, others watch while their dads set off tiny firecrackers in the sand.

"So," Mom says finally. "Should I be worried?"

Ryan looks up at her sharply. "About me?" she asks, then frowns. "No."

"You know we learn this stuff in Parenting 101," Mom says. "If your kid gets sullen and withdrawn, you're supposed to have the 'Just Say No to Drugs' talk."

"Trust me," Ryan says with a smile. "I'm not doing drugs."

Mom stops walking and puts a hand on each of her shoulders, forcing Ryan to look her in the eye. "I know," she says, turning serious. "And I also know you haven't had an easy time of things. But the last few days . . ." She trails off and shakes her head. "I don't know. You've seemed sadder than usual."

"I'm fine," Ryan insists, trying her best to look it.

"I know," Mom says. "I also know you're a good kid. And that freshman year wasn't easy for you."

"Mom . . ."

"But it's not really supposed to be," she continues. "You know what your dad would have said."

The answer comes easily. "Keep your chin up."

Mom smiles. "Always keep moving."

They say the last part together. "It'll all work out in the end."

The beach is now nearly completely dark, the water at their feet an inky color. Ryan digs at the sand with her toe, her shoulders curled forward.

"Hey," Mom says. "It's okay to be unsure about things. That's what high school's all about."

Ryan chooses her words carefully. "I know he was probably right, that if you just push through hard enough, everything will eventually be okay."

"But?"

"Don't you ever wish you could go backward, instead of forward?"

Even in the dark, she can see the smile slip from Mom's face, replaced by a cloudy look, her eyes liquid and far away. For a moment, Ryan thinks that maybe she feels the same way. That perhaps Mom, too, might know what it's like to lose your grip on the moment, one finger at a time, white-knuckled and shaky with fear. But it doesn't take long to recognize the look on her face as one of concern.

"We don't have that sort of choice," Mom says. "Forward is all we've got."

Ryan nods, understanding that she's the only one who's still stuck. But even as she follows her father's words like bread crumbs—what other choice does she have but to try?—she's still clinging to that backward glance, that one last look, that inside-out, upside-down feeling that's less hope than regret. It's a kind of sadness that has lodged itself in the back of her throat like a pill that refuses to go down.

"Are you sure you're okay?" Mom asks, putting an arm

around her shoulders and steering them back up the beach.

"I'm sure," Ryan tells her. The fireworks are starting now, the littlest ones first, red and blue and silver starbursts that light up the sky for a brief moment before disappearing. When they find Emily and Kevin in the darkness, they lie on their backs, eyes to the sky.

"Those are my favorite," Emily says, watching an enormous gold one explode and then fizzle in great dusty streaks, melting into the sky like a weeping willow.

"Mine too," Ryan says, and Mom gives her hand a squeeze.

"They were your father's, too," she says, and they all watch, afraid to blink as one after another brightens the sky, flickering brightly before giving way to the next.

On the way home, they pass Sydney's house, and Ryan sets down the picnic basket she's been carrying to stare at the cars lined up in the driveway. She's listening to the laughter drifting from the backyard, the splashes and high-pitched shouts from the pool, when Mom notices she's fallen behind.

"Parents out of town?" she asks, walking back over.

"Yup," Ryan says, squinting at the fence through the darkness. "I'm sure the whole school's in there."

Mom reaches out and gives her ponytail a little tug. "We're more fun to hang out with anyway," she says.

Ryan looks skeptically up the street to where Emily's turning cartwheels on the grass, and Kevin is staring up at the stars from his perch on the cooler.

"If it makes you feel any better," Mom says, "this kind of thing happens your whole life. It's not just high school. Your friendships are always going to be changing."

"It's not that," Ryan says. "At least not *just* that."

Mom tilts her head. "Well, then is it Nick?"

"Sort of," she admits, looking away. "But probably not what you think."

"Do you want to talk about it?"

Ryan hadn't realized that this is what she'd been waiting to hear, but now that it's out there, now that she has Mom to herself, right here beside her and ready to help tackle any problem, she hesitates. Because what is there to say, really? What they know with certainty has already passed—that he'd had cancer, that he'd beat it—and what might still happen is nothing more than a possibility.

In just a few weeks, Nick will return from Wisconsin, and this is what Ryan thinks about as she steels herself against the sounds coming up over the hedges from Sydney's house. She lets her eyes flutter shut. Right there in the dark, she makes a decision. *He'll be okay,* she thinks, and then thinks it again. *He will be okay.*

And so there it is: a small, wobbly step forward. It is, for now, the best she can do. It's the closest she can get.

When she doesn't answer, Mom asks whether she's okay for the second time tonight. "I am," Ryan says, because it's what she needs to believe, because—if nothing else—she knows how little it would take for her to come undone right now.

There are more scattered cheers beyond the fence, and Ryan gives a little shrug.

"Look at it this way," Mom says, patting her stomach. "At least now you'll have plenty of time to baby-sit."

She rolls her eyes. "Super."

Mom laughs and loops an arm through Ryan's, and they make their way up the sidewalk to join the other two on their slow journey home, four pale figures in the dark, all of them ready for bed.

Chapter Seventeen

WHILE SHE ENDURES THE REMAINDER OF JULY, waiting for Nick's return and avoiding the heat, Ryan makes a project out of the new baby's room, scraping the cakey beige paint from the walls and then using a long roller to cover them in a soft blue. It pleases her how meticulous she's become, carefully taping the corners and using a tiny brush to avoid splattering. It's easy to get lost in the room, to spend long hours escaping into the endless blue of the walls, the dizzying smell of the paint. She tries not to worry as she works, but as August approaches, Ryan grows nervous that things will have changed with Nick when he returns. He'd left just after revealing a part of himself almost too huge to imagine, and secrets like that, once out in the open, have a way of wedging themselves between people. She wonders whether he'll regret having told her at all.

The Cubs, meanwhile, have moved into the second half of the season without any sort of fanfare, closing the gaps in the standings as they inch from fourth place to third, and then on to second in their division. There is a quiet determination to their style of play now, a late season surge that might go unnoticed by anyone not watching closely.

Ryan, however, is watching closely. And she's sure that Nick must be too.

It's been nearly three weeks since they've spoken by the time he finally calls, and Ryan's in the backyard helping Mom water the flowers when Emily runs outside with the portable phone.

"It's your boyfriend," she says, grinning, dancing from one

bare foot to the other, a hand loosely covering the receiver.

Ryan frowns at her—mortified that Nick might have heard—and snatches the phone away, slipping inside the screen door and up to her room. She hesitates before answering, thinking briefly of their last conversations before he left, those grim revelations that had left them both heart-heavy and drained. But when she finally puts the phone to her ear, any worry she felt disappears.

"How's the lake?" she asks, struggling to keep the giddiness from her voice, and when Nick answers—a typically laconic "not bad"—she's pleased that in spite of himself, he sounds equally enthusiastic, the two of them like actors overplaying their roles, booming and eager and altogether thrilled by the fragile trail of wires connecting them across the miles.

"The cottage is like a clown car," he says. "There are a million little cousins running around in swim trunks, and the whole place smells like wet towels."

"Sounds pretty good to me," Ryan says, leaning back on her bed. "Definitely more exciting than my house."

"And cards," he says. "My grandma keeps trying to teach me bridge whenever it rains. Bridge!"

"I could see you being good at bridge."

"I bet you don't even know what bridge is . . ."

"How do you know?" Ryan challenges, but Nick only laughs.

"I just do," he says.

"What else?" she asks.

"My dad's teaching me how to drive the motorboat," he says. "He keeps telling stories about when his dad taught him, and how it was so much harder back then, because the boats didn't have this or that."

"Typical dad stuff," Ryan says, and though she hadn't meant it as anything significant—hadn't at all been thinking about her own dad and all the many things he would never teach her—

they both fall into an abrupt and worried silence. It takes Ryan a moment to rescue the conversation. "I bet you'll be good at it," she says. "Driving the boat."

"Doubt it," Nick says cheerfully. "So what have *you* been up to?"

"Let's see," she says, humming a little. "Yesterday I helped Kevin pull weeds in the front yard, and then Emily and I made orange juice popsicles. And then last night, Mom and I watched a special on surfing in Australia before going to bed embarrassingly early."

"I wouldn't mind being a surfer in Australia," Nick says, then adds, "if being manager of the Cubs doesn't work out."

"You wouldn't be able to watch the games down there, though."

"True," he says. "I guess I'd have to get into cricket. Do you know they have tea breaks? I mean, there's no way it can count as a real sport if they stop for a cup of tea."

Ryan giggles. "It sort of sounds like golf."

There are a few muffled yelps on his end of the phone, and then a vague cheering sound, and Nick groans. "My uncle just threw my cousin into the lake."

"Sounds like you could be next."

"It's possible," he says. "So, I'm back next Tuesday. I'll call you then?"

"Sounds good," Ryan says, leaving the phone pressed to her ear even once he's hung up, imagining his dad and his uncles waiting to pounce, nudging him into the lake—a bit more gently than his cousins, whose arms are not so prone to fractures, whose lives are not so knowingly fragile—and she smiles at the thought of it: Nick pinwheeling off the end of the pier, all pale limbs and freckles and laughter.

On the last weekend before he's due home, Ryan spends an entire day up in the attic, sneezing as she rummages through sagging cardboard boxes filled with books and toys from when she and Emily were little. She carts all of it downstairs to the tiny room at the end of the hallway, and when Mom appears at the doorway, Ryan is sitting cross-legged on the floor, a picture book spread in her lap.

"I can't remember," Ryan says, looking up. "Did Dad used to read these to us?"

Mom lowers herself carefully beside her, a hand on her stomach. "I'm afraid it was usually me," she says. "I had bedtime duty. He was in charge of wake-up calls."

Ryan smiles. "He used to make a bugle out of his hand and march around my room in the mornings."

"Sounds about right," Mom says.

"I'm sorry this baby won't have someone like him," Ryan says, then shakes her head. "I don't mean anything bad about Kevin. I'm just saying that we were lucky to have Dad, and it's sad that he won't."

"Yeah, but he'll have you," Mom says, reaching out to take her hand, and to Ryan's surprise, she pulls it over to rest on her belly. It takes a moment, but when she finally feels it, Ryan widens her eyes. There's the tiniest thump beneath her fingers, a faint hiccup of movement.

"Wow," she says, sucking in a breath. She keeps her hand still, but the baby has fallen quiet again. Ryan doesn't blame him; he still has three more months tucked away from the world in there, three more months to doze in peace. She pats Mom's stomach once before folding her hands in her lap.

"I guess I could probably keep an eye on him," Ryan says, and Mom points to the Cubs pennant taped to the door.

"Just don't get him hooked too early," she says. "No need to crush the poor kid right away."

Ryan's desperate to get out of the house and Nick's eager to avoid unpacking, and so on the day he returns home, they agree to meet at the beach. When she pulls her bike up along the path that follows the water, Ryan sees him standing with his back to her, a flock of kids building sand castles near his feet.

It occurs to her now that despite weeks of overthinking it, she hadn't settled on just what to say once he came back. And despite her rush to get here, she now takes her time locking up her bike, her heart quickening at the thought of this uncertain reunion.

But when Nick turns and sees her, his face breaking into a smile, Ryan forgets everything else. He's sunburned and freckled, and his hair is lighter. He jogs over, weaving through beach towels and picnic baskets, and when they're close enough, he bends to give her a hug.

"I missed you," Ryan finds herself saying before she has a chance to weigh the pros and cons of such a statement. But it's the truest thing she can think to say. She'd missed him even more than she expected she would.

Nick leans back, still half-hugging her, and Ryan can tell from the look on his face that he's about to kiss her. She feels suddenly and swiftly happy—happier than she has in ages—leaning against him with the sun on her back and her feet sunk low in the hot sand. She stands on her tiptoes and kisses him back, managing until the last moment to avoid grinning. Nick pulls away, laughing, and Ryan smiles into his neck.

"I missed you, too," he says, stretching an arm around her shoulders and steering her toward the ledge where the sidewalk meets the beach. "It felt like a lot longer than a month."

Ryan bows her head, suddenly shy. "For me too," she says, and then as if they'd already agreed to it, neither says anything more about the past weeks, the long days behind them, which no longer seem important now that they're here together. It is this way too, with all that had been said about Nick's past. They sit with their feet dangling in the glinting sand, burying it all: the surgery, the chemo, the threat of what could still come. In this—this hesitant march forward—Ryan has found a traveling companion.

"So, our boys are rallying pretty hard," Nick says. "When should we go down for another game?"

"Tickets are impossible to get now," Ryan tells him. "It doesn't take much to get people excited around here."

"Then it's a lucky thing we don't require tickets."

"That's true," she says, sliding off the ledge. Nick follows her down the beach, and Ryan hops from one foot to the other, yelping at the temperature of the sand.

"Put your shoes on," Nick says, laughing, but she ignores him and sprints down to the water ahead of him. By the time he catches up, she's already up to her knees in the lake, her arms prickling with goose bumps. Nick loiters a few feet away, back-pedaling each time a wave rushes at him, and he manages to duck away when Ryan kicks some water in his direction.

"Hey!" he shouts. "What gives?"

She raises one eyebrow at him. "You'll sit outside during the biggest storm of the summer, but you're afraid of a little lake water?"

He rolls his eyes, but inches out a bit farther. There are a few sailboats in the distance, their white sails glowing in the midday sun, and the water is riddled with inner tubes and floaties. Ryan is standing knee-deep in her shorts and tank top, curling her toes against the sandy bottom when she feels the heaviness of two hands on her shoulders, and her feet give out beneath her. When she comes up again, spitting water and clawing away the wet hair from her face, Nick is doubled over, laughing.

"You're toast," she says, lunging at him. He tries running

back toward the beach, but his legs move in slow motion in the water, and Ryan manages to pull him under too. He bobs back up a moment later, blinking indignantly, but now that they're both soaked, they linger out there, floating on their backs until they drift too far and have to paddle back. When they finally decide to swim to shore, they collapse onto the sand, their arms spread wide as they dry out in the sun. Impossibly happy, Ryan closes her eyes and listens to Nick breathing beside her.

"Want to come over for dinner tonight?" he asks, and she rolls her head to look at him. "I'm the world's best barbecuer."

"And modest, too," she jokes.

"It's hard to be modest when you can grill as well as I can."

"Okay, then," she says. "But just know that my expectations are high."

When they've had enough sun and have nearly dried out again, they wheel their bikes up the path that curls out from the beach. Ryan reaches over to swat the back of Nick's shirt, and he whirls around.

"You're still covered in sand," she tells him.

"You too," he grins. "But you don't see me beating up on you."

They're almost out of the parking lot, past the snack bar and the showers, when they pass Lucy and Sydney, sitting in what look like matching bikinis and surveying the crowd. Ryan quickens her pace, hoping to avoid them altogether, but Lucy calls Nick's name and waves them over.

"I know, I know," he says when Ryan gives him a look, and she wonders whether he's also thinking about the dance last spring. Neither one of them has seen Lucy since school ended, and Ryan can't imagine she's not still angry about what had happened that night.

But when they're still a few feet away, Lucy points her Popsicle at Nick. "You're coming to the party tonight, right?"

Surprised, Nick glances at Ryan, then back at the other girls. "What party?"

"Sydney's parents are coming back into town tomorrow," Lucy says, looking almost embarrassed for them. "Last big party of the summer."

Ryan catches Sydney's eye, but she looks quickly away.

"You in or out?" Lucy asks.

"We actually have dinner plans," Nick says, and Ryan can't help feeling the tiniest bit satisfied by the rare display of surprise on Lucy's face.

But she rights herself quickly. "Well, she can come too," Lucy says, then turns to Ryan. "You're into sports, right? There'll be all sorts of drinking games. So even *you* might have fun."

It seems beside the point to mention that she doesn't drink, so Ryan just folds her arms and glances over at Nick.

"Maybe we'll stop by later," he offers, and Sydney nods ambivalently.

Lucy claps her hands. "You should. It's going to be the best party of the summer."

Once they're far enough away, across the parking lot and heading toward home, Ryan shakes her head. "What do you think *that* was all about?" she asks Nick.

"It sounds like it's just going to be a good party."

"Yeah," Ryan says. "Caught that."

Nick laughs. "Maybe she's had a change of heart."

"Or maybe she has sunstroke," she suggests. "We're not really going, are we?"

"Why not?" He shrugs. "The rest of the guys will probably be there, and I haven't seen them all summer. Besides, it could be fun."

"Doubt it."

"You said you've been bored too," Nick points out.

"Not *that* bored."

"Come on," he says. "What else do you have to do?"

She sighs. "Okay, but if it's awful, I'm not staying."

"If we go together," he says, "it won't be awful."

Hard as she tries, Ryan's unable to argue with the logic in that.

Chapter Eighteen

BY THE TIME THEY ARRIVE AT THE PARTY, THE POOL IS already littered with red and blue plastic cups, lit from below by the wavery lights so that they look menacing as jellyfish. Someone had managed to order a keg, and a small group is huddled around the giant garbage can that holds it, thrusting their empty cups blindly toward the guy at the tap. There's a foamy, beery smell to the yard, as if the grass itself has been soaked through, and the song on the stereo—more rhythm than melody—quivers out across the crowded yard and into the neighborhood beyond. Ryan's fairly certain that this is not what Sydney had in mind when she'd agreed to the party. Even the sprinklers have been switched on, creating a trail of muddy footprints in and out of the back door to the kitchen, where she and Kate used to come over after school to bake cookies.

Ryan and Nick exchange a look from where they stand at the top of the driveway on tiptoes, surveying the scene beyond the latched gate. There's a loud cry from just past where they can see, and a moment later, Will O'Malley hurtles himself off the edge of the diving board—a full cup of beer in hand—and attempts a flip into the pool. It ends in a belly flop, and he emerges from the water laughing, then heads straight back to the keg. Ryan hears a few scattered warnings of silence—*shh, the neighbors!*—but this is followed by loud laughter.

She turns to Nick. "We could still go back to your house."

"I see what you're doing," he says. "You're looking for seconds on the burgers."

Ryan rolls her eyes. When Nick moves to unlatch the gate

leading to the backyard, she puts a hand on his arm. "Seriously,"
she says. "What's the point?"

"We're already here," he says. "We may as well go in."

They pick their way among discarded cups and strewn sandals to where a group of Nick's friends are standing around the
barbecue. Ryan automatically hangs back, an instinct she can't
seem to shake. She's grown used to being invisible. But now,
after they greet Nick with slaps on the back and a few good-
natured barbs at his absence this summer, they lift their chins
to Ryan, too. A few months ago, she would have never thought
this possible. A few months ago, she would have been home in
bed right now.

Nick hooks an arm around her shoulders casually—so casually, in fact, that it takes Ryan a moment to realize it's happened
at all. She struggles to keep a straight face, doing her best not to
smile. She wonders if it's possible to jinx something simply by
taking too much joy in it.

Nick spots a deck of cards, sticky with beer, on a picnic
table off to one side of the patio. He motions to Will and a few
other guys, and minutes later, Ryan finds herself sitting with
them at the table. Her eyes stray toward the pool, where Sydney
and Lucy are perched on the edge, their legs tracing circles in
the too-blue water. Neither looks happy that such an important
component of the party has drifted away. Ryan hadn't been to
any of Sydney's other parties this summer, but she's pretty sure
this isn't how they had planned things to work out.

"You in or out?" one of the guys asks Ryan, and she hesitates.
Nick watches her with amusement as he shuffles the cards.

"What are we playing?" she asks.

"How about bullshit?" Lucy suggests as she walks over
to the table, positioning herself directly behind Ryan. "That's
always interesting."

Will shrugs, and Nick cuts the deck. Ryan notices Sydney and Kate and a handful of other girls forming a circle around the table. Nick nudges her shoulder.

"You in?" he asks, beginning to deal. Ryan swallows hard and nods.

When she's been dealt all her cards, she tries to look at each one without fanning them out. Lucy stands behind her making little noises of approval, and Ryan resists the urge to jab her with her elbow.

Will goes first. "I've got one two," he says, tossing a card face down into the middle of the table. He looks stone-faced at each person, daring anyone to challenge him. Ryan swats at a bug near her face. When enough time has passed, the next player, a tall guy whose name Ryan has forgotten, throws in three cards.

During Nick's turn, Ryan's almost certain he's lying. But by the time she musters up the nerve to call him on it, Will slaps a hand down on the pile of cards.

"Bull*shit*," he says.

Nick waves a hand lazily in the air. "Go ahead," he says. "Try me."

Ryan doesn't watch Will as he reveals the card. She's too busy studying Nick's face, trying to see past the mask of indifference, beyond the tactics of the game. She's nearly positive that he's bluffing, but when Will flips the cards at the center, Nick lets out a loud laugh.

"Pick 'em up," he tells Will, who groans as he collects the discard pile.

Nick grins at Ryan's expression. "It's a lot easier to just tell the truth."

"But that's not the game," Lucy points out. "That's not how you win."

Nick seems unconcerned. "There are all sorts of ways to

win," he says, still looking at Ryan. She eyes the cards in her hand, running her thumb over the glossy surface. Behind her, Lucy juts out her hip and sighs, but Ryan isn't paying any attention. She shuffles her cards, flipping them from one hand to the other, staring at them as if a five might somehow materialize. Finally, and with no other choice, she slides a six from beneath her thumb and lays it face down in the center of the table.

"One five," she lies.

"Oh, please," says Lucy.

The guys all look to Nick, as if it were his responsibility to challenge her. He rubs his chin and regards her quietly. After a long moment, he nods at the guy sitting to Ryan's other side.

"You're up," Nick says, and everyone at the table exchanges a look. But then the next player tosses in a couple of cards, and the attention shifts in his direction.

Nick moves closer to Ryan. "You're an awful liar," he says, his breath tickling her ear.

She turns, just slightly, so that their faces are only inches away. "How do you know I wasn't telling the truth?"

"I can just tell," he says.

"Can you?"

He nods. "Your eyes give you away."

Ryan blinks. They sit watching each other, and the smile slips from her face. She feels suddenly too visible, as if he can see straight through her. Her stomach does a tiny flip, and she looks down at her lap, no longer in the mood to joke. The space around the table feels choked with people, the temperature suddenly too warm. She rises from her seat abruptly, bumping her knee on the bench and half-falling into Lucy, who is standing behind her.

Ryan hears the soft splash of the beer before she realizes what happened.

When she turns, Lucy's staring down at her shoes, a pair of delicate sandals Ryan hadn't noticed before—and probably never would have, were they not now drenched in beer, a deeper color pink spreading along the thin straps. Lucy picks up one foot then the other, examining the bottoms of her jeans, now stained a dark blue, and Ryan can almost feel the collective intake of breath from the table behind her.

There is no shriek, no scream, not even a whimper from Lucy. Instead, she looks up at Ryan with eyes hard and angry. "My dad *just* bought these for me."

"I'm really sorry," Ryan mumbles. "I didn't mean—"

"What?" Lucy snaps. "To barrel into me?"

Nick is up now too. "It was just an accident."

Kate appears with a roll of paper towels, and Ryan flashes her a grateful smile then stands waiting for something to happen. The party behind them has come to a rapid halt, and the yard is quiet except for the soft hiss of the barbecue. Lucy stoops to mop at her ruined shoes with a paper towel, and Ryan wonders whether she should help her.

"I'll pay you back for them," she hears herself say, then immediately regrets it.

Lucy rises slowly, wiping her hands. "They were a gift from my father," she says accusingly, as if Ryan had suggested replacing a family heirloom.

Ryan wishes everyone would stop looking at her. She considers just walking away, but isn't sure how to begin so bold a course of action. Lucy's still glaring at her, but by now, she's beginning to lose center stage. Someone has turned the music back on, and behind her, the guys have resumed their card game. Sydney disappears behind the sliding door and emerges a moment later with another stack of cups. Will follows her over to the keg.

Unsure what to do, Ryan remains where she's standing and studies her feet. She puffs out her cheeks. "I'm sorry," she says again.

"Sorry doesn't really do much for my shoes."

"I said I'd pay—"

Lucy cuts her off. "You don't have to pay for them." She smirks, then she leans in close to Ryan, her tone deliberately light. "Isn't that what dads are for?"

Ryan takes a step back as if she's been struck, nearly stumbling again. Nick reaches out an arm to steady her, but she doesn't notice. Her eyes are locked on Lucy's, and she's doing her best to hide whatever hurt might be mixed in with all the anger. She balls her hands into two tight fists, trembling all over and fighting the urge to shoot back at her with something equally spiteful.

But by the time she collects herself, Lucy's already gone, stalking inside to rinse out her designer sandals. Ryan feels nearly dizzy with resentment, with pure outrage at her comment. Nick takes her by the elbow, and she follows him blindly, the music fading behind them, until they're out in the shadowy light of the driveway.

Ryan takes a deep, gulping breath. "I can't believe . . ."

"That was a cheap shot," Nick says quietly. She hasn't ever spoken to him about her dad, and she can tell now by the way he's looking at her that he's unsure of the proper etiquette for this sort of situation.

But Ryan's too preoccupied to care. "I should've dumped another beer on her," she says, still shaking. "I should've done *something*."

"What could you have done?" Nick asks, pacing the driveway in uncertain circles around her. Ryan watches his shadow lengthen and recede in the pools of light from the garage. "You're better off just walking away."

"I always just walk away," she says with a frown. She rests her hands on top of her head and then leaves them there, as if having forgotten to reclaim them. A few fireflies blink yellow in the night, and Ryan watches them until they disappear again. She lowers her eyes. "I hate that I always walk away."

"There's a difference between walking away from a fight, and walking away in general," Nick says. "It's the difference between being smart and being scared."

Ryan considers this for a moment. "How do you know I'm not scared?"

"Because," he says, his green eyes bright as he watches her across the driveway. He stops walking and twists his mouth up at the corners. "Because you didn't get scared off when I told you about the cancer."

Ryan's face softens, and she smiles at him from across the driveway—a grateful, watery smile—before crossing the space between them and circling her arms around his waist. She can feel his chin against the top of her head, and when she looks up, he brings his face low so that their foreheads are touching.

"I'm sorry for making us leave," she says, apologizing for what feels like the thousandth time tonight. "I know you were having fun."

"I'm having fun with *you*," Nick says, then swallows back a laugh. "Besides, that was the funniest thing I've seen in a while."

Ryan manages a weak grin. "Not from where I was standing."

"I'm sorry," he says, though she can feel his ribs shaking with laughter. "It's just that seeing you knock over that cup . . ."

"Okay," she says, stepping back and rolling her eyes at him. "Now would be a good time for that poker face of yours."

Without looking back, Ryan turns to make her way down the darkened driveway, away from the party and the evening's fading disasters. When she reaches the sidewalk, she rounds the corner, moving through the web of shadows and light made by the trees and the stars and the streetlamps.

She doesn't check to see whether Nick is following.

She already knows he'll be there.

Chapter Nineteen

THEY TAKE A SHORTCUT HOME, MEANDERING THROUGH the neighborhood across a chain of linked backyards. Neither speaks, and this reminds Ryan of their first meeting outside the stadium, the way they'd walked so purposefully together without really having any idea where it might lead them. The bluish grass tickles her feet as they pass beneath a large brick house, the lawn spread wide and flat beyond the reach of the patio lights.

Nick pauses to kick at a baseball lying half-hidden in the grass, and Ryan stands waiting a few feet ahead, looking on as he bends to pick it up. The ball is a dull gray, streaked with grass stains visible even in the darkness, and the seams are coming out on one side. He runs his fingers over it, his face unreadable, then tosses her the ball.

Ryan, caught off guard, just barely snags it. "I sort of have a feeling this belongs to the dog," she says, wiping her palms on her jeans after throwing it back to him. The ball finds Nick's hands with a bright smacking sound, the sound of summer, of backyards and dirt fields and dugouts.

"I could never really play baseball as a kid," he says, winding up with the exaggerated motion of a pitcher on the mound. "I was always getting hurt or breaking something. It took forever to figure out why, and then once we did, I was always in the middle of some treatment or another."

This is the most she's heard him talk about his past since he first told her about it, and Ryan wishes she could see his face. They fall into a rhythm with the ball, the back-and-forth motion like something choreographed.

"Little League's overrated anyway," she says, reaching out to catch a wild throw. "I only did it one year, and on the second day, I went to field an easy ground ball and it hit a divot in the dirt and popped up."

"Black eye?"

"Bloody nose," she says. "That was pretty much it for me."

Each time he throws the ball back, Ryan waits for it to emerge from the darkness as if from nowhere.

"It's never really been about the sport anyway," she says. "I never liked wearing cleats and sweaty caps and getting dusty. It was never baseball that was the thing."

"It was the Cubs," Nick says.

Ryan nods, and then, as if they were one and the same, she says, "It was my dad."

He waits for her to continue, but how to begin something like this? It's a bit rusty, this story. Years ago, she'd learned how not to tell it, creating instead a sad and silent fiction all of her own. Talking about him felt like a betrayal of some kind. How else, but through silence, can you prevent memories from turning into memorials?

But to her surprise, the words well up inside her now. "It's hardest in the summer," she says. "Not having him around."

She lowers the ball in her hand, feeling desperately out of practice. For five years, there had sometimes been friends and sometimes not. There had been Mom and Emily and Kevin, but Ryan herself had been absent in some ways, and now she feels like something inside of her is waking up again, something raw and watchful, a hole she'd thought too big to fill.

"When he died . . ." she begins, then hesitates. Her knees are wobbly, and she sinks down onto the cool of the grass without even realizing she's doing it, the forgotten ball rolling to a stop near her foot. "He loved baseball, but not in the way most people do," she says, her voice breaking. "Not the scores or the standings, but just the game itself."

Nick approaches slowly to join her, unfolding himself onto the ground too, and they lie on their backs listening to the low, mournful whistle of a distant train.

"I know it must sound ridiculous, in a way," Ryan says, "only talking about baseball. Because he loved other things too: me and my sister and my mom and our dog, and he loved burnt bacon and new socks and mint toothpaste and cleaning out the garage and planning trips." Here, she trails off, afraid to go on, because what lies ahead is the accident; the scene to be set is a winding river, white-capped waves, rocks like mines in a narrow blue field. And to venture there might be to cry, and to cry would be to let go.

"I bet I would have liked him," Nick says. Above them, the sky is fuzzy and gray, a colorless curtain draped low over the neighborhood so that no stars can be seen. The lights in the house go off, and Ryan stares out into this new shade of darkness.

"Do you believe everything happens for a reason?" she asks Nick, who raises his head and props himself on one elbow to look at her.

"I'd like to think so," he says truthfully.

"But?"

"But what reason could there be for all this?" He waves his hand in the air, and Ryan knows exactly what he's talking about: the long stretches of time he'd spent in the hospital, her father being gone too soon, the breathlessness of being so close to something so final.

She leans back again, the grass tickling her neck. Dad would have had an answer for him, some philosophy about fate or destiny, some profound notion about the strengthening of character through hardship and loss.

"It would be nice," Nick offers, "to have something like that to believe in."

"But you don't?"

He turns away, and after a minute, she becomes certain he won't answer, but then because he's so close and because the night has grown quiet around them, she can hear a soft click in his throat, and he's facing her once more.

"It's like the Cubs," he says. "We say 'wait till next year' so much that it almost doesn't mean anything at all. I mean, do you *really* think they'll win it this year? Or next year, or the year after that?"

"I do," she whispers. "I want them to."

Nick shakes his head. "There's a difference between wanting something and believing something."

Ryan understands this, but to her, the distinction feels murky, the lines blurred.

"There's just as good a chance that they'll never win at all," he says.

This is not a possibility that had ever occurred to her: not when she'd once seen them lose twenty-one to three, not when they traded her favorite player last season, not even when they'd lost eight in a row at Wrigley. About the Cubs, her dad had instilled in her the kind of unshakable faith that doesn't leave room for doubt, a brand of hope known only to romantics and gamblers. And if this had failed her elsewhere, then Wrigley Field was the one place it remained true, this firm understanding that everything would work out in the end.

Nick is looking at her now through such rational eyes, the logic behind them heavy and old, and she fishes through her memory, wishing she had something to offer him right now. But without Dad here, the only words she can think to say are hollow, nothing more than a loose collection of floating letters, impossible to pin down without his help.

"You can't ever count on a win until the final score is posted," Nick says, and realizing they're no longer talking about baseball, Ryan searches for his hand, then slips hers inside once she finds it. "Believing, having faith, all that stuff—it would be nice, but you can't depend on it."

"I do," Ryan says quietly, a little less sure of herself. But what else is there, if not that? Dad had offered her nudges in the form of wisdom, propelled her with words, and this is how she'd learned to move forward. When he died and her world cracked in half, she'd tried her best not to doubt him—to believe that the good things would outweigh the bad in the end—but still it was there sometimes. This tiny, sparking doubt like a trick candle at a birthday party, flickering on and off with alarming persistence. She's found that the best you can do is hope for it not to flare up at the wrong times.

Nick runs a finger over the back of her hand, and she scoots closer, resting the top of her head against his arm. They both lay still, wide-eyed at the starless sky above, listening to the drone of the crickets and the far-off sounds of a car engine.

A few blocks away, their classmates are finishing up a card game, worrying over their shoes, wondering what to do once the beer runs out. It seems unfair to Ryan that she and Nick are the ones left to carry such burdens on their own. Maybe it's meant to make them stronger—as her dad would have said—but what if it doesn't? What if, instead of surviving and enduring and carrying on, they simply sink beneath the weight of it all?

"I wish . . ." Ryan begins, then trails off, feeling silly.

"What do you wish?"

But she doesn't answer. A few scattered lightning bugs wink at them across the yard, and the moon has now emerged above the clouds. It's nearly midnight, and another day is fast approaching. She isn't sure how long they sit there like this, too tired to wonder any further. When they stand, finally, Nick takes her hand, and they walk the rest of the way to Ryan's house in silence. At her front door, he leans in to kiss her once more, and it seems so natural this time, so wonderfully fitting, that it's all she can do to keep from smiling again.

His face is half-lit by the porch lights when he leans back, and Ryan tilts her head to look up at him. "Hey," she says softly, so as not to wake her sleeping family. "If you'd been able to play baseball . . ."

He grins. "I would have been good."

"Yeah," she says. "I bet you would have been great."

Ryan was nine when their dog—a funny-looking white terrier with a penchant for cream puffs and vanilla ice cream cones— died quite suddenly. He was already old at that point, in the creaky, lumbering way that good dogs grow old. But he wasn't yet ancient. He sometimes had trouble making it up onto the couch he wasn't technically allowed on anyway, and he had developed a habit of putting himself to bed before everyone else, but he was small and wiry with years of begging left in him.

She'd been the one to come down that night, negotiating the noisy floorboards of the stairs after everyone else had gone to bed. Once she'd filled her water glass, Ryan tiptoed over to where Addison always slept, his compact body made smaller in sleep, tucked in upon himself, nose to tail, with twitching paws and a quivering nose. But even in the darkness, she could tell he wasn't in his bed, and when she flipped on the light in the kitchen, she saw him in the front hallway. Ryan set down her water glass and approached the dog where he sat with his nose just inches from the wall, his whole body rigid and focused as if there were something beyond it that required his attention.

"Addison," she called softly, but the dog didn't move, didn't flick an ear or wag his tail. She dropped to her knees beside him and placed a hand on his head, and he whined softly—a sound long and low—but remained still, his dark eyes boring a hole in the wallpaper. "Addy," she tried again, and this time, he thumped his tail softly against the floor, but didn't alter his watchdog pose.

Later that night, they took him to the vet, an emergency clinic with fluorescent lights and an empty waiting room. Mom stayed behind with Emily, who had been asleep while they watched Dad lift the dog from the spot in the hallway. Once in his arms, Addison had relaxed, and Ryan wrapped him in a blanket, and they took him out to the car together. She sat with him in the backseat—the dog on one side, and she on the other—while Dad took the back roads to avoid the traffic lights, his mouth set in a straight line. At one point, Addison lifted his head and then dragged himself across the seat to rest his chin in Ryan's lap. For the rest of the ride, he lay still.

When the vet came outside the clinic to help bring him in, her face went grim. Once they'd taken him in the back, Ryan pressed herself into Dad's jeans and cried with great heaving sobs, hiccupping and sniffling and choking on her tears, because it was hard just then to imagine anything sadder in the world than losing something as purely good as her dog.

"We didn't even know," she wailed, tucked, egglike, with her hands clasped around her knees on one of the waiting room chairs, as if she might make herself small enough for it all to go away. "We didn't even know he was hurting."

Dad looped a long arm across her shoulders and drew her toward him, and Ryan buried her face in his shirt until the vet came out to give them the sort of option that really isn't an option at all.

"Do you understand what she means by 'put to sleep'?" Dad asked Ryan, who nodded wordlessly. She didn't, in fact, have any idea what it meant before that moment, but it is moments like this one that reveal themselves with an understanding deeper than words, a sort of reluctant intuition, and so she knew. She knew.

Dad held her hand when they went to say good-bye. Addison lay very still on a shiny metal table, watching them through dull eyes, and when she leaned in close to one spiky ear, Ryan found she couldn't speak. She thought *I'll miss you* and she thought *don't go* and she thought *please*. But what she finally said was simply "Thank you."

Afterward, Dad paused in the parking lot and then stooped down so they were at eye level. "I know this is hard to understand now," he said, his face near hers. "But he was a good dog, and everyone will lose a good thing sometime in their lives."

Ryan wiped the back of her hand across her nose and looked at her feet. Her throat hurt and her eyes stung and she was having trouble catching her breath.

Dad smiled. "Remember the time we came home and found Addy with shreds of toilet paper spread all over the house?"

"It looked like confetti," she said, with a small, wet laugh.

"Well, see?" he said, a hand on each of her shoulders. "You still have a whole collection of memories just like that one."

They walked the rest of the way to the car, and Ryan focused her blurry gaze on him while he fumbled with the car keys. "What do you think he was seeing?" she asked, and Dad turned around. "When he was staring at the wall like that?"

He bent down again, a hand on each knee. When he crooked his finger, Ryan took a step closer, and when she was near enough for him to whisper in her ear, he said, "I think maybe he was dreaming."

"Daydreaming?"

"Exactly," Dad said, nodding.

"Of what?"

"Of what comes next." He smiled. "Sometimes what seems like the end is really only the beginning."

The roads felt different on the drive home, the streets blue and disquieting, the trees haunting in their shapelessness. Ryan stretched across the backseat, her head where Addison had been only an hour before.

Dad flicked his eyes up to the rearview mirror. "Hey," he said, reaching a hand back to squeeze her ankle. "It's important for you to remember this night, okay?"

Ryan looked out the back window, as if she might still catch a glimpse of the grayish building where they'd left her dog, and sniffled. This didn't seem a thing that could be shaken loose, not with tears or time or anything else. Remembering didn't feel like a choice so much as a curse.

"It's how we hold on to things," he said. "Even as we move on."

Later, there would be other things. *Promise me you'll remember this,* he'd say, and wherever they were—the beach or the ballpark, the fire-lit living room or the cool shade of the backyard—Ryan would close her eyes. She filed these moments away like precious documents, wore them smooth with memory, collected them like bits of prayers.

After a while, she began to use her eyes as cameras too. There a leaf-covered footpath and there a man playing the saxophone and there a cloud like a duck. But they piled up too fast and started to slip away, a few at a time, until the worthiest moments, the ones she most hoped to keep close, began to fall away with all the others, the everyday and the ordinary.

When she told him, Dad laughed. "It's not to remember

everything," he said. "You should save room for the ones that are really important."

"But how do I know which they are?"

"You just do," he told her. "You know them when they find you, and then you just squeeze your eyes shut and hold on to them tight."

"What's your favorite one of all?" she asked.

"This one right now is up there," he said, zipping his suit-case.

She bounced a little on the bed, looking around her parents' room. Dad disappeared into the bathroom for a moment and emerged with his toothbrush.

"How come?" she inquired. "We're just talking."

"Exactly," he said. "Talking to you is one of my favorite things to do."

"Top ten?" she asked, handing him his waterproof camera.

"Top five at least," he said with a wink.

"Then it is for me, too," Ryan said, and when he'd finished packing, she took his hand to walk him to the door, to wish him a good trip, and to say good-bye.

Chapter Twenty

THE DREAM COMES IN THE MANNER OF MOST DREAMS, A wispy illusion that should undoubtedly have been forgotten the moment she opened her eyes. But there's a lingering quality to it, and for Ryan, who lies in bed the next morning recapturing it piece by piece, it feels a lot like losing something.

It began with a baseball diamond—grass the color of a green crayon, a sky vast and blue as the lake—and though it could have been anywhere, Ryan knows it was Wrigley Field. Where else would she slip off to at night? What other place has left imprints so deep?

She and Nick were alone on the field, the two of them balanced on the gentle slope of the pitcher's mound, the whole of the stadium opening up before them. Ryan held a ball in her hand—dirty and gray and familiar, with loose seams and various scratches—and she tossed it straight up and down like an experiment in gravity. Nick crouched low beside her as if preparing for a race, and when the ball landed in her hand for the third time, Ryan let it go. It arched through the air at an unnatural pace, sluggish and unhurried. From above, it might have looked like a balloon, the way it coasted so leisurely toward the back wall. From above, it might have looked like the boy running below it was made of speed alone.

They reached the back wall at the same time—the boy and the ball—and Ryan, alone on the mound, watched one fall and the other rise to meet it. But in the brief seconds before the collision, before the ball could hit his hand and his shoulder could hit the wall, something unexpected happened. His left arm—braced to make contact with the ivy, shouldered against the remarkable catch—began to swell. And as if grounded by the weight of it, he fell fast, landing roughly in the grass a few feet short of the back wall. His arm, now nearly twice its normal size, lay at an awkward angle beside him, and the ball—having returned to its original form, all lightness gone, all magic lost—disappeared into the depths of the ivy, only to be forgotten.

It stays with her all the next day. It's there when she helps Mom pick out curtains for the baby's room and when she and Emily set the table for dinner. It becomes duller as the day wears on, fading until it is no longer a memory. It's the memory of a memory, the faintest tracing of a dream.

But still, it is there.

Nick shows up, as planned, at six on the dot. When Ryan meets him at the door, everything in her that had been unsettled melts away. He's wearing a red polo shirt and khaki pants, carrying a plate of cookies his mother baked, and he looks suitably eager for the dinner ahead. Before letting him in, she leans forward to kiss him on the cheek. Nick, looking pleased, gives her a goofy grin.

"You must be Nick," Kevin says, striding through the entryway as though late for a business meeting. "We've heard a lot about you."

Ryan's cheeks color slightly, but Nick gives her arm a squeeze as he steps inside. "And I've heard a lot about you, sir," he delivers his line. "All good things."

In the kitchen, Mom's stirring a pot of rice, and she pulls off her oven mitt to greet him when they walk in. Emily gives him a long look from where she's already sitting at the table, waiting with a fork in one hand and a knife in the other as if she hasn't had a meal in weeks.

Ryan knows this isn't entirely fair. Dinner the night before had been only the two of them, sitting low in wicker chairs out on Nick's back deck, the smoke from the barbecue coloring the dusky sky. They'd eaten burgers off paper plates, talking about school and baseball, nothing and everything, until his parents joined them for ice cream sandwiches as the sun fell behind the trees in the backyard.

When she'd suggested he come over tonight to have dinner and watch the Cubs game, she'd been thinking of ordering a pizza and disappearing into the basement. But in Ryan's house, bringing home a friend qualifies as a rare and special occasion, and so here they are: the egg timer announcing the meatloaf is done and the mashed potatoes burning on the stove.

Nick makes himself useful, shuttling glasses of water from the kitchen counter to the table, and Kevin gives Ryan a thumbs-up behind his back. She rubs her forehead and stifles a groan. By the time they all sit down, Mom has already covered the basic territory with startling efficiency: where Nick grew up, what his parents do, things Ryan never really thought to ask. She realizes that theirs has been a relationship of foggy detail and rough approximations. But it would have been like backtracking, in a way, for them to muse about favorite colors or ice cream flavors as if these things mattered. Instead, they'd gone right to the heart of things and never looked back.

Nick sits across from her at the kitchen table beside Emily, and he watches with interest as she separates the foods on her plate into neat quarters.

"So what brought your family down here?" Mom asks, lowering her fork.

Ryan stares at the bread basket in the center of the table.

"My dad got a new job," Nick explains.

"And do you like it so far?"

"I do," he says, his eyes on Ryan. "Everyone's been really nice."

Emily tucks her knees up beneath her and leans forward on the table. "Do you like Ryan?" she asks Nick, and Mom's eyes go wide. Kevin chokes a little on his water. Mortified, Ryan looks away, holding her breath.

Nick turns to Emily, and with mock seriousness, leans down to consult with her. "Do *you* like Ryan?"

Emily considers this a moment, tapping a finger against her lips in thought. "I guess most of the time," she says finally. "I guess she's okay."

"Then I think so too," he says, turning back to the rest of the table. He winks at Ryan. "We've decided you're okay."

She breathes out. "I can live with that."

Nick turns out to be a master dishwasher, and though Mom tries to shoo them away, they finish in no time, and she sends them down to the basement with bowls of ice cream. Nick pauses at the bottom of the stairs, scanning the room appraisingly.

"It's where my dad and I used to watch," Ryan tells him, though she knows she doesn't have to. "It's a little dusty."

"No," he says, flopping down on the couch. "It's perfect."

She joins him and turns on the game, where they see that the Cubs are already up one to nothing in the top of the third. The sky above Wrigley is a faded purple, and the rows of spotlights make the field glow in the gathering dark. Nick finishes his ice cream and sets the bowl on the table, and Ryan leans back against him.

"I like your family," he says, then gives her arm a little poke. "And I think you're okay."

She laughs. "Gee, thanks."

Beside her, she can feel each breath he draws. How is it possible to be so close to a person and still not know what you are to each other? With baseball, it's simple. There's no mystery to what happens on the field, because everything has a label—full count, earned run, perfect game—and there's a certain amount of comfort in this terminology. There's no room for confusion, and Ryan wishes now that everything could be so straightforward. But then Nick pulls her closer, and she rests her head on his chest, and nothing seems more important than this right here.

"You do realize they're only four games back now?" he asks, his jaw moving against the top of her head. "I mean, we *actually* have a shot at the wild card spot."

"Let's not talk about it," Ryan says. "I don't want to jinx it."

"You don't really believe in that kind of thing."

She swivels to face him. "Have you not been paying attention to the last hundred years of Cubs history?"

"I know," he says. "Curses, goats, bad luck."

"You don't believe in that stuff either?"

"I guess I believe in bad luck."

"But not good luck?"

He shakes his head, and Ryan frowns.

"You can't believe in one without the other."

The noise from the crowd onscreen surges, and they both fall silent as they watch first one Cubs player, then a second, round home plate. Nick shifts, pulling his hand from Ryan's shoulder to rub absently at his other arm.

She turns to him so abruptly that he actually flinches, dropping his hand into his lap. Her dream from the night before crackles now inside her head, a kind of electricity in its recollection. Ryan stares at his shoulder, at the arm by his side.

"Nick," she says, the word leaping out before she has a chance to stop it.

He looks amused by her expression. "What's wrong?"

She points. "Does your arm hurt?"

"A little," he says, then stops. "Why?"

Ryan's thoughts pinball from the previous night's dream to Nick's warning, the awful prediction that came when he broke his arm. She thinks of the dream, of the swollen limb, a thing frightening in its weightiness.

"I'm fine," he says, when he sees her face. "It's just a little sore."

Still, she just looks at him, her stomach wound tight.

"Seriously," he says. "You can't panic every time I have an itch or something. That's not gonna work." He lowers his face so that it's level with hers. "Trust me," he says. "I'm fine."

He gives his hand a little shake as if to prove his point, then tucks Ryan beneath the other arm again, his eyes returning to the game. She tries to focus too, but it's now nearly impossible. The players move from infield to dugout with mechanized precision, swapping places between innings, and the score creeps up in the Cubs' favor. The rest of her ice cream is melting in the bowl on the table, and she watches Nick's feet bob nervously beside it as the pitcher attempts to close out an inning.

But Ryan isn't thinking of any of that. She's remembering—suddenly, and with a sharp stab of regret—the bargain she made that day when she walked out of Nick's bedroom. It had been impulsive and unplanned, a knee-jerk reaction, a deep-rooted instinct to wish away what she'd been most afraid of. But just because she'd forgotten it, doesn't make it any less real. And just because she'd convinced herself he'd be okay doesn't mean it's true.

Nick sits up abruptly, jabbing a fist into the air as the Cubs make a double play, then wiggles his arm unconsciously as if working out a sore joint. His eyes are locked on the screen, his body rigid with focus. Ryan turns back to the game, feeling numb. She tries to remember the exact wording she'd used that day, frantic and confused, desperate to strike some kind of bargain with the world at large.

It's okay if the Cubs never win, she'd said. *As long as he's okay.*

She turns back to the television, where the Cubs have pulled ahead by four. The players trot off the field, their pinstripes fuzzy on the screen.

"I guess they *have* been sort of lucky," Nick says. "At least lately."

Ryan stiffens. What does luck mean, with such terrible consequences? It's her fault, this seesaw of a bargain, and now there's the possibility that it could tilt the wrong way. The Cubs, so dependably hopeless, are coasting through the second half of the season with a playoff spot in their sights.

There's a commercial on now, and Nick's gaze travels around the basement, landing on the wall cluttered with old score sheets. He stands to take a closer look, pinching the edges of papers dating back ten years.

"You and your dad?" he asks, looking up.

Ryan nods.

"Well, if they win tonight," he says, "we'll have to put another one up there."

If the Cubs win, Ryan thinks.

Nick spots the scorebook on the table beside the washing machine, then pulls a new page from it and heads back to the couch. "I've already picked out my spot," he says, pointing to the top left corner of the wall, where an old sheet must have fallen off, leaving a bare patch of paint. He bends his head over the page. "But only if they win."

Ryan closes her eyes. *If the Cubs win,* she thinks, *then what?*

Chapter Twenty-One

THEY SIT ON THE LEDGE AT THE BEACH ONE EVENING, the sun already down, leaving behind a streaky mess of pink and orange. It's the end of August, the last week of summer vacation, and though she has a history of reluctance at this time of year, Ryan is secretly pleased. She's seen Nick nearly every day for the past several weeks, but still, there's something about the regularity of the upcoming school year that makes her happy. She's ahead of herself by days, months, even semesters as she thinks of what the year might bring. Not only will she have someone to eat lunch with, someone to stand by her locker while she grabs her books, someone to wait for at the end of the day, but that someone is Nick. A small and fluttery hope blooms in the center of her chest at the thought of this. She wonders if this is what luck is, finally: nothing more than a haphazard and unexpected swerve in fortune.

Beside her, Nick kicks his feet against the wall. "We should go down for one more game," he says. "Before school starts."

Ryan hesitates, wondering how she could possibly go to a game now, when this ill-conceived bargain of hers might have sealed Nick's fate with theirs. How can she root for the Cubs when the cause and effect of it all might be at his expense? Or perhaps worse, how can she go and cheer *against* them, the look on her face failing to hide all her worries? She's either the world's worst Cubs fan or the world's worst friend. She's not yet entirely sure which.

"Okay," she says eventually, and the word sounds like something broken.

Nick looks pleased. "Let's go tomorrow," he says. "Dodgers?"

"Brewers."

"Know what we could do?" he asks, his face suddenly lit with possibility. "We could go down in the morning, get there really early, and try to get bleacher seats."

Ryan frowns. "They're really hard to get."

"Well, if not, then maybe standing room," he insists. "I mean, worst-case scenario, we hang out at Wrigley for a few extra hours and then sit outside for the game."

"Okay," she says, mustering a small smile. "I'm in."

"I sort of guessed you might be." Nick laughs, and right there, right then, and still somewhat to Ryan's amazement, he leans over to kiss her.

On the way home, they pause at the corner where they part ways, each heading to their own separate home for dinner. Nick promises to come by in the morning to pick her up, and then he's gone again, waving as he rounds the corner, and Ryan hugs her arms and watches him go.

She takes a winding route through the neighborhood, reluctant to return home just yet. There are a few people still out prolonging the day, tossing baseballs or frisbees in their yards. A couple of kids ride past on bicycles, the ticking of the spokes loud against the quiet street.

Ryan finds herself wandering through the nicer part of the neighborhood, where the houses are a bit statelier, the yards well-groomed and endless, the driveways long and curving. She looks ahead to where she knows Lucy lives, a towering brick house that seems straight from the pages of a magazine. What little she knows of the Barrett family is obvious to anyone. It's not hard to gather from Lucy's constant supply of gifts from her father and the quality of the house itself that they're fairly well to do.

She's surprised to hear Lucy's voice beyond the prickly bushes that line the front drive, and she pauses almost instinctively on the sidewalk to listen.

"I thought we were all going together," Lucy's saying, and the superior tone so familiar to Ryan is utterly absent from her voice. "All three of us."

She hears the soft swish of a golf club as it whisks the grass, and then a hollow plunking sound. Through the bushes, Ryan can see Lucy's father lift his club and walk across the small putting green in their side yard to retrieve the ball. Lucy stands with her hands on her hips, watching him with a look of clear disappointment.

"They're great seats, honey," her dad says, twisting to assess the lay of a second ball. "You can take some friends. Drinks and snacks on me."

Lucy frowns and folds her arms. "I don't care about the stupid tickets," she says, her voice softer now, a pleading tone to it that makes Ryan look guiltily at her feet. "We don't do anything as a family anymore."

Ryan takes a step back then hurries down the sidewalk, past the driveway and around the corner, away from the Barrett's house. She hadn't meant to eavesdrop, but even as she's spent so much energy resenting Lucy, there's always been a part of her that's been curious, too. She realizes now that she should know better than to assume that girls like Lucy—girls who are pretty and wealthy and whom everyone adores—coast through life with such effortless ease. Even that kind of existence comes with its own set of problems.

When Ryan gets home, her own family is waiting for her to start dinner. Emily is wiggling around in her chair impatiently,

Kevin makes a stupid joke about sending out a search party, and
Mom looks pointedly at her watch. But Ryan doesn't mind. She
slides into her seat at the table, grateful to be among them: this
version of her family not quite as she'd imagined it, off-kilter
and imperfect, yet somehow—despite all this or perhaps because
of it—happy all the same.

They arrive at the 'L' station early the next morning, still yawning as they wait on the platform, but nevertheless determined
in their mission. The ticket window opens at nine, though the
game doesn't begin until four hours after that. And even though
this is nothing but an ordinary day at Wrigley—though, in truth,
what game *isn't* a kind of spectacle?—they know the line will
be long.

The train is quieter than usual for the trip downtown, filled
with morning commuters rather than rowdy Cubs fans. Ryan and
Nick stand gripping a metal pole, rocking back and forth with the
rest of the car, the snap and rustle of newspapers loud in their ears.
As they near their destination, Ryan has a sudden urge to keep
going, to stay fastened to the train as it snakes its way along Lake
Michigan and into the heart of the city, the buildings that rise like
great railroad spikes on either side of the tracks, the green-blue
river that cuts across it all. She has a swift, ominous feeling about
the day ahead, unfounded yet persistent. But they're already coming to a squealing halt at the Addison Street stop, and Nick rests a
hand on her back to shepherd her out the door ahead of him.

Wrigleyville is just beginning to come to life. Storefronts
are being opened, metal gates clanging up, vendors staking their
corners. It's a weekday, and still morning, but the bars are waking
up too, the rows of silver beer kegs forming lines in the streets
outside. The day promises to be hot for this late in the summer,
and the air is already thick and heavy.

Ryan and Nick join a few dozen other fans in line at the ticket windows, which are still shuttered and silent. The crowd sways restlessly at their backs until a man waving the team's flag runs up and down the line, yelling about the wild-card race and holding a hand to his ear as he waits for a response. Nick reaches out to give him a high five as he passes by, then hops from foot to foot and rubs his hands together, looking delighted by the whole thing: the fans and the ticket line, the day unfolding before them.

"The wild card," he says, shaking his head as if he can't quite believe it.

But Ryan knows just what he means. The wild card spot is the greatest second chance in sports. For the teams that don't win their divisions, there's still hope for the postseason. Whichever team has the next-best record in each league, the wild card is their ticket to the playoffs.

When they added it in 1995, the idea was met with some raised eyebrows. But the season before, the playoffs had been canceled by a strike, and this, to Ryan's dad, represented all that was wrong with the sport. *There's a reason the Cubs don't get involved with this kind of thing,* he had said, referring to the postseason as if it were an invitation the Cubs politely declined year after year. But the wild card was just the opposite: a chance for underdogs, a prospect reachable by even the most frequent losers. It doesn't matter if you started off the season ranked first place or last, if you began as a joke or a team to watch. It doesn't matter if you're the Yankees or the Cubs. *Everyone has a chance,* her dad used to say. *And isn't that all anyone ever wants?*

As the line to the ticket window begins to move, Ryan loops her arm through Nick's and smiles. "After the way this season started, I can't believe they're actually in the running."

"They are," he says, practically beaming. "And don't you almost feel like it doesn't matter what happens after it? If they could just get the wild card, it would already be so much more than anyone expected. And whatever else happens, they'd have that. No matter what."

"It's like small ball," she says. "One step at a time."

"Exactly," he says. "It's easier to think in smaller increments. It's less of a leap."

Ahead of them, a cardboard sign appears in the booth, and Ryan squints to read it. "Bleachers sold out," she says, and Nick tips his cap and shrugs, unfazed.

"I bet we can still get standing room," he says. "It'll be cheaper anyhow."

When it's their turn, they each pay twelve bucks for standing-room-only tickets, where they can jockey for a spot at the way-back section of the grandstand, keeping their toes behind a painted line and craning their necks to see the game. They leave the window clutching their tickets happily.

"What should we do till game time?" Ryan asks, as they veer, almost automatically, toward Waveland Avenue and the familiar stretch of brownstones behind the stadium. When they pass the fire station at the corner, the hydrant is already spouting a thick jet of water, the neighborhood kids in their faded Cubs shirts darting in and out of the spray.

"Let's go in when the gates open," Nick is saying, waving an arm toward the field. "We can watch warm-ups and do some scouting."

Ryan laughs. "Scouting?"

"Don't you know it's critical to the success of the team that we're there to scout the Brewers today?" Nick jokes. "Let's grab some food and hang out till then."

They buy doughnuts and wander around, wiping the powder from their faces. Outside of Murphy's Bleachers, they find an open seat and sit back, enjoying the sun, until game time draws nearer and the manager chases them out to make way for actual paying customers.

Nick looks at his watch and announces it's time to go inside. "We don't want to miss batting practice."

"Right," Ryan teases him. "It would be a huge disadvantage for the Cubs if we weren't there."

They circle around the field, keeping an eye out for their gate. The sidewalks are now crowded with blue-clad fans looking to have a few beers before the game. Nick takes her hand, and as they hurry around the corner of Sheffield and Addison, Ryan stops short, very nearly running into Kate. The two stare at each other for a moment, and then Lucy and Sydney trot over too.

"Hey," Ryan says, unable to hide her surprise. She feels her face go warm and prickly, and she opens and closes her hands, trying to gather herself. Seeing them here outside of Wrigley feels like an intrusion of sorts, as if they've trespassed onto sacred ground. Standing there before her with their little Cubs tank tops and pink hats, Ryan feels somehow betrayed.

There had been a time, long ago, when she would sometimes invite Sydney and Kate to the games. Her dad had been friendly with the guy who owned the two seats beside theirs, and when he couldn't make it, he always offered the tickets to them first. Sometimes, Mom would agree to come, but most often, Dad let Ryan invite her friends.

The three of them would follow him like ducklings through the crowds, holding hands and staring wide-eyed at their surroundings. He'd order three hot dogs, and they'd sit cross-legged in the sticky plastic seats while he explained to Ryan's friends which players to cheer for loudest, the importance of a sacrifice bunt, what happens when the ball gets stuck in the ivy. At these games, Ryan was less her father's daughter, more giggly and prone to discussing the fans sitting around them than anything actually happening on the field. But she always had an eye on the game too, and when the other team made an error or the Cubs managed a double play, she never missed a beat, turning away from the other girls to give her dad a high five.

And so, seeing them here now feels, to Ryan, like being punched in the stomach, like stumbling across an unexpected foe on your home turf. And even before she makes the connection between their presence here and the conversation she'd overheard between Lucy and her father, Ryan is already glaring hard at Sydney and Kate.

"Hey," Sydney says, quietly, cautiously, clearly aware of the delicate mechanics of the situation. "We're just—"

"My dad got me these *great* seats," Lucy cuts in. "And I thought a day at the ballpark might be fun for a change."

Kate shifts nervously, and then looks away.

"We're right behind home plate," Lucy continues. "Where are you guys sitting?"

Nick looks dubiously at the ticket in his hand, as though it might change if he were to stare at it hard enough. "Standing room," he says. "Right field area."

Lucy raises an eyebrow. "Nice."

"Listen, we were going to have lunch before the game," Kate says, her eyes on Ryan. "We'd love for you to come too."

Nick shakes his head. "I think we're gonna head inside early," he tells them. "But maybe we'll run into you again later."

"Sure," Sydney says, bobbing her head agreeably. "That would be great."

Ryan stays still as they walk away, watching their backs, the

light swish of their skirts, the closeness of their three heads as
they lean in to talk. Nick reaches out as if to put a hand on her
arm, but then hesitates and instead asks if she's ready to go. Ryan
looks up at the stadium and nods.

She's ready.

Chapter Twenty-Two

DURING BATTING PRACTICE, THEY'RE ABLE TO WATCH from up close, standing right behind the field with a dozen or so other fans. Ryan leans forward against the railing, looking on as the Cubs players take turns at the plate. Seeing them so close is always a surprise, how large and muscled they look, when she's used to watching them move across the television screen like figurines of themselves. A few of them swing weighted bats, while others stretch with headphones on, oblivious to the crowd gathering behind them. Near the bullpen, the day's pitcher tosses a rosin bag up and down in his hand while he confers with one of the coaches.

The batter at the plate pops a foul ball out into the left field stands, and Nick nudges her with his elbow. "See?" he says. "See how he dropped his arm there?"

"Yeah," Ryan says. "It's screwing up his swing. He needs to keep his elbow higher."

Nick, momentarily speechless, begins to laugh.

"What?" she asks.

"Nothing."

"No, what?"

"It's just that I've always been able to impress girls with this stuff," he says. "With little facts about the game. But you know as much as I do."

Ryan raises her eyebrows. "I'm pretty sure I know *more* than you, actually."

Nick laughs again. "Then I guess I have to work a lot harder to impress you."

When the stadium starts to fill up, they make their way back out into the airy system of ramps and walkways that forms a shell around the field. The designated areas for standing are marked with white paint, tucked behind the grandstand seating so that you have to crouch to follow the high pop flies beneath the overhang of the upper decks. Ryan and Nick shoulder in among the other fans, leaning back against the rails and shuffling their feet while they wait for the national anthem to end and the first pitch to be thrown. Around them, the vendors hurry past, flitting from one person to the next, their voices hoarse, their backs stooped against the weight of their merchandise.

By the fourth inning, the Cubs are ahead by two and playing well, but each time Ryan claps, each time she cups her hands around her mouth to yell, to cheer, to cry out for her team, she remembers. *It's okay if the Cubs never win,* she had said. And so hedging her bets, preparing for the unknown, worrying over the unseen, she lowers her hands and clamps her mouth shut. Just in case they do win. Just in case the flip side of the bargain has consequences, too.

When the catcher for the Cubs hits a home run that lands in a mob of bleacher bums, Ryan's heart bobbles around in her chest. She presses her lips together, and Nick looks at her sideways.

"What's the matter?" he asks.

She shakes her head. "Nothing."

"What?" he tries again. "Are you hot? Thirsty? Hungry? What?"

"Nothing," Ryan insists. "I'm fine."

"Then why aren't you more excited?"

She starts to shrug it away, but sees on his face a look of hurt, having apparently offended him with her lack of enthusiasm. "Sorry," she says quickly. "I must have dazed off for a second and missed the play."

"Look alive, Walsh," he says, smiling once again. He gives her shoulder a squeeze, then raises both arms to cheer as the catcher rounds home plate.

During the bottom of the sixth, Ryan isn't entirely surprised to see Lucy, Sydney, and Kate winding their way toward them, their eyes combing the crowd. She sinks back wearily against the railing and waits for their inevitable arrival.

"Hey," Lucy says brightly, wedging her way in beside Nick, forcing the entire row of people to scoot down. Sydney and Kate press themselves out of the flow of traffic too, and the five of them stand in an awkward cluster.

"How come you're not down by home plate?" Nick asks. "Because if you don't want those seats . . ."

Lucy waves a hand in the air and adjusts her sunglasses, which are perched on top of her head. "We just thought we'd come say hello, since not much is happening."

Ryan and Nick exchange a look. In fact, a *lot* has been happening. Being so close to the wild card spot means that every pitch, every error, every single play counts. It's small ball at its best as the team fights for a chance in the postseason.

At the sharp cracking sound of a bat, the five of them turn back to the game. A player for the Cubs has hit a long ball into right field, where it lands deep in a pocket. Another runner, standing halfway between two bases, dashes back to second before making a break for third, where the coach on the sidelines signals him to stop.

"How come he ran back first?" Kate asks.

"It's called tagging up," Ryan says. "He was cheating forward a little bit, to try to get to third faster if there'd been a ground ball."

"But if the Brewers had caught that ball," Nick continues, "he would have had to run back to second in order to be safe."

Lucy sighs loudly enough for them all to hear. "Too

many rules," she says. "I don't know how you find this stuff
so interesting."

Kate ignores her, and Sydney looks back to Ryan and Nick
with genuine interest. "So that's not stealing?"

"Nope," Nick says. "Fair play."

They all turn their attention back to the field, where another
batter steps up to the box. A breeze from the lake threads its way
between decks to where they're standing. When the hitter con-
nects with the second pitch and safely overruns first base, Ryan
almost laughs to see Sydney hop up and down excitedly, her
pink Cubs hat slipping on her forehead.

At the top of the seventh, the Brewers hit a home run, and
someone in the bleachers tosses the ball back out on the field,
where it rolls to a stop on the grass and a ball boy skips out to
retrieve it. Sydney spins around, but before she can even ask,
Ryan says, "Because it's the visiting team's hit. No true Cubs fan
would keep that ball."

"It's not considered bad sportsmanship?"

"Nah," she says, shaking her head. "It's all part of the game."

Lucy snorts, and they all turn to her.

"What?" Ryan asks coolly.

"Nothing," she says. "You're just so knowledgeable." The
way she says it, the word sounds like something distasteful. Even
Nick bristles slightly. Lucy drapes an arm casually over the rail
and tilts her head. "I guess I wouldn't have thought you'd still
be so into sports."

Ryan's face darkens. "Still?"

Sydney and Kate both look trapped, as if helpless to prevent
what they all know is about to come. The fans around them
are whooping and clapping over a play going on just below on
the diamond, but the little group stands absolutely still, bracing
themselves, ready or not.

Though she looks slightly less certain, Lucy presses on. "Well, now that your dad's not around anymore."

"Lucy," Sydney says in a low voice, a warning to her tone. But Lucy's still watching Ryan, their eyes locked in an even stare.

"Not around?" Ryan says it very slowly. Nick opens his mouth, then changes his mind and closes it again. Kate looks intently at her feet.

"I—" Lucy begins, but Ryan cuts her off.

"He's *not around*," she says, "because he *died*."

There's a long pause. Even Lucy, for once, has been cowed into silence. But Ryan—wounded and hurting—isn't quite finished. She can't look at Sydney or Kate, and she especially can't look at Nick, so it is Lucy alone who she zeroes in on: the target, perhaps fairly or perhaps not, of all Ryan's frustration, all her outrage, all her anger at the burden she wishes to foist on someone else, someone possibly more deserving of the hand she's been dealt.

"At least when he was around," she says, hating the way her voice sounds—petulant and hard, so unlike her in every way— "at least *my* dad didn't mind spending time with *me*."

And more than anything else, it's this that makes Ryan take two steps backward. More than Lucy's horrible insults, it's her own words that unexpectedly have the biggest effect, that are followed by the longest silence. It is this—this awful, petty comment, this unlikely departure from her character—that makes Ryan turn and hurry blindly away from the group. And it is this, above all, that makes her feel very small and very mean and very much alone.

During the seventh-inning stretch, the song—warbling and slightly hokey—brings tens of thousands of people to their feet. There is nothing so unifying, nothing so stirring as the first notes of the organ, the first blaring words of the tune. All those voices braided together, a sea of people with faces lifted, as reverent and humbled as churchgoers.

Ryan has never been much of a singer, self-conscious about the thinness of her voice when set to music, not one to let herself go even in the shower or the car. But at the ballpark, she used to plant her sneakers firmly on the folding seat and rest a hand on Dad's shoulder to sing, loud and unabashedly, reveling in the words, waiting, steadying, building toward that moment when she could cry out—*root, root, root for the Cubbies!*—as if her whole life had been preparation for this alone.

Now the song drifts high up into the rafters as she stumbles out behind the grandstand, her hand skidding along the railing that winds down past the hot dog vendors and soft ice cream carts, the corkboards filled with caps of all colors. She bumps into a man in a Brewers jersey, who asks if she's okay, and, realizing that she's crying, she nods her head *yes* even as she wants so desperately to say *no*.

In a moment, Nick is beside her. "I don't know why I'm crying," she sobs, her face messy with tears, her words watery. "I never cry. And I didn't mean to say that to her. I don't even know anything about her family."

The song ends, and now her voice sounds high and bright on the cool gray ramp, the walkways and hallways like a web all around them. Nick stands with his arms folded, eyeing her as if not quite sure what to say. He sways a little, his hands shoved in his pockets, and then quickly, and with some measure of uncertainty, lowers his face to hers.

"Look," he says. "Remember that day at the Reds game? When I got into that fight?" Ryan nods, and he hurries on. "It's like that."

"What is?"

"This," he says, waving a hand in the direction from which they'd come. "You losing it because of Lucy. It's not just that. It's all of it. How it all just builds up until you can't help being so angry. It's a little bit of everything."

"It's a *lot* of everything," Ryan agrees.

"It is," he says, his face heartbreakingly earnest. "But it's okay. You're okay."

Her throat is tight again, and he puts his arms around her and pulls her close, her face mashed against his shirt, her tears leaving streaks across the Cubs logo. She leans back to look at him. "So you don't think I'm awful?"

"I've told you," he says with a smile. "I think you're okay."

Ryan grins and wipes her eyes. A ripple of noise moves through the crowd, and they both look off toward the field.

"We should go back," Nick says, tweaking her ponytail. "The team needs us."

"I think they'll probably survive if we don't make it."

"Ah," he says. "You *think*. But you're not sure. It's like the whole tree-falling-in-a-forest thing. If the Cubs win and we're not there to watch, do they still make a sound?"

He grabs a napkin from the nearest snack stand, and Ryan uses it to blow her nose. Nick leans against the counter and watches the game on the screen while she collects herself, and once she's ready, they walk back up together.

Ryan knows that Lucy has every right to be angry with her, and that she, in turn, should also be fuming at the things that were said. But there's nothing left in her that wants to fight. All that she wishes is that the truths behind the statements weren't quite so true.

When they find the spot where they'd been standing, a tall man with glasses directs his foam finger at them. "You the kids who were with those girls?" he asks. "The ones who were just up here?"

Nick nods. "Yeah," he says. "Where'd they go?"

"Back to their seats," the man tells them. "But they asked me to be sure to give you the message that they're sorry."

"For leaving?" Ryan asks.

He shrugs. "Maybe. But it felt like a bigger sorry than that to me."

Chapter Twenty-Three

IT WAS ESTABLISHED THE PREVIOUS NIGHT THAT THIS morning—the first day of school for both Ryan and Emily—would go a certain way. Mom would drop Emily off on her way to an early doctor's appointment, Kevin would make sure Ryan was up before leaving for work, and Ryan would meet Nick at his house so they could bike over to school together.

But almost immediately after Kevin knocks on her bedroom door—first at the prearranged time and then twice more—Ryan falls back asleep. She's still tangled in her sheets, one foot hanging off the bed, when she hears Kevin's car start in the driveway. And when she opens her eyes again forty minutes later to look warily at her alarm clock, it seems impossible that so much time could have passed.

She knows she should have laid her clothes out the night before and packed her lunch and arranged her books in her backpack. But that kind of organization isn't Ryan's strong suit, and so now she scrambles around her room collecting her things, cramming stuff into her bag, trying to locate articles of clothing. Down in the kitchen, she rips two brown paper lunch bags because she's not paying attention, her eyes on the oven clock, which says she should have been at Nick's a half hour ago. She reaches for the phone to call, but then decides there's no time, so instead packs an extra cookie for him, by way of apology.

Outside, the garage door refuses to close, stubbornly stopping at half-mast, and Ryan stands impatiently jabbing at the button until it finally lurches shut with a loud bang. The wheels of her bike make sharp skidding noises as she flies down her driveway and takes off toward Nick's.

When she reaches his house, she drops her bike on the lawn and half-jogs up to the front door to ring the bell. She peers through the little front windows, but it soon becomes clear that nobody's home, and though she hadn't expected him to wait, she's still angry with herself for running so late on the first day.

By the time she reaches the school, it's clear by the emptiness of the front lawn and the stillness of the corridors inside that first period has already begun. Ryan pulls the schedule from her pocket, then slinks guiltily toward her history class, sliding redfaced into her seat while the teacher makes a note of her name.

Once the bell rings—only a few minutes after her arrival—she steps out into the hallway and takes a deep breath, feeling flustered and out of sorts already. She looks up and down the long hallway, dismayed that despite the beginning of a new year, despite being a sophomore and therefore supposedly no longer the youngest, the smallest, the most picked on—all things that have always seemed to define her—nothing seems to have changed. She's still dodging Lucy and her friends, still keeping a hopeful eye out for Nick. It doesn't matter that she feels different, because nobody else can see that. She's still just the girl clutching her notebook, her back pressed against the lockers, her brow furrowed as she contemplates her next move.

By lunchtime, Ryan still hasn't seen Nick. This wasn't supposed to be how the day unfolded. He was supposed to walk her to math class, teasing her about how she couldn't possibly pass this year without him as a partner. They were supposed to linger at the water fountain between classes, walk to the cafeteria at lunchtime together. But she knows it's her fault for being so late this morning, for throwing the entire course of the day off-track, and so, as usual, she heads to lunch alone.

In the brightly lit cafeteria, it's not so very different from last year; it's not such a great departure as Ryan stands by herself, scanning the cavernous room. Her stomach wobbles when she sees Kate and Sydney, sitting at a table with their backs to her. She'd known this would happen, of course. It was inevitable that she'd see them today, and Lucy, too. But she'd been counting on having Nick at her side, and right now, alone in a sea of tables, she can't help feeling abandoned.

The girls look up as Lucy joins them, setting down her tray and then dropping her bag on the table before she slides in beside Sydney. They're all sophomores now, no longer cast as lowly and unsure, elevated to new locations and better tables during the lunch hour. But Ryan—always a step behind—is still rooted in the middle of the room, sweeping her eyes around in a final effort to locate Nick.

When she doesn't see him, she squares her shoulders and lifts her chin. She refuses to begin another year the way she did the last. The point was never for Nick to become a safety net. She shouldn't need to be rescued, and she shouldn't want to be saved. And if she has the urge to run, then it should be only because it is *them* that she doubts. Not herself.

Lucy half-stands to reach for a napkin, and as she does, her eyes land on Ryan. For a brief moment, they study each other across the heads of their classmates, the room widening between them. It feels to Ryan like all eyes are on her, though it's really only Lucy's; it feels like minutes, though it's actually only seconds.

In the end, the gesture is a small one. Lucy tips her head toward the empty seat at the table—not beside her, not a place of honor or any great significance—but a few seats down, where there's an unclaimed chair. Ryan doesn't hesitate. There's no big scene, no great homecoming, though when Sydney and Kate turn around and smile, both are—she can tell—surprised and relieved to see her joining them.

Lucy only looks her way once, and even then, the expression on her face could barely be called warm. But then, Ryan doesn't expect much more. There are things that should be said. There are apologies required and mending to be done, and all this only to get back to even, to where they were before. All this, only to make up for what happened this past weekend at the game. Ryan is under no illusion about her friendship with Lucy Barrett. Certain people are meant to be friends as surely as others are not, and Ryan isn't sure she and Lucy will ever see their way there exactly. But it seems now that a quiet truce is on its way to being established, and for the moment, this feels like progress enough.

Sydney leans forward, her fork dangling in the air. "Where's Nick?" she asks, but not as she's asked in the past. She says it so casually, so conversationally, that it takes Ryan a moment to respond. There seems, in the small span of such a short question, to be both a welcome and an apology.

"Probably working out his schedule," she answers firmly, mostly to convince herself that it's true. "He's still catching up from when he switched schools last year."

But when she opens her brown bag and sees the cookie she'd brought for him, Ryan's face falls. Her eyes move to Will's table, where he sits with a few other junior guys, all friends of Nick's. Though she cranes her neck to look for his blue cap, she knows somehow that he's still not there. But each time her thoughts dip too low, veer too close to the darker possibilities running through her head—the ever-present worries that crop up whenever he's late, whenever he's pale, whenever he's tired—she simply shuts them off.

Nobody ever walks into a disaster expecting it to happen. Nobody ever counts on trouble, and nobody expects the worst, despite what they might say. There's too big a part of us that relies on the smaller odds, the outside chance that—however unlikely—when the clouds break, we'll be spared the storm that is so often predicted.

Ryan looks up. "Anyone want a cookie?"

A few of the girls she doesn't know glance over from the far end of the table, arching their eyebrows and smirking. But Lucy says nothing, and through the simple act of ignoring them, they fall silent once again.

"I'll take it," Kate says from a few seats down.

Ryan places two fingers on top of the cookie, then slides it forward across the table as if it were a poker chip. As if she were, by nature, a gambler: bold and brave and not at all worried about her missing friend.

When she knocks on the front door of Nick's house after school, a woman in jeans and a red sweatshirt—a taller version of Mrs. Crowley—opens the door.

"You must be Ryan," she says immediately, stepping out onto the front stoop to join her. "My sister said you might be coming by too."

Ryan nods. "Is Nick—?"

"I drove down as soon as I heard," his aunt says, before Ryan has a chance to finish. "The last time around was so hard on them, and I figure it'll be even harder now, being so far away from the rest of the family."

It takes Ryan a moment to find her voice. "That last time around?"

"All the tests, the waiting," she says, then stops abruptly, her face changing. "You've heard, right? I just assumed, since my sister said you might be stopping by. . . ."

"Heard what?" Ryan asks, though she knows just exactly *what* and isn't sure she's prepared to hear the answer spoken aloud. She takes a step backward, balancing on the edge of the last stair.

"They found another tumor, honey," she says. "His arm was sore earlier in the weekend, and so they took him down to the hospital for some tests."

Ryan's chin is trembling just slightly. "Okay," she says dumbly. "Okay."

"He's downtown now," she says, then looks at her watch. "He's getting a biopsy today, probably right around now, actually. To see how bad it is and whether it's spread."

"And when will they—?"

"In a couple days," she says. "He'll have to stay over tonight, maybe tomorrow, too. It takes a toll." She steps aside to make room in the doorway. "Do you want to come in? I know this must be a bit of a shock."

But it's not, in fact, a shock at all. It feels instead like something she's been waiting for without even knowing it, an inevitable end to the guessing game that has plagued them all summer. In some small and unfortunate way, it's a relief: now, rather than being angry at the world at large, rather than doubting and worrying and waiting, there will be a plan of attack, a course of action. The opponent is no longer invisible, no longer just a possibility, no longer simply a ghost. Now, finally, again, there is something to fight against.

"Do you think I could go down and see him?" she asks, her voice wavering.

His aunt nods. "I think he'd like that very much."

On the train, Ryan holds her backpack in her lap and rests her head on top of it, letting herself be swayed by the motion of the car. It's late afternoon, and the sun sits low in the windows. When the doors open at the Wrigleyville stop, the stadium beyond is empty and quiet, the flags still. For the first time in her memory, Ryan has the urge to look away. She can hardly bear seeing the curved wall of the ballpark, the giant Cubs sign casting a shadow over the outfield. If there's blame to be had for Nick's illness, then here must be its root: a team that has caused nothing but heartbreak, a stadium heavy beneath so many years of disappointment.

When she thinks of the energy she'd wasted, the bargains she'd made, all that she'd staked so fruitlessly on this team, she wants nothing more than to forget it all, though she knows it's not easy to shed a lifetime of allegiance, especially with a team like the Cubs, a team that gets inside of you, stubborn and unshakable.

She glares hard out the window as the doors snap shut, the train lurching forward again while the stadium disappears from view. By the time she gets downtown, the sun has slid behind the buildings to the west, and Ryan walks quickly from the train stop to the hospital after asking directions at a newsstand. The sidewalks are filled with people heading home from work, their feet dragging, their ties loosened. She hurries purposefully toward the blue signs for the hospital, where white arrows give directions to various buildings.

At the front desk of the oncology center, Ryan waits while the receptionist finishes a phone call. Now that she's here, standing amid the orange plastic chairs and the too-bright lights, she can feel a growing knot of worry in her chest. She wonders if Nick's aunt called ahead to let them know she was coming. She wonders if she should have called first. She wonders whether Nick will want to see her at all.

"Can you tell me what room Nick Crowley's in?" Ryan asks when the receptionist hangs up the phone, and she punches a few keys to pull up the information on her computer, then points a finger down a long, grayish hallway. Ryan's sandals squeak on the linoleum as she makes her way to the elevator, then jabs the button for the sixth floor and lowers her head. At the second floor, a woman walks in holding the hand of a small boy—probably no more than six or seven—whose head is completely bald. His eyes are large and round, and he watches Ryan until they reach her floor.

"Have a good night," she murmurs as she steps around them, her heart beating fast. She's imagining what Nick must have gone through before, what so many kids here are trying so desperately to beat. *How many times can you battle this thing?* she wonders. *How much of you does it claim each time around?*

There's a smaller waiting area at the end of the hallway on the sixth floor, and Ryan can see Mr. and Mrs. Crowley conferring with a doctor in a white coat. She stands still, frozen in place, unsure whether to interrupt or just dodge back into the elevator and hurry up the street toward home. It's embarrassing to lose your nerve in a place of so much strength and courage, but Ryan feels suddenly weak-kneed at the reality of the situation. A nurse brushes by, her eyes focused on a clipboard, and when she nears the little group at the end of the hall, the Crowleys look up.

"He'll be so happy you're here," Mrs. Crowley says once the doctor has moved on. She folds her into a long hug, and Ryan stifles the tiny feeling of guilt that works its way through her, the sense that she's the one who landed their son here in the first place. Her and her stupid team, and the regrettable impulse to bargain against them, an ill-advised trading of something too important for words.

"Is he okay?" she asks, then immediately wishes she hadn't. She opens and closes her mouth but can't figure a way to remedy the question.

Mr. Crowley rescues her. "He's an old pro at biopsies," he says with a small smile. "Now it's just a waiting game."

"And will he be . . . ?"

"It depends on how the tests come back," he says, an edge to his voice.

"You should go in." Mrs. Crowley turns to Ryan with red-rimmed eyes. "He's awake now, and he'll want to see you before visiting hours are over."

Mr. Crowley walks her to the room and gives her arm a little pat before leaving her standing alone in the doorway. Nick's head is turned to the side, and she can't tell whether he's awake or not. He looks no different, maybe a little pale, maybe a little thin, but this is as much the setting as anything else. She can see the edge of his bandage beneath the sleeve of his gown, where it covers the stitches from the biopsy. Ryan clears her throat, and he smiles when he notices her.

"Let me guess," he says. "You need me to bail you out in math class already."

"Very funny," she says, taking a few hesitant steps toward him.

"Sorry I wasn't there when you came this morning."

"I think you have a pretty good alibi," she says, moving to the edge of the bed. "Besides, if you must know, I overslept anyway."

"I should have guessed," he says, the last words slowed by a yawn.

"If you're tired, I can go," Ryan says, already inching backward, but Nick curls a finger toward him, and she steps forward obediently, sitting down in the chair beside the bed so that their faces are level.

"Hi," he says.

"Hi," she says back, and then to her great surprise, she begins to cry.

"You know," Nick says as he hands her a tissue from the bedside table, "for all this talk about how you don't ever cry, you sure are spouting a lot of water."

Ryan hiccups, then laughs. "I don't usually . . ."

"Cry," he says, smiling. "I know. I've heard."

She wipes her face with the back of her sleeve, taking a deep breath. *When is the time to ask questions?* she wonders. They've never spoken much about the specifics of the cancer, preferring to tread in other waters, sometimes safer, sometimes not. But now, Ryan feels like she's moving with blinders on, unsure where her next footstep might fall, not knowing whether she'll hit solid ground or not.

"Are you okay?" she asks, wanting to know exactly what they saw on the scans, the story behind the films she'd seen the doctors studying, the black-and-white tracings of bones and lungs. She'd like to know when they'll hear back about the biopsy, what happens after that, a rundown of all the medical possibilities, and within those possibilities, a list of anything unforeseen that might still occur, and on and on until there are no dark corners, nothing left on which to shed any more light.

Nick lifts his shoulders. "Hard to tell," he says. "We'll see, I guess."

Ryan stares at him, stricken by his voice, which sounds so empty of hope in the quiet of the hospital room. She's reminded of his words from the summer, which come back to her now with renewed meaning. *Do you really think they'll win?* he'd asked about the Cubs, looking doubtful as they lay sprawled outside on the grass that night. Ryan couldn't understand then how it was possible to watch every game, to cheer as though it mattered, and to do all this without truly believing. *Isn't that a requirement in this unreliable pastime?* she had wondered. *A certain amount of faith that things will work out in the end?*

But now that she, too, has given up on their team, Ryan sees that she's gone through life in the very same way: moving forward without conviction that it's going to take her anywhere.

She stands and walks to the window, letting the silence between them grow. The truth is that she has little to offer him right now. In a way, she realizes, she's been no better than he has.

Nick's hair is uncombed and his eyes are glassy from lack of sleep, a paler shade of green in the brightness of the room. Ryan flips the switch, and the room goes from white to gray, a wedge of light from the window stamped across the end of the bed.

Her eyes fall to his Cubs hat, which sits on the bedside table, and out the window just beyond it, she sees the scattered pinpricks of light that mark the harbor below. When she closes her eyes, she can almost imagine they're elsewhere—on the lawn beneath a nighttime sky, or lying on the couch in her basement—but the high sound of a beeping machine goes off behind the curtain that separates the room, and there's a flurry of footsteps as the doctors and nurses move in and then back out.

"Do you know who it is?" Ryan asks after a moment, her eyes on the curtain.

Nick shakes his head. "It was somebody different this morning."

She's about to ask something more, but he's watching her with pleading eyes, a look that suggests just how little it would take to topple whatever composure he's managed to cobble together. And Ryan knows how that feels. So she does the only thing she can.

"Hey," she says, her voice gruff. "How many games back are we now? For the wild-card spot?"

Nick looks visibly relieved. "We're only one behind Houston," he says. "So the St. Louis series is really important. But it's definitely doable."

"As long as we don't start acting like the Cubs."

"True," he says, smiling. "There's a game on tomorrow night. Would you want to come down here after school to watch?"

Ryan hesitates, glancing up at the little television suspended from the ceiling and angled toward his bed. She's not sure how to answer the question, designed to be easy, but now suddenly a challenge.

"I could try," she says, feeling like a fraud, because you don't *try* to make it to the hospital when someone you know is sick. You just do it. And perhaps even more important, you don't just *try* to make it when someone invites you to watch a Cubs game. You put on your cap, ready yourself for battle, and you cheer until your voice has left you. There should be no such thing as *trying* in either of these propositions, but for Ryan, all the rules have recently changed, and now she feels turned inside out. She stands from the chair and paces the room while Nick watches, frowning and confused.

"You don't have to," he says, not bothering to hide his disappointment. He shakes his head and looks at the ceiling. "I just figured you'd want to."

Ryan rubs her eyes, not sure how to fix this. But something inside of her has shifted, and the team that has carried her through so much has now let her down. And not because of the tally of losses, the endless blunders, the perennial disappointment. But because she'd been foolish enough to bet against them, to play a dangerous game with stakes she had no business setting, and however illogically, she now feels let down. And it's nobody's fault but her own.

But maybe even worse is the thought that strikes her now: if she's given up on them, and if Nick never believed in the first place, then what's the point? If neither one of them cares anymore, if neither can muster up the kind of enthusiasm that first brought them together, then what's the point of any of this?

"Why do you cheer for them?" she asks quietly, and Nick

looks over, surprised. "If you really don't think they'll ever win, why bother watching at all?"

She can tell he's annoyed with her by the way he's scowling at his hands, but the question seems important somehow.

"What does it matter?" he asks, shrugging. "You already made it pretty clear you don't want to come watch anyway."

"It just does," she says. "It matters."

"Why?" he asks, but Ryan isn't sure how to answer. Right now, she feels further away from him than ever before, just a few feet between them in the tiny room.

"I'm sorry," she says, unsure what she means exactly, though it feels like there's plenty to be sorry about. And then, because it's the only thought that keeps persisting, and because it's the only thing she knows with any certainty, she says, "I just want for you to be okay."

Nick shrugs, punching at the remote control to the bed, which whirs up and down beneath him until, satisfied, he leans back.

"You don't have to come tomorrow," he says. "It's just a ball game."

"I'll be here," she tells him, a hollow note to her voice.

"Sure," Nick says, then rolls over so that his back is to her, and there's nothing left for Ryan to do but walk back out into the bright yellow hallway alone.

Chapter Twenty-Four

IT'S RAINING WHEN THEY EMERGE FROM THE HOSPITAL later, a shower with a hint of autumn to it, chilly and biting in the gray dusk. Ryan follows Nick's parents to their car, her backpack hanging off one shoulder and her collar pulled up to her ears in a useless attempt to ward off the rain. Her stomach is churning as they pass out of the hospital parking lot, the full weight of the situation only now hitting her.

She knows that Mrs. Crowley called her mother while she'd been in with Nick, and everything before her now seems suddenly daunting: the long car ride home, the discussions to follow, the slight shifting of those around her in response to this new information. How Nick must feel, Ryan can't even begin to guess. Because even her tangential role in this new turn of events makes her want to run, to bolt, to crawl into a hole and fall asleep and not wake up until—when? When they find out he's okay? When they find out he's not? When the ending to his story has already unfolded, for better or worse, and whatever might befall him—tragedy or triumph—has made itself known?

They drive home in silence, Ryan huddled in the backseat near the window, her knees close and her head low as they pass beneath a bruised and purpled sky, the rain loud on the windshield and the wipers singing out in the growing darkness. A few times, Mrs. Crowley swings her head around between the seats as if to offer a few words of reassurance, but it's a hard thing to break a silence that thick, and so she turns back again and again without speaking. Ryan breathes a circle of fog onto the window, then rubs at it with her thumb, unable to bring herself to voice any of the questions that are clouding her head.

By the time they pull off the highway, the headlights do little more than illuminate the layers of rain, and Mr. Crowley's back is curved as he hunches over the steering wheel. Without the rush of the expressway, the world around the car has fallen silent, and Mrs. Crowley turns the radio to the first clear station, a too-cheery oldies song that quickly fills the car.

"This isn't an easy thing," Mr. Crowley says over the music, and Ryan sits up in the backseat. "But we've gotten through it before, so . . ."

Mrs. Crowley lays a hand on his arm, but his eyes stay focused on the blurry road ahead as they turn off into their neighborhood. She leans between the seats again, and this time, clears her throat. "It's okay if you're worried," she says to Ryan. "And it's okay if you have questions or don't understand all of it."

Ryan nods, but she wants to tell them that the problem isn't that. The problem is that she *does* understand. The problem is that Nick is there and she's here, and that none of this is how anything is supposed to happen. Nobody has said any of the usual things—*he'll be just fine* or *don't worry* or *he'll be better soon*—and this is what Ryan is thinking about as they pull into her driveway. She can see Mom's face peering anxiously through the kitchen window, and she puts a hand on the car door, unsure what should happen next. Should she thank them for the ride? Do such rote manners still apply in times like this, when the world is crumbling to pieces all around you?

She runs up to the house beneath a ragged curtain of rain. Inside, it's strangely quiet for this time of evening—the hour of clanging forks and noisy television, the daily recounting of stories at high volume—and when Mom moves swiftly around the corner and sweeps her into a hug, Ryan has to remind herself to breathe.

"I'm so sorry," Mom says, murmuring into her neck. "We didn't know."

"Don't," Ryan says, and Mom pulls back, bringing both hands to the curve of her stomach. They stand studying each other, only the welcome mat between them, until Ryan notices Emily hanging over the banister at the top of the stairs. Kevin pokes his head out of the bedroom and motions her back inside, and Emily—close-lipped and distressingly obedient—disappears from the hallway.

Ryan fixes her eyes on Mom, who shakes her head. "I'm sorry," she says again. "I just thought maybe you and I could talk alone."

"I don't really want to," she says, shrugging her backpack to the floor where it lands with a wet thump. This is not true in the least, but the theatrics of it all—the careful choreography of the moment—make Ryan feel somehow worse. Nothing has happened to *me*, she wants to shout. No need to tiptoe around *me*. No need to feel sorry for *me*.

But instead, she ambles off toward the kitchen with Mom following at a safe distance, and pulls a tin of cocoa from the pantry. Mom sets a kettle boiling on the stove, and Ryan takes a sweatshirt from a pile of laundry and pulls it on over her damp clothes. The lights in the kitchen flicker from yellow to brown then back again, and the house sighs at the drum roll of thunder out beyond the windows.

When it's ready, they take the cocoa into the den, where they sit on opposite ends of the same couch listening as the windows tremble against the weather.

"You didn't tell me," Mom says, lowering her mug. "How come?"

'You're busy," Ryan says, looking away. "There's the new baby and everything." They both know this isn't the reason, but

neither makes a move to say anything further. Ryan stares hard
at the mug in her hand.

"Is it because you didn't want it to be true?" Mom asks
gently, and there's nothing left to do but nod, a miserable, weary
little tilt of her head. Rather than move to hug her, rather
than close the space between them on the couch, Mom looks
thoughtfully out the window at the storm, and Ryan is grateful
for this. She feels dangerously unglued, mere inches from falling
to pieces. Outside, a jagged fork of lightning brightens the sky,
and at the exact same moment—as if by some previous agree-
ment—the lights in the house fall suddenly dark.

"Mom?" Ryan says, her voice small in the blackness, and
then there are a few confused moments as they feel their way
to the kitchen and fumble through the drawers to find a match-
book and a few candles. When they manage to get them lit, their
fingers slow in the absence of light, the flames are close and
orange, and Mom's face is wavery behind them. Every so often,
the room flashes white and the thunder makes them draw closer
to the candles. Ryan hugs her knees and shivers.

"Well," Mom says, laughing softly. "This isn't dramatic at
all."

The comment sounds so much like Nick's pronouncement
that day at the game—the day of the last big storm and the even
bigger announcement—that Ryan has to blink fast, working
to stop the tears that are hot against the backs of her eyes. She
wipes her nose and sniffles.

Mom scoots over on the couch and rubs her back. "It's okay
to be scared."

"I'm not," Ryan says, staring ferociously at her lap.

"Then it's okay to be upset."

She shakes her head.

"You're just like your father," Mom says eventually, and

Ryan's jaw tightens. How can she explain that it's too much to live up to, this weighty comparison between them? Even after all that he'd been, all that he'd stood for, all that he'd taught her, Ryan now stands before a trial greater than any ball game, not tall and straight and ready, but cold and scared and alone.

"I'm not," Ryan mumbles. "I'm not as much like him as you think."

Mom smiles faintly. "You are."

"Then I don't want to be," she says, and the words come out with a force she hadn't expected. But somewhere inside of her a small knot of anger is twisting itself tighter. All she could think when she saw Nick in the hospital earlier was *how could you?* and *why him?* and *it's not fair*, over and over and over until she was no longer certain who she was even talking about. It was Nick she was looking at, but a part of her thoughts were—as they always are and ever will be—on her dad.

The branches of a tree scrape at the window, and Ryan watches the shadows across the ceiling. Mom dangles a hand over one of the candles, her fingers waving like a magician's, scattering smoke and splitting flame. When the light is steady again, she looks up at Ryan. "I remember your father used to have this horseshoe hanging above the garage door," she says, shaking her head at the very idea of it.

"What for?"

"For luck." Mom smiles from behind distant eyes. "He had it hanging upside down to catch as much of it as possible. Then one day, he shut the door too hard and the thing fell right off. Your poor dad looked like a kid whose last cookie just hit the floor. But he bent down, picked it up, and brushed it off. Then he went right out to get his toolbox so he could hang it up again. And you know what he said?"

Ryan shakes her head.

"He said that it's not a bad thing to have to start from scratch every now and then."

"With the luck?"

Mom nods. "*That's* what he meant when he told you to always keep moving forward. It didn't mean you always have to know exactly what to do or where to go. All he meant was that when your luck runs out, you just have to pick yourself up, brush yourself off, and make some new luck for yourself."

"But how?" Ryan asks.

"Listen," Mom says, moving closer to her on the couch. "Nobody's asking you to be Dad. But you *should* know that you *are* like him in the ways that are important. Don't confuse baseball with life, okay? When Dad said to be brave and keep your chin up and always keep moving, he didn't mean you can't ever be scared. And when he said everything works out in the end, he didn't mean it would come easily. And he didn't mean it wouldn't be tough."

Ryan's voice, when she speaks, is very small. "I'm not sure . . ." she begins, then breathes in and starts again. "What if it's not enough?"

Mom wrinkles her forehead, waiting.

"What if I can't hope enough for us both?"

Even in the dark, she can see Mom's face change, the lines around her eyes going soft and slack, the shape of her mouth loosening. There's a long silence. The wind rattles the beams of the house with a rhythm of its own that blends with the rain.

"You don't have to," Mom says, placing a closed hand against her heart. "You don't have to do anything alone, and you don't have to be so brave."

Ryan bows her head but doesn't say anything. After a moment, she looks up. "Where is it now?" she asks.

"What?"

"The horseshoe."

Mom smiles through the dark. "He gave it away years ago."

"To who?"

"Someone who needed more luck than he did."

"Who?" Ryan insists.

"Who do you think?" Mom says, her smile widening. "He left it at Wrigley."

Chapter Twenty-Five

IN THE MORNING, RYAN STANDS BEFORE HER CLOSET for a long time. Outside her bedroom window, the sun breaks free of the clouds, and the smell of waffles from the kitchen winds its way up the stairs. The night before, she'd slept fitfully, twisting the covers into knots. She hadn't meant for her conversation with Nick to snowball the way it did yesterday, to turn into an argument of sorts. But everything had felt so terribly bleak: with Ryan, guilt-stricken over the bargain she'd made, and Nick, so frighteningly void of all hope. She had no idea how to possibly reassure him when she herself was so completely unsure. How would he ever be okay if she couldn't even find the words to say it?

She bites her lip and stares at her closet door. It takes her a few minutes to finally step forward, standing on her tiptoes to feel along the uppermost shelves. She pushes aside scarves and mittens, shoeboxes full of photographs and sweaters she hasn't worn in years. When her fingers finally brush the brim of the cap, she closes her hand around it.

A thin layer of dust has settled along the top, and Ryan curls her lips into a small *o* and blows until its original color has more or less returned, a comforting shade of blue. She traces the stitching, running a finger along the curve of the red *C* that stands out so boldly in front, already feeling somewhat better. Just having it close to her again after so many years is heartening, and she suspects this is how most kids must feel about blankets and teddy bears. Before tucking it into her backpack, she curves the brim into a half-moon shape, the way her dad had once taught her.

But by the time she gets to school, Ryan still feels overwhelmed and unprepared for the day ahead of her, weaving toward her locker with her head down, shaky from the previous night's revelations. In the faces of her classmates, she notices a few creased brows, a handful of worried looks, and the occasional slow and knowing tilt of the head. This, she tells herself, could mean anything. But by lunchtime, she has no doubt that some version of the news about Nick has made the rounds.

As she makes her way to the cafeteria, Ryan has the sense that things are moving too fast, and she wishes for something steady to hold on to. When they see her, Kate and Sydney wave her over to their table, and Ryan breathes out, relieved not to have to worry over seating arrangements today. Lucy looks up from her salad and flashes a distracted smile before turning her attention to a bottle of dressing. It's the same table as yesterday, long and rectangular, with two rows of normally unfriendly girls who now direct sympathetic looks at Ryan as she slides in between Sydney and Kate.

An uneven hush falls over the table as, one by one, people begin to notice her, nudging one another with their elbows. Ryan lowers her face, flustered by this type of attention, suddenly visible for all the wrong reasons. She wishes that Nick were beside her, then remembers with a start that his absence is the cause of it all: the whispering and sympathetic looks, the sidelong glances and bent heads.

One of the girls sitting across the table clears her throat. "I'm sorry about—" she begins, but Sydney doesn't give her a chance to finish.

"April!" she says sharply, widening her eyes at her.

Looking surprised, April leans back in her seat. "I didn't mean to—"

Sydney shakes her head, and the other girl falls silent. The table is quiet but for the sounds of the lunchroom around them, the rustle of paper, the clattering of trays, a distant ripple of laughter. Ryan looks gratefully at Sydney, and on her other side, Kate reaches out to give her hand a squeeze.

It's true they'd abandoned her before, but isn't that part of moving on too? Forgiving those who find their way back? Now, when she needs them again, when it counts the most, they're here, sitting on either side of her like a couple of security guards, backs straight and eyes sharp. It had been this way after her dad died, too, when the playground had begun to seem a dangerous place, filled with difficult questions and undisguised staring. Ryan had preferred to stay inside at recess, and even when the teacher insisted they go out with the others, Sydney and Kate had been adamant about staying behind to keep her company. Some days they drew pictures, some days they talked, and others they just sat quietly, the three of them together.

Too much else has happened to Ryan for her to hold a grudge. There have been too many other things she's had to worry about surviving, and long ago she'd stopped seeing friendship as anything more than a simple expression of patience, rising and falling like the seasons, circling back on itself in the most surprising of ways.

For the remainder of lunch, the other girls at the table discuss homework and teachers, upcoming parties and weekend plans. But Ryan remains quiet. For the moment, at least, her worries have slowed, lightened by the presence of her friends beside her. And all the motion—the spinning and spiraling of all that's passed and all that's yet ahead of her—has, for the time being, grown mercifully still.

Later, when she can't take any more talk of rocks and minerals, Ryan slips out of science class with the bathroom pass and takes her time crossing through the now-empty hallways. When she opens the door to the bathroom, she sees Lucy in front of one of the sinks, studying herself in the mirror. She's standing absolutely still, not combing her hair, not fixing her lipstick, not even washing her hands, which are balanced on either side of the sink so that her whole body is pitched forward, her nose near the silver glass of the mirror. Ryan hovers uncertainly, one foot in the bathroom, the other still out in the hallway. She considers backing away, gently closing the door behind her and returning to class. But right now, Lucy looks the way Ryan feels—pale and quiet and faraway—and so instead, she lets the door fall shut behind her and clears her throat. Lucy turns around, then takes a step back from the sink, looking vaguely suspicious.

"Listen," Ryan says. "About what happened at the game the other day—"

"Don't worry about it," Lucy says shortly, and when Ryan opens her mouth to continue, she whirls around. "Seriously, we don't have to talk about it."

Ryan nods, unsure what to do now. All of a sudden, she *wants* to talk about it. Because if they were to hash it out right now—a fight so completely and wholly trivial compared to all that's happened since then—it might make everything else seem just a little bit less scary. All day, people have been talking around her in great funnels of words, and now, when she least expects it, she has something to say. Right here in the bathroom, surrounded by the murky blue tiles and the faint smell of disinfectant, Ryan feels like talking. And to Lucy Barrett, of all people.

But before she has a chance to say anything, Lucy reaches into her back pocket and pulls out a tissue, then simply stares at it as if working out a difficult puzzle. There's something about the way her shoulders are curved that suggests a sort of mounting sadness, and perhaps because Ryan herself is so terribly and utterly sad—better versed in the uneven terrain of such sorrow—she recognizes it before even Lucy does, and she's beside her when she starts to cry. Ryan reaches out instinctively to put an arm around her shoulders, because what else is there to do when a girl dissolves into tears in a bathroom? What else can you do but the very thing you'd want if it were you?

"I'm sorry," Lucy says, her hands cupped over her face as if this might make her invisible. "I know you've got much bigger things going on right now."

Ryan takes a step back, trying not to look so astonished at seeing Lucy go to pieces. "What's wrong?" she asks, her voice low and echoing in the empty bathroom.

Lucy, realizing she's still holding the tissue, blows her nose noisily. "I can't believe I'm crying," she says, looking at Ryan as if only just now registering her presence here, the unlikely scenario they'd somehow stumbled into. "This is so stupid. I never cry."

Ryan smiles. "It happens."

"My parents are getting divorced," Lucy says with a small shrug. "I guess it sort of feels like they've been on their way there for most of my life, but they only just told me last night."

"I'm sorry," Ryan says, remembering that day in her yard, Lucy's father brushing her off as he concentrated on his next putt.

"Oh, please," Lucy says, but not unkindly. "I'm sure this is the last thing you need to be worrying about today."

Ryan shuffles her feet a bit, but can't think of anything to say to this. Outside, they hear footsteps, and then the door to the boys' bathroom opens and closes. Lucy balls up her tissue and tosses it into the garbage can, and Ryan assumes that whatever this had been is now over.

"You know," Lucy says. "In a weird way, I used to be jealous of you."

"Of *me*?" Ryan chokes.

Lucy doesn't laugh. "I know this sounds awful," she continues, "but I was jealous that your father died, because it meant he wasn't around anymore to disappoint you. All you had left were these great memories, all the things you did with him as a kid, when dads are at their best."

Ryan is too surprised to speak.

"There was never really a chance for him to let you down, you know?"

But he did, she almost says, thinking of that last April morning when they'd walked out to the car together. He'd bent down to cup her chin in his hand. "I'll be back soon," he had told her.

"Not for Opening Day," Ryan pointed out.

"No, that's true," he said. "But Mom will take you."

"It's not the same."

He struggled to keep from smiling. "I know," he said. "But we'll go the following weekend, okay?"

Ryan considered this. "You promise?"

Dad pulled her into a hug, then straightened. "I promise," he said, crossing his heart with two fingers, then giving the bill of her cap a little tug. She stood on the edge of the curb, her toes pointed out in the direction he'd driven, and even after he was gone, she didn't move until Mom called her back inside.

Now, Ryan looks at Lucy. "It's too much to ask of anyone," she finally says. "Not to ever let you down. That's all everything is. Just a whole series of disappointments."

"Well, that's cheery," Lucy says, and in spite of herself, Ryan laughs.

"I guess I mean that even with the best intentions, things can sometimes backfire," she says, thinking not only of broken promises, but also of the bargain she'd made that day this summer, when she'd walked into Nick's bedroom and had a feeling and managed to curse them all.

The bell rings, tinny and metallic by the time it reaches the bathroom, but neither one of them moves. Lucy looks at the door, and Ryan can tell she's also reluctant to return to the world beyond it. She tries—as she so often does—to think of something meaningful to say, some token of wisdom from her father, but her mind is now on Nick, and the words are caught in her throat.

"Have you ever heard of small ball?" Ryan finds herself asking. The color rises in her cheeks when Lucy wrinkles her brow, but she pushes on anyway. "In baseball, it means instead of trying to hit every ball out of the park, you try to collect a bunch of smaller plays to move the runners forward and score."

They can hear their classmates out in the hallway, the scuffling of shoes, the muddled voices just beyond the door. Lucy looks unsure whether to stay or go, but Ryan rushes on before she has a chance to say anything.

"It doesn't mean you don't want to win," she says. "It only means it's sometimes easier to do it a little bit at a time."

She realizes suddenly—and with a small start—that for all his talk about not buying into any unfounded optimism or superstition, Nick is not, in the end, that unlike her father. Because for all his balking, for all his reluctance to give in to faith—to allow himself to hope—Nick is still a believer in small ball. And even if you have a hard time counting on the big win, even if you won't stake anything on the chance of a game-winning home run, there still must be a part of you that is open to the smaller possibilities. Even the tiniest hits can sometimes carry you home.

Lucy is watching her now with something like confusion,

and Ryan struggles to find her way back to the conversation. But she knows, suddenly, where she should be. And she knows exactly what she needs to say.

"All I mean is that things can sometimes get better a little piece at a time," she explains, thinking of Nick.

"Well, they can't get much worse," Lucy says, and they both smile. The bathroom door opens and a few older girls walk inside, and Ryan can feel the moment flickering. She hands Lucy another tissue.

"Good luck with everything," she says, as if they'd been talking about a math test.

"You too," Lucy says, nodding gravely, and then Ryan hurries out into the hallway, around the corner, and out of the building.

Chapter Twenty-Six

B Y THE TIME RYAN APPEARS IN THE DOORWAY OF NICK'S room after the seemingly endless trip downtown, everything else has fallen away. When he sees her standing there—flushed and anxious—he looks first surprised, then confused, glancing at his watch to confirm that it's only two o'clock: not quite the end of the school day and hours still before the start of the game. Ryan doesn't say anything as she walks over to his bed, then sits beside him and puts her hand on his.

"Yesterday was my fault," she says. "I'm sorry."

Nick swings his legs over the side of the bed to sit up beside her. He's wearing an old Cubs shirt and sweatpants instead of a gown, and looks better today: the color has returned to his cheeks, and the bandage on his upper arm's been changed to one that is smaller and considerably less frightening.

"Can we just skip this part?"

Ryan stares at him. "What?"

"This." He points at her, then back at himself. "Apologizing, explaining. We shouldn't have to go through the motions like that. We understand each other a lot better than all this."

It would be easy, now, for her to agree. To rest her head on his shoulder and pass the afternoon in this way, lingering until the game begins, forcing everything else to wait. But Ryan came here for a reason, and so she shakes her head and takes a deep breath.

"Please," she says, when he starts to speak again. She shakes her head and a few pieces of hair come loose from her ponytail; already, she can feel herself coming undone. "I really need to explain something, okay?"

He nods, waiting for her to continue.

"My dad and I used to make these bargains," Ryan begins. "About the Cubs, mostly. Just stupid things like if they hit a home run, I'd have to be nice to Emily for a week. Or if they won a game, he'd come home early from work one night."

She ventures a look at Nick, whose face is unchanged in the harsh hospital lighting. Out in the hallway, a nurse is lecturing someone on submitting paperwork, and on the other side of the curtain that splits the room, another patient is softly snoring. Ryan pauses to listen, half-hoping someone might knock, but nobody does.

"They didn't mean anything," she continues, then feels immediately terrible, because they had, of course, meant something. To her and her dad, they'd meant everything.

She closes her eyes, then starts again.

"That first game of the White Sox series," she says, choosing her words carefully. "They won, remember? And after the game, I ran over to your house to see if you'd been watching." She glances down at her hands, embarrassed. "The front door was open, so I just went upstairs, but you were asleep with the TV on."

Nick looks somewhat amused, but says nothing.

"I didn't know then, not for sure," Ryan says, waving her hand around the hospital room. "It was just a feeling, I guess, that maybe you were sick, and I just . . ."

"What?" he asks, when she trails off.

"I made a bargain that it was okay if the Cubs never won again," she says. "As long as you'd be okay."

The floor of the hospital is a patchwork of linoleum squares, and Ryan traces her foot along the width of one of these as she waits for Nick to register this information.

When he finally speaks, his words are slow and deliberate. "So you think this is your fault?" he asks, his face unreadable.

"That I'm back in the hospital now because the Cubs are winning, and it's your fault?"

"Sort of," Ryan says, nodding feebly.

"Which is why you've been so weird about the Cubs lately,"
Nick says, then laughs. "Are you really *that* superstitious?"

She shakes her head. "Not anymore."

"Good," Nick says. "Because even if it *were* possible to curse
someone by accident, I'd sort of hope that fate has bigger things
to worry about than me and the Cubs."

Ryan leans into him as he puts an arm around her. "Nothing
seems more important than you and the Cubs," she says quietly.
"But I realized that you were right about all of it, anyway."

"All of what?"

"Curses, bargains, all that stuff," she says. "And about small
ball, too."

"What did I say about small ball?"

"It's not so much something you said," Ryan tells him. "It's
just that you believe in it at all. You might not believe in good
luck, but you *do* believe in something."

She can feel him smiling against the top of her head. "So?"

"So, it's hopeful," she says. "It makes me think things will
be okay."

Nick leans away, and when Ryan turns to him, his face is
serious. "You asked me yesterday why I bother cheering for
them if I don't believe they'll ever win," he says. "But there's a
difference between not believing and not caring."

She waits for him to go on. His eyes are on the blue square
of the window, where the clouds are bottoming out over the
lake, and he looks energized again, his back straight and his
hands busy as he speaks. "It's not about winning or losing, really,"
he's saying. "It's just the showing up every day. It's stepping up
to the plate and whiffing, and then doing it over and over again,

whether you get a hit or not. It's getting up every morning and failing and being disappointed and getting beat up and being let down, and then doing it all over again the next day."

"I get that," Ryan says. "Any Cubs fan gets that. But you still want them to win, and you still have to believe they can do it. Or else what's the point?"

Nick shakes his head. "Being a championship team, winning the World Series," he says. "Those aren't the kinds of things that give you shape or substance. I'd rather cheer for a team with a hundred losing seasons than one that wins every year. That gets boring. Losing never does."

"Because there's always a chance they'll win," she says, but she realizes as she does that this isn't the answer Nick is looking for. It's clear to her now that although he lives and dies with the Cubs each summer, though he memorizes the lineups and checks the standings in the papers and rarely misses a game, a part of him—whether he realizes it or not—*likes* the fact that they never win. There's something in him that has come to appreciate them for what they represent, and he depends on them for the very things that disappoint so many others. It is, in a twisted way, the ultimate form of hope. He doesn't love them *despite* their losing streak. He loves them *because* of it.

"But how can it be both?" she asks him. "How can you cheer for them so hard without believing they'll ever actually win?"

"You just can," he says. "It's like anything else. Not everything is so black and white. It's okay to have doubts, even as you hope. You don't have to choose. You can be both things at once."

Ryan lowers her eyes. Just last night, Mom had tried to tell her the same thing. *When Dad said to be brave*, she'd told Ryan, *he didn't mean you can't ever be scared.*

She understands now what she, in all her worry, had forgotten. That even as she hesitates and wavers, even as she thinks too
much and moves too cautiously, she doesn't always have to get it
right. It's okay to look back, even as you move forward.

It's okay to have doubts, even as you hope, Nick had said.

It's okay to be scared, said her mom.

Ryan spreads her hands over the blanket on Nick's bed, then
sits in the chair beside it, and lays her head down on the covers.
She feels a swift rush of weariness, and Nick, too, is yawning,
blinking away the last of the afternoon light in the window. He
runs a hand through her hair and kisses her forehead, then scoots
down so that their faces are close.

They're both tired: tired of thinking, tired of worrying,
tired of wishing. Nick falls asleep first, and Ryan can feel her
breathing matching up to his, the faint rise and fall of his chest,
the occasional twitch of his fingers near her neck. She buries
her nose in the fabric of the sheets, feeling like she's ten years
old again, on the day before the day the world ended, on the
day before a new baseball season began, and a different kind of
season drew to a close.

And so they sleep.

Hours later, when they finally wake—first Nick, then
Ryan—their hands are braided together, and Nick untangles his
fingers from hers and then nudges her gently.

"Hey," he says, as she finds her way back. "The game'll be
on soon."

The lights are still off in the room, though they can see that
the nurses have been by to draw the curtain over the window,
which glows in its efforts to hide the moon.

"I guess now I can cheer for them again," Ryan says ruefully, rubbing her eyes and stretching. "Since you don't believe
in curses."

"I believe in some curses," Nick says, and she looks at him sideways. "That's why it's so easy for people to love the Cubs. Everyone loses sometimes. Everyone is a little bit cursed."

"Especially us," she murmurs, looking around the darkened hospital room.

"Not us," he says. "We're lucky."

On the way home, Ryan steps off the train at Addison Street almost without thinking, slipping out just before the doors snap shut. She stands with her hands on her head, breathing hard as she watches the train rattle around the corner and then disappear entirely. She'd promised Mom she'd come straight home after the game, but she's suddenly gripped by a need to be alone, to walk or be still, to think hard about all that's happening or perhaps briefly forget it. All she wants is a small wedge of time in which to collect herself.

The streets around Wrigley Field are now mostly empty. Ryan and Nick had watched earlier as the Cubs beat the Cardinals, evening up the wild card race in one breathless game. Though there's still a month left of the regular season, a win tomorrow night would put them in the lead. And even in something as uncertain as baseball, even with a team as uncertain as the Cubs, something like that might just be enough to carry them forward into the playoffs.

But now, the fans have gone home and the stadium sits low beneath a star-strewn sky. Ryan passes the main entrance, the metal grates pulled down to hide the turnstiles and ticket booths. A few pieces of litter tumble up the street—plastic bags and empty soda cans, ticket stubs and crumpled programs—but otherwise, the world is still.

She crosses to the corner of Waveland Avenue, then pauses. The narrow brownstone is tucked shoulder-to-shoulder among

its neighbors, dark and silent as the street surrounding it, and
Ryan starts up the path without thinking. She puts a hand on
the cool stones of the building, then lowers herself onto the
porch. The lights around the stadium flicker and buzz, casting
shadows across the empty shell of the field.

Ryan tucks her chin into her jacket, feeling strangely distant
from the scene before her, as if part of her had been left behind in
the hospital room up the road. She closes her eyes—just briefly—
and then opens them again, thinking of her dad and the last game
they'd gone to here together, of the time he caught the foul ball
and the time the Cubs won a doubleheader in the sweltering heat
and a thousand other games on a thousand other days.

Promise me you'll remember this, he'd always said.

But it was never a question of remembering. How could
she possibly forget?

Since he died, Ryan has learned to read silences like a map, to
study them for the spaces in between, predicting and forecasting
the gaps. Because it's within these moments of quiet that she can
almost hear him, a sound like a whisper, like the last murmurings
before sleep. She knows he's always with her, but never more so
than in those dips between words. It's a feeling like falling, though
not in a scary way. It's like hoping for hope itself.

She digs through her backpack for the hat he'd once given
her, holding it carefully between stiff and chilly fingers. A siren
calls from somewhere beyond the stadium, and the lights color
the sky momentarily red before disappearing again. She looks
out across the street, then closes her eyes, and the stadium is
wrenched from view.

It's how we hold on to things, her dad had once said, even as
we move on.

She lets her eyes flutter open again, then sets the cap down on
the porch beside her. When the wind picks up, it nudges it along

the stone floor, past the spot where Nick had once sat—where they'd talked and not talked, where they'd shouted and whispered and feared and dreamed—and after a little while, it goes skidding off the end of the porch entirely, cartwheeling down the steps toward the stadium like an offering of some kind.

Ryan blinks out into the gathering darkness. Before her, the world carries on as it always does. There are cars and trucks and taxis, a handful of people out for an evening stroll, all beneath the pale lights of the stadium, which looms like a monument in the bluish sky above. But Ryan sits unnoticed—a stolen moment as night falls over the street—huddled in a corner of the porch as if searching for shelter from a storm.

Chapter Twenty-Seven

RYAN'S POKING HOLES IN A SHEET OF GRAPH PAPER THE following morning when her math teacher pauses to ask, for the second time, that the boys in the back of the room remove their caps during class. When she twists to look, Ryan sees that they're all wearing Cubs hats, which they now doff with great formality, making little bows to one another before tucking them under their desks.

The teacher shakes his head. "This is getting ridiculous," he says with a grin. "The whole city's practically hysterical."

This pronouncement is met with scattered claps and deep cheering, a flurry of anticipation over tonight's big game. Once the noise from the back has died down, the discussion returns to slopes and coordinates. But when the teacher looks back over his shoulder for an answer to the question on the chalkboard, his eyes land on Ryan, who has gone white at the reminder.

She hadn't planned to come to school today. Even Mom and Kevin had agreed it might be better to be at home when the call came, but Ryan had promised Nick she'd pick up his homework, and it felt important to carry on as usual, to not appear overly concerned. Optimism seemed as promising as anything else today, on a day when they'd learn whether the cancer was back, and whether or not it had spread beyond his arm.

But the mention of the Cubs triggers something in Ryan beyond just the memory of last night's win or the excitement about today's all-important game. There's an odd prickling in the tips of her fingers, and her mouth has gone chalky and dry.

"Ryan?" the teacher says, making his way between the desks to more closely examine his suddenly pale student. "Are you okay?"

Ryan nods, though she isn't at all certain. She takes a few breaths, trying to steady herself. "Can I go to the water fountain?"

"Maybe it would be better if you saw the nurse," he says. "Do you want someone to take you there?"

She shakes her head and accepts the hall pass with wavering hands. Once outside the classroom, she walks a little ways, then pauses to lean her forehead against the cool of a metal locker, breathing hard. Ryan's rarely ever sick, and though she knows this has to do with more than just sweaty palms and a churning stomach, she's still surprised by the power of her worry.

When she feels sturdy enough, she continues downstairs and through the long front corridor to the nurse's office. She's made it a point to avoid this place since the fourth grade, wary of the starched white cot and jars of cotton balls and bandages. But now she sits obediently, feeling too weak-kneed to protest as the nurse shoves an oversized wooden popsicle stick into her mouth. Ryan gags and coughs until she pulls it back out to make a few notes on a pink chart.

"Have you been feeling dizzy or faint at all lately?" the nurse asks, the lines in her face collapsing into a frown when Ryan only gives her head a mournful little shake. "Nauseous?" she asks, trying again. "Queasy? Shaky?"

The answer to all these remains *no*, and the nurse sighs and clicks her pen, then brings a hand to her forehead. Ryan wiggles her eyebrows unhelpfully and looks around at the room, the Q-tips and Band-Aids and wispy pieces of gauze, the posters for various illnesses and support groups and hot-lines, and she thinks of the last time she was in an office like this one. It had been during those endless, hourlike minutes when she'd sat wondering about the particulars of the accident, trying unsuccessfully to nudge the clock back to the exact moment when her father died, wishing she could have somehow known, wondering what it meant, all those lost seconds when they should have already been missing him.

And she realizes now—with a sense of desperation that wrenches her up from the paper-covered cot—that this must be a similar kind of moment. What else could this have sprung from—this sudden wooziness, this curious spinning of her throbbing head—if not that? Those leaden moments of time that pass in such terrible ignorance before the unexpected arrival of bad news.

The nurse calls after her as Ryan slips out the door of her office, but she doesn't turn around. Her head is bent when she returns to the brittle stillness of the empty hallway, where she isn't the least bit surprised to see the figure of her mother standing just outside the principal's office.

Ryan doesn't need to ask what she's doing here. She doesn't even think to question whether the phone call from the Crowleys had been good news or bad, whether the cancer is back or not, whether it's finally—quietly, stealthily—made its way to Nick's lungs. And she doesn't, when she crosses the space to her mother, ask when the news had come, because they must surely have learned of it during those dizzying moments when Ryan groped her way along the rows of lockers to the nurse's office, the sight of disappointments past and present.

When she reaches the end of the hallway, Mom draws her into a hug, and Ryan buries her face in her sweater and lets herself be held. She presses her lips together and closes her eyes, and she doesn't ask, because she already knows.

Though it's not quite September, the leaves have already started to lose their grip on the trees lining the road downtown, and one by one they skitter across the pavement, drifting alongside the breezes from the lake. Ryan leans back from the car window to look over at Mom, whose belly is by now nearly too big to fit beneath the steering wheel, and who's driving toward the hospital with a look of such concern it makes Ryan want to hug her all over again.

There's a lull in the music on the radio, and the DJ mentions the event on the minds of all his listeners: this afternoon's game against the St. Louis Cardinals, the deciding factor as to which team will take the lead in the wild-card race.

"Pretty big game," Mom says, flicking her eyes from the road to look over at Ryan, who nods. "You guys must be excited."

"We are," she says, but the words sound empty, and they both go quiet again as they pull off onto the exit for the hospital.

"Mrs. Crowley said she can drive you home later if you want to stay for the game," Mom says when they pause at a red light. "But if you don't want to stick around here that long, everyone would understand."

Ryan shakes her head. "I should stay," she says. "I *want* to stay."

"I thought so," Mom says, reaching across the car to put a hand over Ryan's.

Once she drops her off, Ryan stands outside the hospital for a moment before going inside. Behind the sliding doors, the waiting room is filled with people, faces drawn and hands clasped. There's a woman holding a bouquet of daisies, a man worrying a handkerchief between his fingers, two little girls playing musical chairs. There's a boy who looks too young to be in a wheelchair, and a moment later, a man seemingly too old in the same kind, his robe trailing behind as a nurse pushes him through the busy room. Ryan takes a deep breath before walking inside, toward the now-familiar nurse's station and the bank of elevators that lead to Nick's floor.

Upstairs, she looks around for his parents, but doesn't see them, and so she knocks once on the open door to Nick's room. A woman brushes by with a balloon for another patient, and Ryan wishes she had thought of something like that, something to lift his spirits on such an otherwise miserable day. But when Nick calls her inside, she finds him looking exactly as he had the day before—sitting up in bed, watery-eyed and so obviously pleased to see her—and she relaxes.

"Hey," he says, waving her over, and Ryan stands at the side of his bed and leans to kiss him. The small television set in the corner of the ceiling is already tuned to the pregame show, and Nick scoots over to make room for Ryan to lie down beside him. He puts an arm around her shoulders, and she can feel him breathing beside her, a movement so steady and natural that it's almost hard to believe anything could be wrong with him.

They don't talk about the prognosis or the test results or the course of chemotherapy he'll soon be starting. They don't say anything about his lungs or his arm or that terrifying word—cancer—that hovers and looms and threatens to make itself felt in even the most remote conversations. They simply don't talk about it. Even when the nurse comes in and hands him two large pills and a glass of water. Even when his parents return and then, noticing Ryan's arrival, announce they'll be back later on. An orderly delivers a blanket, and outside, instructions are related and pages are turned as one shift of nurses gives way to another. But Ryan and Nick aren't listening. They are somewhere else entirely.

Ryan presses herself closer to him on the bed, and they whisper about the day's starting lineup, their voices lowered as if it were a great secret between them. They sit up a little when the first pitch is thrown, and duck their heads when the Cubs make an early error in the outfield. They grip each other's hands when they gain a shaky lead over the Cardinals, and then clap until their palms are sore when they widen it with a two-run homer. At the end of the third inning, they make toasts to the Cubs with Styrofoam coffee cups of lukewarm water, and then turn up the volume until a nurse asks them to please lower it again. Nick takes a get-well-soon card from the table beside his bed and writes GO CUBS across the back of it with a blue pen, which Ryan tapes along one side of it with some Band-Aids to create a flag, and they take turns waving it each time their team scores.

And they do, often.

The Cubs play so beautifully it almost hurts. Ryan finds she's digging her nails into Nick's hand as the game progresses, as the runs pile up and the other team starts to crumble against the team that invented crumbling, the lovable losers, the hundred-year choke artists. On the screen, the sun is setting behind home plate, and the ivy on the back wall of Wrigley Field looks gold in the autumn light, the tips already beginning to turn an impossible shade of red. The crowd is on their feet—on their tiptoes, even!—as each inning comes and goes and the unlikely leaders of the game continue to pull away from their opponents. They are playing now with a kind of perfection, a flawless state where later doesn't matter and before is nothing more than a memory. There is only now, this game, this dusky evening at Wrigley, and nothing else can possibly exist until the last pitch is thrown. It's the kind of game that makes your forget about everything else—yesterday and tomorrow, the world around you and your place within it—everything but the endless green field and the dusty bases and the red-laced ball as it cuts through the air.

The sky out the window of the hospital room matches the one on the television screen—a blurry confusion of red and orange—and Nick brings his mouth low to Ryan's ear. "If the Cubs win . . ." he says quietly, then trails off without finishing.

It seems too big an *if* to ever end the sentence.

Chapter Twenty-Eight

FEW WEEKS LATER, RYAN'S BETWEEN CLASSES WHEN she once again sees a familiar figure in the hallway just outside the principal's office. But this time, it's Kevin, looking uncharacteristically flustered, and when he sees her, he practically lopes down the hall.

"It's time," he says, his eyes wide and his face flushed. "Your mom and sister are in the car, and it's almost time!"

Ryan stares at him, trying to work out the date. "She's not due for two more weeks," she says, and Kevin puts a hand on her back to hurry her along, the two of them skidding down the corridor of the high school and toward the front door. Ryan looks up at him, her throat tight. "Is she okay?"

Kevin slows down and smiles. "She's fine," he says, patting her shoulder. "They're both fine. Just early."

Ryan breathes out, relieved. The car's still running where Kevin had parked it just outside the entrance, and Mom gives Ryan a reassuring wave from the window. Emily throws open the back door and crawls across the seat to announce, in case Ryan hadn't yet gathered it, that the baby is now on his way.

The drive downtown isn't all that different from others they've taken as a family, with Kevin sitting stiffly at the wheel, navigating the highways with the care of someone transporting valuable goods. Mom takes deep breaths in the front seat and explains to Ryan and Emily that it might take hours for the baby to come, and that they're to behave themselves in the waiting room, since Kevin will be inside with her.

"We can't watch?" Emily asks, her lower lip already jutted out.

"We'll be fine, Mom," Ryan says, feeling suddenly very much older. "You don't need to worry about us."

The maternity ward of the hospital is just a few blocks away from the oncology building that she's come to know so well. Ryan runs in ahead of Kevin, who's busy helping Mom out of the car, and asks someone to bring a wheelchair outside, and then she and Emily trail behind as they check in. Mom gives them each a hug before disappearing down a long hallway with a nurse, and Kevin hands them a few dollars for the vending machines before trotting after her.

"Is it bad that it's early?" Emily asks as they take a seat in the waiting room.

"Nah," Ryan says. "Maybe the new baby's just impatient."

"Like you," she says.

"Like *you*," Ryan shoots back, smiling.

Every now and then, Kevin returns to give them an update, and in between visits, Ryan and Emily pass the time by trading thoughts about the baby, what they might name him, what he'll be like when he's older.

"Will we have to change diapers?" Emily asks, wrinkling her nose.

"Maybe," Ryan says. "It would be a big help to Mom."

"Did you help with my diapers when I was a baby?"

Ryan shakes her head. "Dad did a lot of that stuff."

"Kevin will, too," Emily says, and Ryan's surprised by the force of her voice.

"Of course he will," she assures her. "He'll be a great dad."

"He already is," Emily says.

Ryan puts an arm around her little sister, and Emily looks up at her, surprised.

"What's that for?"

"Nothing," she answers truthfully. "Just everything."

They keep an eye on the clock above the nurse's station as the first hour passes, and then the second. Emily flips through the various magazines on the table before them, and Ryan picks up the sports section of a newspaper, leafing through it idly. There's an article warning of all the Cubs are up against in the coming series as they attempt to buck a century of history and tradition, and Ryan's glancing over it—all the many milestones of failure, the numerous reminders of defeat—when she hears a man talking to his young daughter across the room.

"This is no small thing," he's saying. "For them to have gotten the wild-card spot, to even be going to the playoffs at all, well . . . it's just not something that happens every day."

He's wearing a Cubs hat, which he takes from his head and twirls on his finger. The girl leans against his shoulder to watch, smiling when he places it on her head.

"One hundred years," he says, and she lifts her chin to look out from under the brim of the too-large cap. He laughs, a sound of sheer amazement. "What's one hundred years, anyway?"

Ryan smiles and sets down the newspaper. Someday, when the Cubs finally *do* win—this year or next year, or one of the many more to come—people will say it had to happen at some point. That *eventually* has to have a finite ending. That every *if* must find its pair in a *then*.

But Ryan knows differently.

There aren't just two kinds of endings. It's not as simple as winning or losing. There's a space in between, and this is where most of us tend to live.

Soon the playoffs will begin, and Wrigleyville will come alive in October. The sportscasters will be laughing and the gamblers scratching their heads, but either way, the streets around the stadium will be thick with crowds, an ocean of blue caps and raised fists, a great and noisy mob of fans stunned by such good luck.

And just a few miles farther down the lakeshore, Ryan and Nick will watch from his hospital room, each thinking of the first day of this strange and incredible season, when they had wandered those very streets together, pushing their way among vendors and fans, straining to hear the first stirrings of music from the press boxes and waiting for something to cheer about on the kind of spring afternoon that only Opening Day can provide.

Already Ryan is thinking about slipping out of the hospital later, walking the three blocks between buildings, tracing a familiar path to Nick's room. They'll sit together—as they will for the weeks to come—and watch the light changing in the window, the patterns shifting across the floor.

Soon enough the days will become muddled by medication and blurred by tears. Ryan will begin to wonder whether her hand ever existed outside of Nick's, so long does she sit by his side, their fingers knotted together on top of the covers. Sometimes, they'll talk, but mostly not. The silences contain all they'll ever need to know about each other, a fluency born of trial and trust.

And when the time finally comes to say good-bye, she'll swallow hard against the tightness of her throat and the weight of her heart. She'll think *I'll miss you* and she'll think *don't go* and she'll think *please*. But what she'll finally say is simply *thank you*, and it will mean all of these things—everything promised and remembered, everything wordless and spoken and understood—and so much more.

But all that is still to come.

For now, Ryan's thoughts are on new beginnings. And when she looks up, Kevin has appeared in the waiting room once more, this time wearing a hospital gown and plastic booties pulled over his shoes, his face lit by an enormous grin.

"Want to come meet your new brother?" he asks, and Ryan and Emily spring to their feet to follow him down the hallway.

When she sees the baby in her mother's arms, Ryan hesitates. What had for months been little more than an idea or a promise now appeared in the world as a howling pink baby, his fingers working through the air as if already desperate to be a part of things. None of them says a word—each overwhelmed by this new member of their family—until Emily steps forward to run a finger across the back of his tiny hand. Kevin leans to kiss the top of Mom's head, and from where she's still standing by the door, Ryan is overcome by a wish to be a part of it too.

She walks over to the bed and Mom reaches out to squeeze her hand. Kevin puts an arm around her shoulder, and Emily laughs as the baby wiggles his nose and then opens his mouth in a miniature yawn. There's a certain joy to all this that Ryan hadn't expected, not just for the new baby, but also for the way he's brought them all here, the five of them together in perfect stillness, in mute and wondrous awe.

Chapter Twenty-Nine

MONTHS LATER, ON A FROZEN NIGHT JUST BEFORE Christmas, Ryan wakes to hear the baby crying. She lies still for a few minutes, listening to the sound of his wailing, the heartrending sobs that echo throughout the upstairs hallway. The moon is bright through her curtains, reflecting off the steep drifts of snow in the front yard. Ryan rubs her eyes and sits up, resting one foot tentatively on the cold wooden floor as if testing the water.

Out in the hall, Mom's door opens at the same time, and they smile at each other, both tiptoeing in the direction of the baby's room, where the crying has grown louder, a series of howls punctuated by the occasional hiccup.

"I can get him," Ryan whispers. and Mom—bleary-eyed and rumpled from the last few times she was up tonight—squeezes her hand gratefully and makes her way quietly back to her room.

Ryan peers over the edge of the crib at her little brother, whose face is red and blotchy. He thrusts his fists in the air and kicks a few times before she reaches over to pick him up. His small body is warm against her pajamas, and she holds him close and makes a few slow circles around the room, moving in and out of the shadows. Outside, the snow has begun to fall again in large, unhurried flakes, and they stand at the window, looking out over the pale and muffled world. The baby twists and sniffles in her arms, his eyes wide and alert.

"You're not tired either, huh?' Ryan whispers, rocking him back and forth as she walks him out into the hallway.

The floorboards are old, but she knows which stairs creak and which can be trusted. Downstairs, the snow is banked up against the windows of the family room, and Ryan takes a seat on the couch, holding the baby close and switching on the television.

One of the sports networks is replaying classic baseball games, and Ryan leans back and smiles, seeing the pinstriped uniforms she knows so well. Though the picture is fuzzy and the game's nearly ten years old, she still flicks her eyes up to the corner of the screen, anxious to see the score. The catcher for the Cubs is arguing with the umpire over a questionable call, and Ryan realizes with a start that she'd been there that day.

"Look," she says softly, holding the baby up to see. "We were at this game."

He makes a gurgling noise and blinks at her as the previous decade's Chicago Cubs finish off the inning. Ryan's eyes fill with tears when the camera follows the players into the dugout, moving just below the seats on the third base line where they'd been sitting that day, and on so many others.

She remembers that the Cubs had been losing badly in the eighth inning. The whole stadium was pulsing with heat, restless beneath a blistering sun, and she'd been tired and sweaty and faint. But when she'd tugged on Dad's hand to ask whether they could go, he looked at her sideways.

"It's not over," he said, lifting her so that she was standing on the seat beside him. Ryan had leaned an elbow on his shoulder and sighed mightily.

"But we're losing by so *much*."

"That's the fun of it," Dad said. "You never know when there might be a comeback."

Later, after a series of batters had failed to do anything to remedy the declining situation, Ryan had tapped him on the shoulder. "We're still losing," she pointed out.

"True," Dad said, smiling. "But there's an art to losing. It's just as important to know how to do that as anything else."

"How come?"

"Because that's how you learn," he'd said, cupping her chin in his hand. He studied her with pale gray eyes. "It's how we learn to keep going. It's how we survive."

On the field below, the Cubs hit a double, and Ryan began to cheer in earnest, hopping up and down on the seat and clapping for her team. Dad put an arm around her waist, and she could tell he was proud of her. It took a certain kind of person to love the Cubs, he always said, and Ryan was happy to be one of them.

And in the end, he was right, of course. It took four extra innings, but there'd been a comeback after all.

Now, as the Cubs begin their rally on screen—an echo across the years, a distant and welcome memory—Ryan's brother curls his tiny hand around her finger.

"Don't worry," she says to him. "I'll take you too, someday."

She watches for a while with the volume turned low, the baby dozing on and off, his eyelashes fluttering against her arm as he shifts in his sleep. Sometime in the eleventh inning, the sound of the game is suddenly muted by a series of bright beeps. This is followed by a scrolling ticker that runs along the bottom of the screen like a ribbon, a warning about the worsening weather outside. Ryan looks to the window, where the flurries are coming down hard and fast now. The windowsills are caked with snow, and when the wind picks up, a row of icicles falls from the roof with a sound like a dozen tiny bells going off at once.

The lights flicker, once and then again, and the room goes suddenly dark. The television screen fades to black, and Ryan sits very still, bathed in the ghostly light of the snow outside. The silence that follows is charged, almost electric, and the baby stirs, letting out a few hesitant cries. Ryan holds him tighter, closing her eyes and waiting in the deep hush of this blue-cold night. Her heart is loud in her ears, and she thinks of Nick, a memory so powerful it almost feels real, as if he were right here beside her, his socked feet propped on the table, his arm slung lightly over her shoulders.

"This is it," he'd be saying, half-trying to rile her as the Cubs struggled to finish out the game. "It's all up to chance now. Nothing left but jinxes and curses."

"And . . ." she'd say, prompting him.

"And bargains," he'd tease.

Ryan would shake her head in mock exasperation. "And *hope*."

And then Nick, smiling that familiar smile of his, would have pulled her a bit closer. "Okay," he'd have said, relenting. "Hope, too."